THE UNRIPE GOLD

THE UNRIPE GOLD

GEOFFREY JENKINS

BOOK CLUB ASSOCIATES LONDON

This edition published 1983 by
Book Club Associates
by arrangement with William Collins Sons & Co Ltd

Printed in Great Britain by
Richard Clay (The Chaucer Press) Ltd,
Bungay, Suffolk

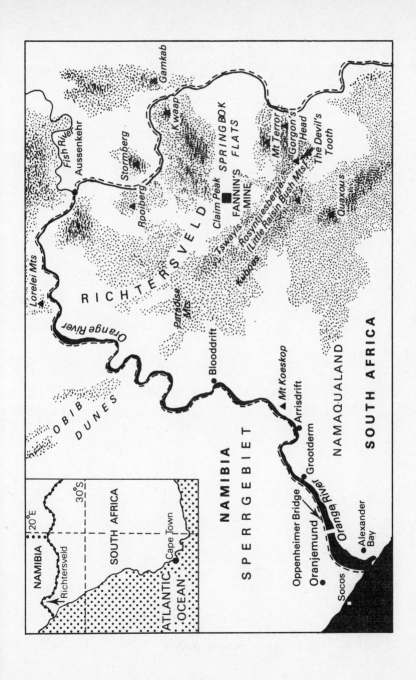

I

The blackness. Hell, the blackness! It was as thick here inside the barge's hull as the fog outside on the river. It broke like invisible surf over the kneeling man. It washed across the Browning Kapitän automatic readied in one hand, and over the unlit flashlight in the other. It drove on against the long object in front of which he crouched. It could have been a coffin or a log. Only his torch would show. He seemed to hesitate to use it for fear of giving himself away.

The blackness. The silence. The macro-value of sound at two a.m. He thought he could almost hear the rough breathing of the guard he had slugged on the deck above, though he had dragged him clear of the barge out of sight under one of the ore-lorries parked on the roadway to the jetty.

The blackness. His pants and jerkin were black, to match the night.

John Keeler swung his head to-and-fro like a radar scanner searching for some danger blip of sound in the silence. The motion was a practised one. It should have been. It had saved his life before tonight. So had the Hi-Power 9mm parabellum automatic with its special lightened trigger and combat-version safety catch. The gun was a man-stopper, a killer, poised now on a hair-trigger of tension as was the man himself.

Was there another guard? A few minutes before, Keeler had been the hunted instead of the hunter. A slight tell-tale sound of his own careless making had been enough to part that frail curtain of silence and alert the sentry. That warning put an extra thumb-screw on his tension now. Keeler had

7

used the row of half a dozen lorries to cover his short approach to his objective, the barge-train on the river. One of them – the craft in which he now lurked – rode high and unladen at the jetty's end. Ahead of it, its presence only perceptible in the fog because of a mooring rope which vanished ahead, was another empty barge. Ahead of it three more units of the barge-train were anchored somewhere near in the murk.

Keeler had dodged behind the giant wheels of the ore-lorry closest to the barge. He had waited, watched, listened. Wraiths of fog had stolen by, as soundless as the condensation which dripped from the tarpaulin-covered hump amidships of the barge. There had been nothing.

Keeler had straightened up to make for the gangplank connecting barge to jetty. As he did so, his flashlight – still doused – had struck the truck's chassis with a metallic clink. He had frozen.

The guard had been cunning. He had shown no light on which to give the intruder a firing bead. But the sounding-board of the empty hull had relayed the sound of his footsteps to Keeler's straining ears. Then – a movement, and Keeler had spotted a blur of the man's red hair in the fragmented darkness. Allowing even for distortion due to the fog, the guard had seemed a giant.

Adrenalin pumped through Keeler's veins. The sight of the sentry and his obvious professionalism told Keeler two things – first, that there must be something more than mere innocent copper ore aboard the barge to merit such vigilance; second, if that were so, his hunch had paid off, and he was on the trail which he had come halfway across the world to find.

Keeler had willed the man to come closer, turn, and then start back aboard again. That would be his moment.

The red-head nosed forward across the gangplank until he was on the jetty. Keeler was scared he might hear his own breathing, he was now coming so close. Close enough to make out that he grasped a rough wooden blackjack with a head big enough to crush a man's skull.

Keeler knew exactly where and how he would hit the man at the moment he re-crossed the gangplank. He palmed the Hi-Power Kapitän, barrel-first, into his fingers and slid his index finger forward to check that the adjustable backsight was projecting just the fraction he needed for a precision blow at the killer-nerve at the base of the neck.

The guard turned. Keeler struck.

The backsight, weighted by the near-kilogram mass of the pistol, was spot on target. Keeler's victim pitched forward untidily like a collapsing Rugby scrum. The blackjack – knobkerrie, they call it in Southern Africa – shot from his hand, banged on the steel decking, and splashed into the river. To Keeler in the silence, it sounded as loud as a mortar bomb.

He dropped into a firing crouch to meet any follow-up.

He waited.

Two minutes.

Five minutes.

No sound came, except the gasping of the unconscious man.

Keeler then hefted the inert body out of sight under a truck. He crept aboard the barge, one step at a time, eased aside the tarpaulin, and found himself in the big hold of the barge. He still did not dare risk the flashlight. Before trying it, he dropped on his knees to present the minimum target. For the first time in a career which had made him FERRET's most feared and respected operative, he wished for a silencer for the Browning. A shot would be heard in the silence almost as far as the security posts flanking the great bridge across the river, let alone by the crew aboard the strange craft at hand.

Now!

Keeler flicked on the flashlight. The beam streaked across the dusty hold.

Keeler – and his firing reflexes – had been prepared for almost anything but what he saw: the long object wasn't a coffin or a log. It was a sea-going kayak.

It stood propped on two wooden boxes in the centre of the hold. Another similar kayak was stacked against the barge's side. Both craft were painted deep purple-blue ocean camouflage; both had skegs, small stabilizing fins at the stern, for deep-sea work.

Keeler drew in his breath, sharp with excitement. His mind raced like a supercharged computer. Kayaks – what was the link between these two and that other one which had first roused his suspicions? After all, a sea-going kayak is not the sort of craft one would expect to find in a desert place which fronted on one of the most dangerous coasts in the world. The sea off the river mouth wasn't the sort of place you go for Sunday afternoon jaunts. Yet here were two fine kayaks – Keeler's admiration as a skilled kayaker himself was aroused – apparently ready for sea. To compound the mystery, there was a third kayak – rather inexplicably damaged – at a riverside camp a couple of kilometres away on which great effort was being expended to repair it to meet a secret ocean-going deadline. The bite was on the men who would be using the kayaks; the breakthrough had come for his mission.

Keeler was so excited as he made for the twin cockpits of the nearer kayak that his footsteps kicked up puffs of copper ore dust from the floor of the hold. He deliberately slowed in order not to sneeze. The gear which Keeler found stacked in the rearmost cockpit raised his suspicions. It was not only deep-water gear; it was cold-water gear – blue nylon caps with ear flaps, anoraks, woollen undergarments and sweaters, thin neoprene gloves, waterproof overpants and boots. The sort of thing a kayaker would need off the coast where the icy Benguela current draws in close to Africa's southernmost landmass after its long journey from Antarctica. There were also spare paddles, a couple of lifejackets and buoyancy aids as well as two Yachtshutes – used as international rocket distress signals which fire 300 metres up into the air – and some smaller flares. Keeler's fingers frisked the kayak expertly. But all that he found was not in itself incriminating for his purpose. He aimed the flashlight again to make sure he had missed nothing. The blues, oranges, reds and purples of the gear flashed by in the hold's sombre light.

Keeler shoved his hand deep under the rear decking and his searching fingers came in contact with some brown paper, roughly wrapped round a heavy object. He drew it out, pulled aside the wrapping. It seemed to be some sort of electrical instrument. He could not identify it. The connections were not wired up. It certainly had nothing to do with kayaking. He decided to search further.

Keeler investigated the second kayak. Its A1 gear was a duplicate of the first's. In its forward cockpit was a waterproof bag made of thick brown plastic material. Keeler might have passed it by as merely another item of equipment had he not been attracted by the elaborate double lashings of nylon cord securing its neck. The bag wasn't heavy – a kilogram or two. The contents felt like small stones. He untied the neck. Inside was a second waterproof polythene bag.

Deftly and swiftly Keeler undid the securing double drawstrings and shone his light into the bag. There seemed to be a collection of marble-sized stones. Why, Keeler asked himself, all this waterproof protection? He selected one which, considering its size, was remarkably heavy. Some sort of metal? Lead perhaps? Keeler slipped it into his pocket, replaced the inner polythene bag in the larger one, and started to re-tie the drawstrings.

Then, as if his keyed-up senses were acting on two distinct separate levels – his ears caught a sound from the gangplank above.

Keeler acted like lightning. In a flash he had put out his torch, thrust the waterproof bag back into place, and ducked

11

out of sight between the kayak and the barge's side.

The Browning's blue muzzle tracked the direction of the sound in the blackness.

Was the guard coming back? He could not credit that he would have revived so soon. If not him, then who? His relief?

There was no time to work it out. From above came the cautious pat of another footstep on the gangplank. The Kapitän tracked the advance.

The newcomer knew his job, Keeler conceded. Next he heard the faint rustle of the stiff tarpaulin at the entrance to the hold. He guessed he was standing there, as he himself had done, straining to catch any untoward sound before risking a light.

A torch beam cut across the dusty hold, rested inquiringly in turn on the kayaks, and swivelled across and about the entire interior. Keeler crouched down, safe. The intruder was not to know that he was only a trigger-press away from a magazineful of heavy shells.

The beam returned to the centre kayak. Keeler risked a quick glance. He saw the sharp eye of the light, nothing of the man behind it – except a hand. And that hand held something that made him go cold. His finger tightened on the Kapitän's trigger. It was a six-inch fighting blade with a double quillon guard and a handle large enough to give its operative the purchase he might need in a hand-to-hand duel. The blunt end had a skull-crusher taper which – as Keeler himself could bear witness – could deal a stunning blow to an opponent. Keeler noted, almost subconsciously, that there was not a gleam from the knife's metalwork – it had been specially treated with gun blue to prevent the shiny parts giving warning in night work. The sight of that disembodied hand told Keeler that behind that weapon was a pro, a killer who had taken all the precautions. All, except his giveaway footstep.

A combat knife versus the Kapitän! Both weapons had their advantages, depending on the circumstances. Yet the knife, the silent knife, implied that the newcomer was as furtive as Keeler himself, that he was no sentry, but a searcher, like himself. Keeler debated quickly whether he should strike first and kill him as he stood.

Before he could decide, the man moved forward as swiftly and purposefully as a cobra striking. One moment he was in the entranceway, the next he was bending over the kayak cockpit where the instrument parcel was.

He obviously saw it, for he put down his flashlight on the cockpit's bottom-boards as a preliminary to examining it.

The light reflected upwards, etching and emphasizing his lower face and jaw with its scar along the left side. Full lips were terminated at the corners by two rat-trap lines which were pronounced enough to look like a cartoonist's sketch of a mouth meant to keep secrets.

Keeler gasped inwardly and blinked over the gunsight to make sure he was not seeing things.

The man in his gunsight was his friend. He was camped with him on the river bank nearby. He had left him asleep after the party tonight. His name was Ross Gressitt. He was an American. He called himself a professor, a fossil-hunter. Keeler eyed the quick-release sheath hanging upside down from Gressitt's belt for deadly ease of reach and the paratrooper's cut-throat in his hand.

His mouth hardened, and he slid silently from concealment in the darkness into an attacking position.

2

Keeler eased sideways on his belly past his own kayak's sheltering bow. He felt the dusty grit under his hands. He kept the Kapitän clear of the steel decking, using his wrist as a lever to propel himself along. He was safe from any incidental light from Gressitt's torch and heading to take the kneeling figure from the rear. Gressitt was as tall as Keeler himself, six feet, lean and hard, a fact which he had laughingly attributed to the result of living at a dinosaur fossil site. Keeler smiled grimly when he remembered the remark now in assessing his chances of attack. He needed no light to recall what the rest of Gressitt's face was like – a curious paradox. It might have been cast in two moulds – below nose-level that tough mouth, and above it a rather soft playboy handsomeness. Like his face, Gressitt was a split personality, all right.

There was a rustle of paper as Gressitt concentrated on the instrument parcel. Keeler wormed his way behind him, stood up cautiously, the gun pointed. Any second Gressitt's attention might switch from the parcel, although for the moment he seemed completely preoccupied.

Keeler edged into position, and from arm's length rammed the Kapitän against Gressitt's neck. He had no intention of risking a backhanded sideswipe from the deadly blade by standing closer, or an equally lethal upswipe from its skull-crusher haft.

Gressitt went rigid at the touch of the metal. The nudge of the Hi-Power's barrel was enough to say 'drop it'! He knew enough to obey.

14

Keeler edged far back to get in a shot if Gressitt tried anything silly.

He did not. He swivelled slowly, reluctantly, away from where his salvation lay with the knife, into the blue-black eye of the Kapitän.

'*Keeler!*'

'Shut up!' Keeler whispered savagely. 'There may be more guards about! Out!'

'*More . . .?*' He was on his feet now.

Keeler gestured for silence. He indicated the exit.

Gressitt made a mime of asking permission to pick up his flashlight. Keeler was too old a hand to fall for that one. He motioned the other man aside and warily retrieved it and the knife. He kept Gressitt semi-blinded all the time with the light.

He pointed the beam at the way out. Gressitt followed it.

'Quiet!' ordered Keeler again between his teeth as they reached the gangplank. 'There is a guard under that truck – out cold. He could come round any time.'

Keeler gestured again with the gun for Gressitt to take the short unmetalled roadway leading from the jettyhead. The two men sneaked ashore past the line of parked lorries along the dusty road that hugged the Orange River.

If they could have made out anything at more than a hand's distance away in the fog, Keeler and Gressitt would have seen on their left the 1½ kilometre-wide channel of the Orange dotted with innumerable small reedy islands, sand-banks and shoals. The two men were on the southern bank of the river where there were no security restrictions. On their right was the large Alexander Bay airport, serving the diamond fields. Keeler smiled grimly to himself as he threw a glance in the direction in which he knew aircraft must be parked on the runway aprons like those great fossilized wonder birds called teracorns Gressitt had gone on about over the riverside camp fire. That was when he still believed Gressitt to be a genuine professor of palaeontology. The recollection irked him. He jabbed his captive unnecessarily in the back with the barrel of his Browning.

'Keep going!' he snapped harshly.

'Where the hell to?'

The threat of Keeler's gun certainly hadn't cowed Gressitt's spirit. Keeler reminded himself to keep the tightest watch on the American. If he slipped into the fog he would never find him again. That fog was as much a feature of the Diamond Coast as the Orange River itself. Every night for a million years it had swept in and covered the coast for about 30 kilometres inland – a dense, impenetrable, moisture-saturated curtain. Here, close to the river mouth, it did not simply spill over from sea to land. It swept up-river blanket-thick, perfect cover for dark doings. And both he and Gressitt had used it for just that.

'Keep going – you'll see soon enough,' retorted Keeler.

Keeler knew where he was taking Gressitt for questioning – interrogation would be a better word – at gunpoint. It was a ruined house – on the way to their riverside camp – at the junction of the road they were on with another main south-bound one used by the ore-lorries. Hundreds of kilometres away was the railhead, where the ore was transferred to rail transport.

To Keeler, shrouded in fog, it was like a walk down a mental tunnel back into boyhood. He knew the road well. He had spent happy boyhood years in Oranjemund where his father, a Canadian mining engineer with itchy feet, had held a job for several years.

The surface of the road was slightly better now than then, but the dust was the same. So were the dunes endlessly trying to encroach; even the trees, each one an individual with distinctive trunk, twisted like sugar-candy from the continual attrition of the wind, had not changed. Since he had landed at the airfield two days ago the time-warp of the years since his youth seemed to have evaporated. Except, he reminded himself grimly, for what was now going on in the middle of the night between two men, one armed with a knife and the other with a gun. What it was all about, he meant to find out.

In the murk, the only way Keeler knew he had reached the ruin was the fact that the road divided, one arm forking away sharply right.

'Inside!' he ordered.

Once in, Gressitt seated himself on a piece of ruined brickwork and reached for a cigarette.

'Hold it – *professor*!' Keeler checked him. 'No lights.'

He kept the Kapitän aimed; he felt Gressitt's movement was too casual to be safe.

'What were you doing aboard the barge?' demanded Keeler.

'I might tell you when you tell me what you were doing there.'

Keeler kept the Kapitän on the American, and turned on the flashlight, revealing a pair of searching brown eyes above that tough, rat-trap mouth and a jaw solid enough to take a professional's punch.

Keeler indicated his gun. 'I am asking the questions.'

'Through the barrel of a gun.'

'Yes,' Keeler replied tightly, 'through the barrel of a very light-triggered gun. Now – what sort of fossils did you expect to unearth aboard that barge – with a paratrooper's knife?'

Gressitt bridled at Keeler's tone. 'My credentials are one hundred per cent. You can check with the Smithsonian Institution in Washington. I am a professor of palaeontology.'

'Skip it,' snapped Keeler. 'The Smithsonian is a long, long way away. I'm in a hurry. This . . .' Keeler switched the gunsight from Gressitt's chest to his head, '. . . is an excellent means of short-circuiting long-distance communication.'

Outwardly, Gressitt remained relaxed. His voice was edged with sarcasm. He nodded at the gun. 'For a so-called agate salesman gum-shoeing around in the middle of the night, you don't do badly, John.' His voice became abrasive. 'What sort of agates do *you* expect to find in a consignment of copper ore, Keeler? Sneaking about like a heat-packer with a Browning and laying a guard out cold!'

'The fact that you can identify my gun puts the spot on you further, Gressitt – or is this kind of hardware part of your palaeontology curriculum at the Smithsonian?'

'You are phony, Keeler,' Gressitt fired back. 'You're not in agates. The company you claim to represent – Agate Enterprises – is a dummy. It does not exist. Your Hong Kong address likewise is a phony.'

Keeler felt himself go as cold inside as the fog seeping through the broken windows and doorway. Had Gressitt, he asked himself, managed to break his cover? More significant, and if so, how had he managed to do so in only one day? Hong Kong is on the other side of the world from Oranjemund. It presupposed – and the thought made Keeler doubly wary and suspicious of the man in front of him – that Gressitt had access to an ultra-fast means of communication and an organization capable of checking out facts anywhere within hours. The cover had sounded so safe, so unbreakable, when it had been hatched up at FERRET's Hong Kong headquarters.

Keeler's cover was, in fact, Agate Enterprises Ltd., Victoria Gardens, Hong Kong. As an executive of that company he was visiting Oranjemund to explore the possibilities of buying agates for the Far East market. These are to be found in conjunction with diamonds, but were not regarded by the only diamond company which operates the entire Namib fields, Consolidated Diamond Mines, as having much market value by comparison with diamonds. FERRET had expanded his field of activity by providing him with the further task of visiting Namibia to buy rhino horn, available through culling in the Namibian game reserves in the far north. Rhino horn, a valuable commodity in the Far East, has for centuries been regarded as an aphrodisiac. It is literally worth more than gold.

FERRET was an underworld nickname for FERIT – Far Eastern Regional Investigation Team. It was a grudging tribute to the crimes the organization had dug up from holes as murky as any which involve big money and low characters. FERRET's Hong Kong headquarters were not listed in the Hong Kong telephone directory; nor would you find a FERRET accreditation to Interpol, or to the International Association of Airport and Seaport Police; nor, closer to home, to the Commercial Crimes Bureau of the Hong Kong Police. Yet all these powerful forces of the law had drawn on a crime data bank which Keeler himself had helped to establish, and followed up missions which FERRET operatives had trail-blazed – where the price of failure was a knife in the back or a corpse floating in a sleazy backwater of some Middle East or West African port.

FERRET had been established some five years before Keeler's present mission to Oranjemund, in an attempt to smash a new marine-fraud racket which consisted in some unscrupulous ship-owners staging fake shipwrecks in order to claim insurance. The stake was worth it – up to the time Keeler had joined FERRET, some 65 million dollars' worth of highly profitable cargo had simply vanished.

The method used was as follows: a ship carrying high-value cargo would leave port on its lawful occasions and then be reported lost on the high seas by its owners. Keeler had traced the fraud pipeline through obscure ports of the Eastern Mediterranean (a favourite haunt was war-torn Lebanon) to West Africa. Once under way, the ship in question would change its name, paint-job and port of origin time and time again, as well as its crews. And while the owners would claim it as 'lost', the ship with its cargo intact would finally reappear at some remote port, and a handsome profit would result.

FERRET had been established originally by a group of marine insurance associations in the Far East, based in Hong

Kong, who had become increasingly worried about their soaring claims. Western insurers inevitably became involved. So did Keeler – at FERRET's own invitation. His legal background at the Admiralty in London had been a recommendation. But it wasn't the legal experience of the 34-year-old Canadian that FERRET wanted; it was that of a clever, tough, strong-arm operative who would go in and literally ferret out the facts about missing ships from rotting ships' holds, from waterfront dives and brothels, or grim dockland warehouses in which might be salted away anything from Hueys to micro-chips.

The razor-edge type of life suited Keeler's temperament. Unmarried, with no ties, he had become FERRET's Number One operative. By establishing a unique computerized data bank he had put the finger on a number of small, independent syndicates who had been inter-changing the latest 'ringing' techniques. Keeler had also worked out a computer system which had uncovered a definite pattern in the type of loss for which insurance was claimed: an alleged sinking in deep water involving old ships with relatively modest hull values but carrying high-value cargoes; no loss of life amongst the crew; often in weather which Keeler established later to have been fair. With these ingredients, FERRET could practically smell the stink as the claim envelope was opened.

FERRET and Keeler considered they had the 'ringing' racket taped; they knew how and where to look, and what to look for.

Then, the racket had taken on a different and more dangerous character. Lengthy investigation of so-called facts presented in shipowners' claims revealed that small syndicates had given way to a single, high-powered outfit. This outfit had brains, ruthlessness and, above all, money.

At the same time the focus of the racket had switched away from its previous happy hunting grounds in the Far East to the Middle East and West Africa, the critical area being pinpointed at the mouth of the Orange River, off the coast of

Namibia. The dreaded Sperrgebiet, or Forbidden Diamond Coast.

Several big ships sailing under tow down the Diamond Coast had gone missing and their owners had alleged that the tugs had been obliged to cut their tows in the Sperrgebiet's wild waters.

FERRET had now set a trap. And Keeler was sent to spring it. A tanker of about 50,000 tons was on tow from West Africa to breakers in the Far East. She was the *Rigel Star*; the tug was the japanese *Sumarai Maru*. The tanker typified the type of vessel which had gone missing in previous cases off the Orange River mouth. Keeler's job was to find out the mastermind behind the racket. Although the *Rigel Star* was under tow, FERRET believed her engines to be still sound, and that they would be used for the getaway once the tow had been cut. The *Sumarai Maru* was scheduled to refuel at Walvis Bay, the major Namibian port some 900 kilometres north of the Orange mouth, for the tough haul round the Cape of Storms.

A 12,000-kilometre flight from Hong Kong via Cape Town had brought Keeler to his target area. FERRET had given him complete freedom to act as he judged fit.

It wasn't FERRET's computer which had brought him face to face with Gressitt tonight. It was Keeler's own sudden hunch to case the copper ore barge-train. The pay-off might be sitting in front of him. Despite Gressitt having blown his cover, Keeler believed he had landed his first hard clue – apart from the kayaks.

3

Kayaks are as Canadian as a maple leaf, though the word kayak itself is Eskimo. Keeler could not remember the time when he had not paddled his own canoe. The type of craft he had found aboard the barge owed its origins to the skin-covered, decked-in kayaks used by the Eskimo off the coast of Canada and in the Arctic. Keeler drew a clear distinction between a kayak and a canoe which was the open river and lake craft, traditionally used in Canada and the USA and propelled by a single-bladed paddle. The kayak was bigger, decked, intended for ocean use, and driven by a double-bladed paddle. It also had a steadying fin or skeg at the rear.

The two kayaks aboard the barge were of the latest fibre-glass construction. Their toughness and length – slightly under 5½ metres, decked, with double cockpits – would enable them to face the wild seas of the Sperrgebiet.

Two days before his present confrontation with Gressitt, Keeler had been flying north from Cape Town to Oran-jemund in a Piper Chieftain. In the seat next to him there was a deeply tanned man. He had obviously been exposed to the sun for a long time and the process seemed also to have cauterized his wispy beard. He guessed him to be about five years younger than himself, in his late twenties. Keeler had been immersed in his newspaper, when suddenly the plane had dropped like a stone in an air pocket and had thrown passengers and hand luggage in a heap.

Keeler had found himself on the floor of the gangway; there was a smell of perfume, and a brush of soft tawny hair blocked his view. He guessed it must be the pretty woman passenger he had been sitting across the aisle from. She had pushed herself into a sitting position; Keeler had looked into a pair of grey-blue eyes. The fear had not quite gone out of them, but it had been overtaken by laughter at their abandoned posture.

'That's one way of getting introduced,' she had remarked breathlessly.

She had got up and back to her seat; Keeler had been left to pick up his newspaper and could not help but recognize the picture of the man on the page where it had fallen open. It was his sunburned fellow-passenger. There was an accompanying interview with Peter Herington who, the article said, had just completed a 1,600-kilometre marathon journey by kayak, the entire length of the Orange River from source to mouth, a record-breaking achievement.

When the passengers had sorted themselves out, Keeler had shown the newspaper to Herington. Kayaking had been an immediate bond; they both took to one another right away. Keeler had admired Herington's courage and determination in accomplishing the notable journey. Herington had received a festive welcome on its completion at Oranjemund by the 3,000 inhabitants. The great two-kilometre long Oppenheimer bridge, a landmark near the river mouth, had been lined with well-wishers as Herington had paddled past.

That finish, Herington had confided to Keeler as the plane continued north, had been on a paddle and a prayer. About 90 kilometres upriver from the bridge, Herington had damaged his kayak's bow by hitting a rock in some rapids. Keeler had noticed Herington's guarded reticence about the incident.

With the help of an American professor of palaeontology named Ross Gressitt who happened to be camped at a riverside dinosaur site about halfway between the rapids and the finishing line, he had managed emergency repairs. Herington was enthusiastic about Gressitt who was now

23

camped with him near Oranjemund itself on the river and would be meeting the 'plane. Herington went on to say that he had flown to Cape Town to buy supplies of fibreglass mat, resin, and other materials to repair the kayak's bow.

Suddenly, Keeler's interest had switched to self-interest. He had flown to Cape Town with no fixed plan of campaign as to how he would – or could – intercept the *Rigel Star* and her tug off the Orange River mouth. Now – the kayak! It would be the ideal craft for the job – swift, silent, so low as to be almost undetectable in a seaway.

Keeler had offered to assist Herington repair his damaged kayak. He was well versed in such operations. Herington had then invited him to join him and Gressitt at the camp. Keeler had readily accepted.

Then – the first cloud of suspicion had crossed Keeler's mind. Herington had confided that he was in a big hurry to get the kayak seaworthy. He then swore Keeler to secrecy about his reasons for haste. His marathon trip had been only the first leg of a still more ambitious one, a hazardous sea journey by kayak from the Orange River mouth to the small Namibian port of Lüderitz, about 300 kilometres along the length of the Sperrgebiet coast. It had only once been attempted before – by the German pioneer of Namibia, Adolf Lüderitz, who had founded the port of the same name nearly a century before. Lüderitz, Herington had informed Keeler, had attempted the trip in a primitive canvas canoe, complete with mast and sail. After putting to sea from the Orange River in a rising gale, he had never been heard of again.

Why the secrecy? Keeler had asked.

Because the territorial waters of the Sperrgebiet, like the diamond territory itself, are out of bounds, Herington had explained. Consolidated Diamond Mines operated a tight and extensive system of security. In enforcing this, CDM (as it was popularly known) flew plane and helicopter patrols daily over the diamond territory, patrolled the desert wastes by Landrover and on foot, checked and rechecked every entry and exit, and backed it all by a highly efficient network of secret radio communication posts, scattered along the coast and hidden in the desert. There was a total ban on landing on the 300-kilometre coastline. Summary arrest of trespassers, followed by stiff fines and/or imprisonment, could be the consequence.

Herington told Keeler that he was prepared to risk all this in the interests of emulating Lüderitz's historic, abortive voyage and attaining his objective. He had made great play of the fact that he wished his going to sea in his repaired kayak to coincide with Lüderitz's starting date. Come hell or high water, he intended to risk the security precautions and be off in five days' time.

Five days! At once Keeler had realized he was on to something.

In approximately five days, the *Rigel Star* and her tug were due off the Orange mouth.

4

'Rhino horn – that's shit for the birds!'

Gressitt's contempt was as penetrating as the cold outside the paneless windows of the ruin. It was three a.m. It would be morning in a few hours' time, Keeler reminded himself, although the light would not come until the fog cleared.

Gressitt, Keeler thought, was mistaking his brief silence for confusion; his thoughts had been with the *Rigel Star* trap and the kayaks.

'You are a phony, Keeler,' Gressitt repeated. 'You acted phony from the moment when you stepped off that plane and pretended not to know of the security regulations requiring you to notify the authorities in advance of your visit and your business in Oranjemund. You lied when you claimed you weren't aware of the lack of hotel accommodation in Oranjemund town. You lied all the way down the road.'

'It used to be different . . .' began Keeler, trying not to reveal too much of his earlier association with Oranjemund.

'Bullshit!' snapped Gressitt. 'You simply latched onto Herington so he could make things easy for you – like a goddam leech. You spent your time at the party tonight chatting up Rill Crous – for the same purpose, I guess. God knows what sort of line you shot her. The only person you haven't conned is me. I was right about you, all the way.'

'So you searched my kit back at camp to find out who I was.'

'Of course.'

Keeler felt he was losing the initiative, despite the fact that the gun was in his hand. He decided to bluff it out.

'Listen – I don't have to answer to you or anyone else,' he snapped. 'The heat's on you. You tell me what you, a so-called professor of palaeontology, were doing aboard that ore barge and perhaps – perhaps – I may clear up some of your queries about myself.'

Gressitt brushed aside Keeler's words brusquely. 'Characters like you have a way of running into trouble in this part of the world,' he said. 'You are right on the boundary-line of the world's richest diamond fields. The company doesn't care for jokers like you on its doorstep, I assure you.'

'At this moment we are on the southern bank of the Orange,' Keeler retorted. 'That means outside the diamond area and CDM's jurisdiction. The Sperrgebiet begins across the river on the northern bank. I have every right to be here, and to do as I wish.'

'True,' he remarked, 'yet I have only to report you to CDM and Major Rive's men will dog your every movement from now on, outside the diamond area or not – it's only within spitting distance!'

Major Rive was head of Security in the Diamond Territory. Keeler had met him. Major Rive had been at Alex Bay airfield to collect some film canisters when the plane had landed with Herington, Rill Crous and Keeler aboard. Major Rive had overheard Gressitt offering Rill a lift to Oranjemund in his Landrover. Since the Gressitt-Herington camp was in the opposite direction, Rill had instead accepted a second lift offer from Major Rive, a short, dapper man with the kind of tan which comes from constant polishing by Oranjemund's wind. He was the only man Keeler had seen so far wearing a suit. Keeler had felt Major Rive's keen probing eyes all over him when he had given out his cover story of being in the agate business. Perhaps one got like that in the diamond game.

Or, Keeler had speculated inwardly, had his ignorance of Oranjemund's changed security checks aroused the suspicions of Major Rive?

27

Major Rive had pointed out politely but firmly that Keeler would not be permitted to enter Oranjemund because he had failed to comply with the advance notification regulations to Security. Even a party of international VIPs now visiting Oranjemund, including six Japanese, had had to comply with this rule.

Oranjemund is totally owned, and was totally designed and built, by the mining company CDM. Everything, from power station to post office, from supermarket to social club, belongs to and is operated by CDM. Oranjemund is also the antithesis of the customary mining town concept. As his plane had come in to land – the runways stretch almost to the Orange River bank – Keeler had caught his breath at the sight of the place where he had spent happy boyhood years. Situated about eight kilometres from the Oppenheimer bridge, Oranjemund is pure suburbia imposed on the face of a pitiless desert. Its blossoms, green gardens, green lawns, flower-lined streets, green trees, parks, are all fed by life-giving water pumped by the mining company from the river. Its tarred, grid-pattern streets with modern overhead lights and traffic islands intersect neat villas, a school and a hospital. Like waves against a sea-wall, the white sand dunes of the Namib lap at the man-made amenities. CDM operates its own security force – there are no police, no military, in Oranjemund. Only Major Rive knew how many men his strength comprised, several hundred was probably not wide of the mark.

Gressitt's point about the security force making a marked man of him was true, Keeler conceded to himself. With Security tailing him, his freedom of movement would be severely restricted. The *Rigel Star* trap would be in danger – Keeler would never be able to carry out his plan to obtain use of Herington's kayak and slip out to sea if the ever-vigilant Rive had the spot on him.

Keeler pointed the Browning between Gressitt's eyes. 'Two can play this little game of yours, Gressitt. You, too, would have a lot of explaining to do if I told Major Rive about your activities tonight. Moreover, I hear there is talk on the Oranjemund grapevine about your overlong stay at the dinosaur site at Blooddrift. If you are what you claim to be, a professor of palaeontology, you could have seen all there was to be seen at the site in a matter of days. The place has been worked out for years – there is nothing left. What is *your* game, Gressitt?'

Keeler's words seemed to strike. Gressitt started to his feet, but Keeler ordered him to keep his seat.

Rill, the party, Oranjemund – all were relegated to memories at the back of Keeler's mind as he tried to browbeat the big American into an admission. The ruined house in the fog looked like a location for a werewolf movie, with the monster about to climb in through one of the shattered windows. It was three a.m.; two tough determined men faced one another across a pistol barrel.

Gressitt, Keeler could see, wasn't afraid of a gun. He would have to change his tactics.

'How does the *Rigel Star* figure in your books, Gressitt?'

If Keeler had expected any reaction in Gressitt's grim face, he was mistaken.

'*Rigel Star?*'

Keeler was watching his man closely. Against his expectations Gressitt's puzzled repetition of the ship's name seemed ingenuous.

Keeler changed tack. 'Yes, *Rigel Star*. Listen, Gressitt, I'll tell you something. You're right, I'm not in the agate business. I am a marine insurance man. The part about Hong Kong as my base is correct. That's where I come from.'

'Marine insurance.' The way he repeated the words could have meant anything – or nothing. 'What have river barges got to do with marine insurance?'

'You tell me.' Keeler made a gesture with the Kapitän. 'You know.'

'I've never heard of the *Rigel Star*,' Gressitt answered. 'Is it a ship?'

'It *is* a ship. It is due off the Orange River mouth tomorrow night. It is going to disappear – I want to know why. I think you can tell me.'

Gressitt's answer was in a completely changed tone. 'I swear I don't, John. If I did, I would tell you, for sure.'

Keeler wasn't going to be conned by the tough-mouthed American. 'Tell me anything – I'll listen.'

There was a pause, then Gressitt said, 'I was also looking for something aboard those barges.'

'You're telling me nothing!' snapped Keeler. 'I found it out for myself. What was that electrical instrument in the one kayak?'

'It is a laser rangefinder – designed for integration into a helicopter sight. French-made. Name of TCV 115.'

'That tells me you are not a professor of palaeontology.'

He shrugged resignedly. 'Okay, I'm not a professor, so what?'

'You're merely supplying me with negative information. I came to that conclusion before.'

There was a tight pause. 'What is that laser sight meant for?' Keeler wanted to know.

'It is a highly sophisticated piece of equipment,' answered Gressitt. 'I can't imagine any use for it in a place like the Namib.'

'That copper-mine boss, Reutemann, has a helicopter,' Keeler pointed out. 'It is no secret that he uses it for ore-carrying.'

'That instrument has no civilian application,' replied Gressitt. 'It is military.'

'Bomb-sight?'

'Yeah, maybe – but it is only part of a gyrostabilized helicopter sight. It couldn't be used by itself.'

'Was this the sort of thing you were hoping to find aboard the barges – professor?' Keeler asked.

'Listen,' said Gressitt. 'Why don't you and I make a deal? You know now that I'm not what I pretend, and the same goes for you.'

Keeler saw in Gressitt's offer the first sign of a break-up of the impasse.

He said warily, 'What kind of a deal?'

'Mind if I smoke?' asked Gressitt. 'That gun in my face makes me nervous.'

'It's meant to,' retorted Keeler.

Gressitt said cautiously. 'My guess is that Reutemann and Trevenna are riding the beam over their ore cargoes.'

'Cover, you mean?'

'Yeah. Playing innocent.'

'Who is Trevenna?'

'Reutemann's Number Two; red-headed guy. Big as an ox.'

'He went down like one.'

There was a note of admiration in Gressitt's response. 'That the guy you laid out?'

'The description fits.'

'You must have hit him mighty hard, that is all I can say.'

'Maybe.'

'Did he see your face? If he did, you're a marked man when he comes round.'

'I can look after myself.'

'I'll say you can!'

'What made you look into those ore cargoes?'

'This is the fourth weekly shipment of Reutemann's that I've checked out. It's clean, like the others. I've double-checked further down the transportation line also. There has been nothing suspicious.'

'You may have been looking right at it and not recognized it.'

'What do you mean?'

'The two kayaks, for example.'

'It's the first time they've been aboard.'

31

Keeler felt for the heavy nodule he had taken from the waterproof bag aboard the second kayak. He balanced the flashlight carefully before holding it out to Gressitt.

'You missed this tonight.'

The way Gressitt took it and made no attempt to grab his pistol made Keeler feel better.

'What is it? – it's goddam heavy.'

'You tell me.'

'Where'd you get it?'

'There was a bagful of them in the kayak you didn't get round to searching. The way it was waterproofed made me think its contents must be valuable.'

Keeler added derisively. 'You say you're a geologist – you should recognize it.'

Gressitt appeared uncomfortable for a moment but recovered quickly. 'Rill's the person to identify it. She's a rock expert and is very smart.'

Keeler deliberately flew a kite. 'Why not rather ask one of CDM's geologists? They have laboratory facilities which Rill has not.'

'No, CDM is out,' replied Gressitt decisively. 'The fewer people know about you and me and the barges tonight, the better.'

'Who *are* you, Gressitt?'

He dodged the question and stared at the nodule. 'This is the first hard clue I've had to back up my suspicions. I think we're at the wrong end of the racket here at the river's mouth. I believe it starts upriver somewhere. Aussenkehr, maybe. Or Fannin's Mine. I mean to find out.'

'It depends what you are looking for – or at.'

'This nodule could be the key for us both. At this stage, we simply don't know. Is high-value, small-size contraband being smuggled downriver? Out to sea? Is that what the *Rigel Star* is all about?'

'The racket I am after involves the disappearance of ships at sea,' replied Keeler. 'Smuggling doesn't enter into it.'

'What does enter into it?'

'Marine insurance fraud. There seem favourite areas of the high seas where the practice erupts. Right now it happens to be the Forbidden Diamond Coast. The *Rigel Star* is a sort of test case.' He did not mention the trap FERRET had laid, or the name FERRET itself.

Keeler considered that if he threw Gressitt enough scraps without revealing the scope of FERRET's operations, he might in return extract more from Gressitt. Gressitt himself was still concentrating on the heavy nodule in his hand as if trying to wring its secret from it.

Keeler said, 'Listen, Gressitt. Even if smuggling is going on – whatever commodity is involved – why should you be interested? You're an American. You're not a customs officer. You're not a South African or a Namibian. What the devil has it to do with you?'

Gressit spoke slowly and gravely as though he was reciting a prepared speech. 'Namibia is the fourth largest mineral producer in Africa, if you except fuel,' he said. 'South Africa has 73 per cent of the world's reserves of the platinum group metals; 68 per cent of its chrome ore reserves; 48 per cent of its gold; 37 per cent of its manganese; 19 per cent of its vanadium . . .'

Keeler broke in impatiently. 'Fine, fine. I can't check your figures, but I accept them. We're dealing with copper ore right now.'

'Are we?' The way Gressitt said it made Keeler reflect. 'Are we? That's just what I want to know. The copper coming downriver from Fannin's Mine is probably the purest in the world – over 80 per cent pure – but what the hell? There's plenty of other copper in other parts of the world. Nor does copper rate fancy transportation methods like a helicopter and hovercraft.'

'What are you implying?'

'Already we in the West rely heavily on Namibia – more so than we care to admit. The world's biggest uranium mine is at Rossing, in the north of the territory near Swakopmund. It produces no less than 5,000 tons of U-308 a year. Close Rossing, and the nuclear power stations of Britain, France and Germany would grind to a halt. In energy terms alone, Rossing's output equals about five hundred million barrels of oil – two-thirds of the world's yearly consumption.'

'Oranjemund is nowhere near Rossing and its uranium.'

Gressitt's voice took on a still more emphatic note. 'No, but we have something bigger – the Richtersveld. The Richtersveld is one huge mineral treasure-house, and it is largely unexplored and unexploited.'

'Except for Fannin's Mine.'

He weighed the nodule in his hand. 'Outsiders can't get to Fannin's, even if they want to. You yourself couldn't get to Aussenkehr, even if you wanted to. They're tight shut to all but Reutemann and Co.'

'Which means you've tried?'

'Yes – and failed. I mean to attempt it again.' He shot the question. 'Why are you so interested in Herington and his kayak?'

'It's the craft I need to check on the *Rigel Star*, fast, low-profiled, almost invisible, and at the same time able to negotiate the sort of seas I can expect at the mouth.'

'For a different purpose I'm also interested in Herington's kayak. To case Aussenkehr.'

A silence fell between the two men. Keeler felt that both had given the other enough rope to hang him by.

Then Gressitt said quietly, 'Listen, John. I think our interests converge, although our objectives remain different.'

'If that's a market bid, I'm passing.'

'Meaning?'

'You're a convincing talker, Gressitt. Unless you tell me more, I'm not buying.'

Gressitt got up and paced the ruined room as if the place were too small for him. Keeler no longer tried to stop him.

Then he faced Keeler. 'We are at war, John, and in war it is a good thing to sort out your friends from your enemies.'

'War?' echoed Keeler puzzled. 'What war?'

'A silent war, the sort that leads to a shooting war. The Richtersveld is our battlefield.'

'What the hell are you talking about?'

'This war is one in which the material pre-empts the weaponry,' he went on animatedly. 'It is called the Resources War. The term was coined by the former US Secretary for State, Alexander Haig. He should know – he commanded NATO once.'

'Go on,' Keeler answered. 'I still haven't bought your story – Richtersveld battlefield?'

Gressitt nodded. 'As modern weapons become more sophisticated, so the demand grows for more of the hard-to-get metals.'

'That's just a generalization, a media cliché. It doesn't explain what you're doing here.'

Gressitt emphasized every word of his answer. 'The focal point of the Resources War between West and East, between the United States and the Soviet Block, is Namibia and South Africa. Plus the Richtersveld. Geologically, if not politically at any rate, the Richtersveld is part of Namibia.'

'I get it!' exclaimed Keeler. 'You're CIA!'

'No, not CIA, which catches all the blame for America's foreign policy sins,' he answered. 'I'll tell you, if you have to know, for the sake of my bona fides. But I warn you, the knowledge will not make your own life any safer.'

Keeler shrugged. 'I'll take that chance.'

'Okay,' Gressitt replied. 'Here, I'll spell it out for you. When Carter moved out of the White House, the National Security Agency decided that the time was overdue for America to do something positive about securing long-term supplies of strategic materials to ensure arms supremacy for the USA.'

'National Security Agency?' asked Keeler. 'Is that a branch of the CIA?'

For the first time, Gressitt grinned slightly. 'Don't let NSA hear you say that! The CIA has always enjoyed the limelight and the publicity, but NSA was in existence a long time before it. It has done the job as such a job should be done – in secret, away from the spotlight of the media or the glamour build-up the CIA enjoyed. NSA is, simply, America's top ultra-secret security agency.

'Now – within this super-secret organization, the Reagan Administration set up a still more secret outfit. They gave it a name which would delight any Washington bureaucrat – Southern Africa Minerals Exploitation. SAMEX for short.'

'I wouldn't have thought you could keep SAMEX secret for long in a place like Washington.'

'Our headquarters are not actually in Washington itself but nearby – at Fort Meade, about 20 kilometres away. Even in Fort Meade, no one knows of SAMEX's existence. Our brief is simple – SAMEX will buy, bludgeon or bully any nation or individual who has minerals vital to American weaponry into supplying them. We are easy in what we use – the dollar or the deringer, whichever is best suited to the particular case. SAMEX became interested – interested only but not involved – when Reutemann started using fancy equipment such as a helicopter and hovercraft. Clearly he was super-capitalized. However, it was the discovery a couple of months ago by a SAMEX agent of a laser cutter en route to Aussenkehr – and presumably onward-bound for Fannin's Mine – that alerted us. That put the clincher on our earlier suspicions. I got here as quickly as I could and used Blooddrift as my cover. The rest you know.'

Keeler in his concentration on what Gressitt was saying neglected the oldest rule in the book – never allow the enemy to come close. He'd already relaxed by allowing him to pace.

Gressitt's strike was so swift that Keeler scarcely realized that the Browning had been snatched out of his hand and he himself was looking into the barrel.

Gressitt said, 'I forgot to mention, SAMEX is a para-military body. Meet Colonel Ross Gressitt, if you want my full handle.' He went on menacingly. 'I've been doing all the talking up to now, Keeler. Now you do some.'

'If I don't?'

'If I killed you now, who would know? You are without friends, contacts or credentials. I could push your body into the river. Trevenna, not me, would have to do the explaining.'

'You bastard, Gressitt.'

'At least my Smithsonian cover wasn't as phony as your agates and rhino horn,' he jeered.

'It was very smart, breaking my cover so quickly,' Keeler said. 'I didn't realise SAMEX was behind you, of course.'

Gressitt laughed, but he was very wary. 'There's a powerful radio in one of my Landrover's lockers,' he said. 'You practically sat on top of it when you borrowed the Landy to go to Alex Bay. Every day I make a fixed time report to SAMEX headquarters in Namibia. Our operatives have naturally infiltrated the territory – I am the field boss. It took Fort Meade only a couple of hours to check you out once they had my request.'

'What I said about marine insurance fraud is kosher,' said Keeler. 'My outfit also has a name. FERRET . . .' He outlined briefly the *Rigel Star* trap, the deadline, the urgent need for him personally to investigate what was going on off the coast.

When Keeler had finished, Gressitt reversed his grip on the Kapitän and handed it back to Keeler by the barrel.

'We both have too much to lose by not working together,' he said. 'I help you with the *Rigel Star*, you help me with Aussenkehr? It's a deal?'

Gressitt's grip was like iron. 'Fine,' replied Keeler, 'that makes two of us. But it still doesn't account for Herington.'

37

Gressitt eyed Keeler narrowly. 'What do you know about Herington?'

'Come hell or high water, Herington is determined to put to sea tomorrow night,' Keeler replied. 'The reason he gives is that he wants his trip to coincide with the day his hero Lüderitz made the same journey in a primitive canoe nearly a hundred years ago.'

'He didn't tell me all this,' remarked Gressitt. 'I only know he is in a big hurry.'

'He brought special resin accelerator from Cape Town so that the fibreglass patches would set fast, in time for his deadline. He's as edgy as hell. He's deliberately steered clear of CDM because the coast is strictly out of bounds. His deadline happens to coincide with the *Rigel Star*'s arrival date.'

'Your requirements and Herington's over the use of his kayak seem to clash,' Gressitt observed.

'I hoped to persuade Herington that the *Rigel Star* is the more urgent.' Keeler laughed without humour. 'The use of force is not unknown in FERRET either, Ross.'

'I believe you, fellah.'

'I mean to find out what is going on off that coast,' repeated Keeler. 'It also seems to me very significant that Herington's kayak and two others belonging to Reutemann should all arrive more or less together – all three sea-going craft. Note also, Herington was apparently allowed through Reutemann's security net at Aussenkehr.'

'He couldn't have faked the river marathon,' said Gressitt.

'No, but it could have provided excellent cover. Did SAMEX check him out also, Ross?'

'Never thought he wasn't 24-carat,' replied Gressitt.

'Look here, Ross – you need Herington's kayak to scout Aussenkehr and I need it to scout the coast when the *Rigel Star* arrives,' Keeler said. 'FERRET's man in Lüderitz has orders to monitor the ship and its tow as it passes the port. It is three hundred kilometres from there to the Orange River mouth – we can work out a fairly precise ETA once we know that,' Keeler eyed Gressitt. 'You seem to be concentrating on Aussenkehr – why? If your suspicions are correct, Reutemann's secret originates not there but at Fannin's Mine.'

'Sure,' replied Gressitt. 'You don't think I would have sat on my ass at Blooddrift for a month if I'd been able to get to Fannin's Mine?'

'Why not?'

Gressitt laughed. 'The entire Richtersveld is state land. There is not a road, not a track, through those godawful mountains. The nearest approach to one is a jeep track which leads from the river to the base of the escarpment. There it ends. I *know*.'

'You could fly.'

Gressitt answered half ruefully, half in admiration. 'This guy Reutemann's got his security wrapped up in a way you can't believe. There is a total ban on overflying the Richtersveld. The authorities imposed it many years back. The reason for it is simple: if a plane crashed in those mountains, the search-rescue effort involved would be colossal – and dangerous. An overflying ban is the simpler solution – there's hardly a human being in the territory, anyway. So Fannin's Mine is included in the overflying ban.'

'Yet Reutemann ferries his copper ore from Fannin's to Aussenkehr by helicopter.'

'When he reopened Fannin's and the authorities noted the high value of the copper involved, they granted him a special dispensation. He is permitted to fly along an air corridor above the Throughway.'

'Why not use that route yourself?'

'The permission is for the ore helicopter only. Other aircraft are banned. Again, I *know*. I tried.'

'I suppose then you attempted by legal means to have a sight of Aussenkehr from the air?'

Gressitt snorted. 'From two thousand metres up – yeah. What did I see? A building on a cliff through a dust haze. A few lorries and a jetty in the river at the base of the cliff. A space next to the fort could have been a helipad, but I was too high to make out details. The trip told me nothing of what I really want to know. I need to case the place on my own tugboats.'

'Tugboats?'

'Feet to you – and kayak!' grinned Gressitt.

'*We must have Herington's kayak!*' exclaimed Keeler.

'Let's go ask him.'

'Here's your persuader.'

Keeler handed Gressitt back his paratrooper's knife which he had retained during the short time Gressitt had held the pistol on him. He kept the Browning free in his belt.

5

When Keeler had first spotted the string of barges coming down the river the previous day, he had never seen anything like it, and did not yet connect these river craft with the legendary Copper Mountain and Fannin's Mine. In the days of his boyhood in Oranjemund there had been little talk about it, perhaps because no one had ventured near the place since the German days before World War I. It was Gressitt who later held forth about the legend on Keeler's first night round the camp fire. He had been surprised that Gressitt, an American, should be so familiar with an obscure story that had taken place a century and a half ago in this equally obscure part of the world.

According to Gressitt, the British explorer Sir James Alexander had made his way upriver from the Orange mouth in 1838. At a place called Arrisdrift, some 30 kilometres upstream, Sir James had met an old coloured man who had set the Copper Mountain legend in motion when he had shown the explorer some samples of copper ore. When later assayed, they had turned out to be very rich indeed.

The legend snowballed when Sir James returned to England and wrote in a book on his travels that there was a mountain of pure copper deep in the heart of the wild Richtersveld mountains. The story led to a mining company being formed and a man named Thomas Fannin made his way into the Richtersveld and claimed to have found the site. Fannin started to mine the copper ore, which was indeed very rich. However, the remoteness of the area and insuperable transport problems had killed the venture. Fannin's

Mine folded up after about a year. Fannin killed hundreds of oxen trying to move ore across the mountains to the Orange River, from where he floated it downriver on barges and rafts to its mouth. These were more frequently grounded on the sandbanks and islands than afloat during the course of the river journey.

The present barge-train's link with the legend was brought home next day to Keeler a few hours after Gressitt's campfire story. He had been in Gressitt's Landrover on the river road when suddenly the air had been filled with the noise of an aircraft.

It wasn't an aircraft, however. It was a hovercraft.

A hovercraft was acting as tug to a string of five copper ore barges. Ostrich-plumes of creamy chocolate water were being thrown up in every direction as the pilot sheepdogged the barges into the main inshore channel of the jetty. Keeler had been fascinated. The end of Gressitt's recital of the Copper Mountain story had told of Fannin's Mine being reopened by a concern headed by a German named Reutemann. Reutemann, Gressitt had said, had licked the deadly cross-mountain haul of the ore by using a heavy-duty helicopter as a ferry. Space-age technology was succeeding where Fannin had failed.

Gressitt's story and the sight of the barge-train led by its hovercraft tug had provoked Keeler's hunch. He had decided to case the barges after the Oranjemund party that night.

It was at seven thirty p.m. when Keeler, Gressitt and Herington walked into the crowded foyer of the Social Club, entertainment heart of the diamond town, for a gathering in honour of the group of visiting international diamond VIPs – American, Dutch, British, Belgian, Swiss, French and Japanese.

Rill came forward and held out her hand. 'Welcome!'

Keeler could hardly believe the change in Rill. That morning when she had intercepted him on his way to telephone the FERRET sub-agent in Cape Town for news of the *Rigel Star*'s progress, Rill had appeared a boyish figure in jeans, red polo-necked sweater, crumpled blue windcheater, floppy blue cricketer's hat, and dark glasses. She had flagged down his Landrover and invited the three men camped on the river bank to the party. Keeler had immediately raised the question of his entrance to Oranjemund – Gressitt and Herington had Security clearance. Rill had flushed and dismissed the problem by saying she had vouched for him with Major Rive. It gave Keeler a pleasant feeling towards her. Now at the party Rill wore a low-cut full-length green dress which offset the beauty of her Titian-tawny hair, turning her into a beautiful, desirable woman.

Keeler relaxed. He had been keyed up at the prospect of his foray into the barge-train. He had decided to carry out his cloak-and-dagger operation after midnight when the fog would be thickest. He planned to slip away from camp after he was satisfied that Gressitt and Herington were asleep, and make his way along the river bank to the jetty.

Keeler was returning to the place of his boyhood, a place where he had been happy. Gressitt drove his Landrover across the Oppenheimer bridge, the only one spanning the river for hundreds of kilometres. They drove past the tree windbreaks guarding the town and down its famous avenue of wild olives, along the main thoroughfare. Behind hibiscus hedges and showers of yellow Spanish broom were the comfortable suburban villas and lawns fronted onto streets lit by overhead lighting, grass verges and traffic islands ablaze with roses and petunias. The children's play-parks and so-green sports fields, watered by non-stop pumping from the river, added a further dimension of contrast with the sterile desert sand so close by. It was all as Keeler remembered it – a symbol of enduring serenity and pleasure.

Keeler had noted a certain nervousness in Herington and Gressitt. It seemed to him that since the arrival of the barge-train Herington had intensified his efforts to repair his kayak. Keeler felt he was getting in his way when he snappishly told him there weren't enough old clothes and gloves to cope with the messy resin, fibreglass and remoulding. Finally, he had left Herington alone. Gressitt had gone off for a couple of hours in his Landrover; on his return there was a certain coolness, calculation even, in his attitude towards Keeler.

But Rill's smile had dispelled Keeler's tense, thoughtful mood. 'Come and have a drink at the bar, all three of you. You look like you need one.'

The Social Club was another part of Oranjemund that had not changed for Keeler either, except that it had been refurbished. The long curving bar near the main entrance was the same, and so was the reception area beyond, thick with people and drinks and tobacco smoke.

Keeler turned to Rill and said, 'I thought you said it was casual. Look at that crowd and all those dressed-up VIPs.'

Keeler himself had worn the special dark jerkin he usually wore 'for the job', with its double slits at the sides for easy gun-reach, and a built-in knife-sheath.

Rill laughed and brought Gressitt and Herington into her warmth in a way which thawed the reserved mood Herington also was in.

'You're wrong, John – the evening's top VIPs are right here with me. A marathon kayaker and a dinosaur expert from the Smithsonian.'

No VIP rating for Keeler. Yet, Rill's attraction to Keeler had been evident in that she had come looking for him that morning to invite him to the party. This had made him feel good – plus a little guilty for what he planned after the party.

'Go on massaging my ego, honey!' grinned Gressitt. 'For another fossil-hunter like me, you sure have a social technique!'

Keeler found it more difficult than ever to credit what Gressitt had told him during their drive from the airfield, that Rill was a palaeontologist busy excavating at a dig near

44

Arrisdrift – the place where the Copper Mountain legend had originated, and which was inside the Forbidden Diamond Territory. Arrisdrift, Gressitt had emphasized, was completely unlike his own dinosaur site further upriver. Rill, he had added, lived in Oranjemund with the blessing of CDM and commuted daily the 30-odd kilometres to Arrisdrift.

The drinks came and Keeler drowned his whisky with water. He disliked drinking on an assignment.

The move was not lost on Gressitt. He said lightly to Rill: 'Don't understand this guy, Rill. You had better watch out. One moment he's drinking it straight out of the bottle – my bottle – and the next he's killing good Scotch stone dead.'

Rill had a rock shandy and Herington timidly lurked behind a beer.

However, a plump little woman swooped down on the four of them with a smile as wide as her girdle. Rill introduced her as the chairwoman of the women's committee organizing the party. She swept Herington and Gressitt away. 'Celebrities! Celebrities!'

Keeler was grateful that his low social rating left him alone with Rill.

She said ruefully, 'Sorry, but she's near the top of the pecking order in Oranjemund, along with the General Manager and Chief of Security.'

Keeler had held back to everyone about his early association with Oranjemund. Now, it seemed irrelevant to do so with Rill.

'Still the same as it ever was.'

'As it ever was?' Rill echoed in surprise.

Keeler took a small sip of the whisky.

'The social ladder used to drive my father screaming into the desert.'

'You mean to say, you've been in Oranjemund before?'

'Yes – as a boy. Coming here tonight was like coming back home. Something special. Oranjemund has always rated plus with me. I grew up here. It was my father's longest job-hopping stop. He started off as a mining engineer in a Canadian nickel mine. He had the wanderlust all right. We trekked all over the world, from Namibia to Nigeria, from South America to Siberia. However, nowhere had the same meaning as Oranjemund.'

Rill leaned forward and spontaneously touched Keeler's arm innocently revealing the exciting plunge of her breasts under the thin material. Her steady grey-blue eyes were warm. 'I'm glad – so glad. That makes two of us.'

Their eyes locked. They exchanged something neither of them understood. There was a small pause, the prelude to two people having too much, rather than too little, to say to one another.

Then Keeler went on. 'I thought you came from Cape Town and that your job here was merely an interlude.'

'I've been here eighteen months,' she replied. 'I love it.'

'You are less like my preconceived idea of a fossil-hunter than it is possible to imagine.'

Rill laughed. 'What was your mental picture?'

'Skin burned like leather, to start with . . . and older. There must be something more compelling to keep you here than your fossils, Rill.'

'I've tried to explain to myself why I stay,' she interrupted. 'When I was in Cape Town a few days ago I continued to wonder. My friends say I am crazy to bury myself in an unknown dump in the desert while the years whizz by . . .'

'I see the grey hairs quite clearly,' Keeler quipped. 'You must be every bit of 25.'

'Not a bad guess – 24,' she smiled back. 'My friends regard Oranjemund as a prison.'

'There is no barbed wire. The restrictions are far easier than they used to be.'

'No physical wire, of course. But the sense of confinement is always present. I would hate to have to undergo the old security checks twice a day on my way to and from Arrisdrift.'

46

'You really seem to have made a notable find there, Rill, from what Gressitt says.'

'Gressitt . . .' Suddenly there was a quick, abstracted intensity about her, leaving her face with a kind of inscrutability, the reflection of mental reserve about the American. Then she replied incisively. 'There is no comparison between Arrisdrift and Ross Gressitt's dinosaur site at Blooddrift. Dinosaur sites are common throughout the world – there are others not so far away in northern Namibia. Arrisdrift is far younger by comparison – it's only fourteen to eighteen million years, whereas Blooddrift is about sixty-five million. Blooddrift dates from the time the dinosaurs vanished abruptly from the face of the earth.'

Keeler looked into her eyes and wondered how they would soften under passion. 'I'm more interested in what makes someone like you spend time searching for old bones.'

'I wasn't involved in the original Arrisdrift discovery which shook the scientific world in 1976 when bones were spotted in a prospecting pit near the river bank,' said Rill. 'At least twenty-seven extinct types of creatures, some of them never recorded before in southern Africa, have been taken from that one small pit. Two of the most exciting finds were true bears and bear-dogs, which were animals with the characteristics of both bears and dogs. These had become extinct south of the Sahara millions of years ago. There was also a creature from which evolved the true elephant of modern times.

'Two years after the first strike, the main excavation had been completed and material sent off to Cape Town for cleaning and identification. That is the stage at which I came in. I was a student at the time. There are still more fossils deeper down at Arrisdrift, but they're embedded in a concrete-like matrix and very hard to get at. That – and the geology of Arrisdrift – are my interests.'

'Geology?'

Rill flushed and shook her head diffidently so that her fine hair partly obscured her face. 'I'm a geologist also. Anyway, Arrisdrift caused a sensation because it provided the sole source of fossil material of that particular period of antiquity in southern Africa.'

'And so you go on living the life of fourteen million years ago, commuting daily, checking, digging?'

Even as he said it, Keeler realised that he had put too much inference into his remark. Rill turned away and flushed again.

'There's a saying in Oranjemund, if you have an ugly sister, send her to Oranjemund and we'll marry her off within six weeks. It's a male-orientated society, is Oranjemund, except for the wives. Males outnumber females by five to one.'

'You've survived eighteen months,' Keeler went on gently. 'Tell me what keeps you here, Rill.'

She turned to him and said with surprising vehemence, 'How many years is it since you have been in Oranjemund, John?'

'Could be twenty. A lifetime.'

'And you've come back!'

Keeler went on. 'Do the gemsbok and the jackals still come into the streets at night in the fog?'

She stared at him for a long moment. He knew he had been without a woman – a proper woman – for too long. The bustle and chatter round the bar was as remote as Piccadilly Circus.

'I was prepared for a let-down tonight,' she said. 'I felt that after rushing out and inviting a stranger, that all I'd get was small-talk and a salesman's jokes, a slick chatting-up.'

Don't get conned into making confessions to a pretty face, Keeler. FERRET is your business here. Don't you forget that, Keeler reminded himself.

'What have you found?'

'I'm trying to make up my mind. The last thing I would have expected, is to discover that you have an understanding of the mystique of the Namib.'

There was another pause in the conversation, positive, not negative. Then Keeler said, 'You haven't yet answered my question, Rill. Do the gemsbok still come into the streets at night?'

She looked at her watch and answered a trifle shyly. 'It's too early still, but we can go together later and see, if you wish.'

'I wish,' replied Keeler.

Rill got up from the bar.

'Let's go through and dance meanwhile, shall we?'

6

They danced. In the desexualized romp which goes by that name, Rill came close and Keeler could feel the softness of her body against his. As they moved round the big room, Keeler noticed a dozen or more men and women in a group. Herington amongst them, looking like a Rugby scrumhalf, desperately looking for an escape route on the blind side. Rill smiled at Keeler's unspoken comment.

Among the VIPs were six black-suited Japanese. They attracted Keeler's attention not because they were Orientals – he was accustomed to them and had not the Westerner's usual inability to distinguish individuals – but because of their marionette-like pose. All six had uniform smiles stencilled on their faces, their gestures were as synchronized as a corps de ballet, and their curious stillness was equally stylized.

'Those are Japanese engineers who have come to study CDM's diamond extraction processes,' explained Rill. 'The method has been evolved at Oranjemund – there is nothing like it anywhere else in the world, I'm told.'

'And who are those other visiting firemen?'

'They – and the Japanese – are what tonight is all about,' she answered. 'Tycoons, every man of them – American, British, Belgian, Dutch, French, German, Swiss. There is enough money among them to rock the world's diamond markets, if they cared to, which they don't. Would you like to be introduced? I can arrange it.'

'Me? What could I find to say to *them*?'

A faint smile pulled down the corners of her generous mouth. She stopped dancing and stared at Keeler. She gave a shiver. 'Let's go and have another drink, shall we?'

Keeler and Rill did not get as far as the bar. They were intercepted by Major Rive, the Security chief. There was no reason. Why, Keeler thought quickly, should the top man on the totem pole in Oranjemund want to engage an agate salesman in conversation? The thought made him cautious – and apprehensive. So did Major Rive's steel-blue eyes. Here was the spider at the centre of the invisible security web which could vibrate, if threatened, from a corner of the vast territory under his control. His super-efficient civilian organization made a police presence redundant in the Sperrgebiet; the confidence with which governmental authorities viewed his activities – despite an international boundary – was reflected in the fact that the nearest military bases were hundreds of kilometres away to the south and east.

'How are the agate sales prospects shaping?' asked Major Rive suavely.

Keeler replied with forced, cheerful bonhomie. 'I'll get down to business when I've got over my jet lag and I've finished helping Herington with his kayak.'

'How long will that take?'

'Four – maybe five, days,' Keeler lied.

'Herington should have taken up CDM's offer – he could have worked much better and quicker in our workshops.'

'That is what I told him.'

Major Rive didn't expect that; before he could pursue the matter Rill intervened.

'I've invited John to come and see the dig at Arrisdrift tomorrow,' she said. 'Is that okay with Security?'

It was the first Keeler had heard of it; he realized that Rill was protecting him from Major Rive's probing.

'If you vouch for him – again,' replied Major Rive blandly. The way he smiled at her made Keeler realize that she held a special place in his affections. But the mailed fist in the velvet glove was visible in his next words. 'But I'm afraid he'll have to check through Security inside the diamond area both on his way to Arrisdrift and on the return trip.' Keeler felt the

Security chief's eyes boring through him like X-rays. 'Is that clear?'

Major Rive's next words showed that he did not intend being sidetracked entirely from his purpose in intercepting them.

'CDM's agate expert is somewhere here tonight, Mr. Keeler, you should meet him. But if you are to be with us tomorrow, there will be time enough.'

It was a tight little trap; Keeler could see no way out but to be gracious about it. 'I'd like that.'

Major Rive went on. 'There are some other guests I would like you to meet – our Japanese friends.'

'I know nothing about diamonds,' Keeler stalled.

As he replied, Keeler glanced automatically at the Japanese group. It was not on them, however, that his attention fixed. It was on a hard-looking man of medium height standing apart from the Japanese and yet, by some association he could not define, he seemed to belong with them, although he was not conversing with them. He had a peculiar air of controlled power as if his reactions were being held in check. He sucked at a corncob pipe which served to enhance his brooding air. The sun-tanned face with its prominent nose, tough chin and powerful line-structure resembled a gothic figure on a painting looking out, unperturbed and with relish on a scene of men being drawn and quartered.

Major Rive ushered Keeler towards the Japanese.

'Diamonds don't matter – perhaps coming from Hong Kong as you do, it may help them to feel a little more at home, if you see what I mean?'

Keeler did not. The men's response in stilted English was reserved and puppet-like. He wanted to pitch a rude Chinese word amongst the politeness and see how they would react as humans – if indeed they understood it. As it was, he passed down the line with a grin on his face as stereotyped as theirs.

Major Rive passed on from the Japanese to the man with the corncob pipe. He had shown no awareness of having heard the exchanges with the Japanese but subjected Keeler to a penetrating look.

'Ah, Dr Reutemann,' said Major Rive. 'I'd like you to meet Mr John Keeler from Hong Kong – I think you already know Miss Crous.' Rill nodded, said nothing.

'Hong Kong?' Reutemann's interest was as perfunctory as his handshake. The hand was square, hard and calloused.

'Dr Reutemann operates the old Fannin's Mine in the Richtersveld mountains,' Major Rive went on. 'The barge-train of copper ore came downriver today from Aussenkehr, an old fort about a hundred kilometres upstream dating from the German colonial days.'

'That is correct,' Reutemann replied shortly, as if the facts had been thrown in question.

This was the man whose barges Keeler intended to search when the party was over! He looked as tough as teak. Keeler found himself mentally measuring the powers of Reutemann's shoulders in case they should ever have to tangle.

Reutemann went on in an assertive tone. 'Unfortunately Aussenkehr is not a public place or a museum. It is a working establishment which I now own. I have restored the fort. It is the loading-point for the barges after my helicopter has ferried the copper ore across the mountains. No one except my workers is permitted – it is a protected area.' Reutemann spoke perfect English apart from a Teutonic difficulty in pronouncing his 'th's.

The circuits meshed in Keeler's brain. Upriver, one prohibited area – off the river mouth and out to sea another prohibited area! Did the two add up to a connection with the *Rigel Star*?

He asked, as casually as his surge of interest permitted.

'Could a visit be arranged?'

'Ask Major Rive – he knows,' replied Reutemann offhandedly. 'No, I will tell you myself. Aussenkehr is strictly *verboten*, unfortunately, as is its surrounding area which is a game reserve. When I first came here some years ago I discovered that in the Cheating and Abaharib mountains behind Aussenkehr there was a herd of some of the rarest animals in the world, the Namib elephant. It is an endangered species. There were only about eighty of them left, and poachers were at work to get the ivory.'

'What is so special about the Namib elephant?' asked Keeler.

'They are the tallest elephant in the world and are so adapted to the desert that they can live practically without water. They have evolved a special "sandshoe" type of foot to negotiate the sand.' He addressed Rill. 'Who knows, they may be the direct descendants of the creatures you have unearthed in your dig at Arrisdrift?'

'They could be,' murmured Rill. She clearly had no wish to be drawn into the conversation.

Reutemann went on with a touch of arrogance. 'I think it is likely. The herd enjoys the special attention of the Southern Africa Nature Foundation and the International Union for the Conservation of Nature.'

'That's a lot of nature,' Keeler interjected flippantly, trying to lighten the heavy Teutonic tone of the conversation.

Reutemann ignored him and continued. 'Both these august bodies were delighted when I offered to protect and patrol the whole area of the elephant habitat. A security fence extends near the fort itself. It is strictly policed by my armed rangers, because only bullets will stop poachers.'

Keeler noted the relish with which Reutemann said this. He wondered if any of Reutemann's so-called rangers would be guarding his barges tonight.

'But can you stop people from using the river?' asked Keeler.

Keeler didn't care for his laugh. 'No one passes up or down the river near Aussenkehr unless he has my express permission.'

Herington! How had Herington managed? Keeler asked himself. Had he been allowed free passage because he was a friend of Reutemann's? Keeler made a mental note to ask Herington.

'Then one can only see the elephants by air, I suppose,' remarked Keller. 'I reckon that shooting them up from the air would not be very practical.'

'You have come from abroad so you probably don't know that all flying is prohibited over South African game reserves' air space,' retorted Reutemann. 'Severe penalties are enforced for contraventions.'

'Isn't the Orange River an international boundary?' objected Keeler. The swarthy German's personality had drawn him into an unexpected verbal clash. 'How can you enforce an overflying ban over an international water-way?'

Reutemann eyed him. 'For a stranger who has been in the area only a couple of days, you seem to know a great deal, Mr Keeler.' He went on in the same arrogant tone as before. 'I myself recognized the problems of overflying international waters. The previous minimum altitude allowed for aircraft was five hundred metres. I am happy to say that at my instigation and with the backing of the environmental bodies I have just mentioned, the authorities raised the minimum altitude permitted over Aussenkehr to two thousand metres. That also applies to the river for a distance of thirty kilometres both up and downstream from the fort. Except for ore-carrying helicopters, of course.'

'Naturally,' murmured Keeler.

The conversation died in its tracks. Major Rive left Keeler and Rill, who made their way towards the bar.

When they were alone Rill gave a slight shiver.

'Cold?' he asked.

'No. Reutemann. He worries me.'

'Why?'

'Woman's intuition, I suppose. I've met him before. I feel he's evil.' She turned and faced Keeler directly. 'Let's skip the bar and get ourselves outside. It's almost Gunga Din's witching hour.'

7

'Gunga Din?' Keeler exclaimed.

For an answer, Rill took him by the arm and made for the entrance. 'I call my gemsbok Gunga Din because he is a water carrier – like the slavey in the poem.'

Keeler fell in with her change of mood. 'I like the name but I don't get the allusion. There's no water in the Namib.' He liked the way she held his arm tighter as they emerged from the lighted club into the gloom of the fog. 'That's just it, John. Reutemann's elephants have the same sort of adaptability as gemsbok in the desert – they can go for ages without a drink of water. So I call mine Gunga Din because I reckon he must have a year's water supply stashed away inside him.'

They laughed. It was good, Keeler felt, to have her with him. It also made him think of all the women who had been closer physically, yet light years more remote than she was.

'Where do we begin?' he asked.

'This way. Gunga Din usually has starters on the lawn outside my flat before casting around for an open garden gate to provide a more substantial course of flowers and shrubs.'

The fog grew thicker as they went further from the club.

'How far is your flat?'

'A block or two away. In front of it there's a big green open space which I call my lawn. When Security is feeling charitable, the patrol helicopter uses the lawn as a helipad to land and give me a hitch to Arrisdrift. It saves a long hot dusty journey by road.'

Keeler listened to the sound of the big diesel which drove the stand-by generators of the town's power station. Usually the power came from a grid source on the South African side of the river but when problems arose Oranjemund switched to its own supply. 'Without the thud of that engine in Oranjemund, I'd feel the world had come to an end. It used to go all the time when I was a boy.'

'You really feel at home in this place, don't you, John?'

'Did,' he corrected her. 'I remember lying in bed and feeling reassured by the power station's diesel.'

'You still need to be reassured?' she said.

Keeler thought of the barge-train and how a lone man trapped aboard might fare.

'Yes, maybe I do.'

She did not miss his tone. She drew very close to him. Then he felt her body stiffen.

She whispered urgently. 'There he is – Gunga Din!'

The animal was grazing within twenty paces of them. The fog distorted it to twice its normal size.

'It's not a gemsbok – it's a unicorn!' Keeler whispered back. 'Look, he only has one horn!'

She put her mouth against his ear. It was cold from the fog, her breath warm from her blood. 'He probably lost the other horn in a fight – you can tell him anywhere.'

The splendid creature must have picked up the faint sound of their voices. He reared upright and in a flash vanished into the fog with a clatter of hooves.

They stood. Both wanted the moment to go on forever.

Rill finally broke the silence. 'I've got the fossil skull of an extinct antelope in my flat. It inhabited the Namib millions of years ago. Would you like to see it?'

Keeler's mind was not on Climacoceras, Rill's deer-like animal of the Miocene age, but on her.

He asked casually, 'What does Gressitt think of it?'

'He's only interested in dinosaurs,' she replied.

The sharpness of her tone jerked him back to the consideration of fossils.

'He's a professor,' observed Keeler.

'The dinosaur site at Blooddrift was worked out years ago,' she answered. 'Geologically it is uncomplicated and an expert can see all he wants to in a day or two. Ross Gressitt has been there a month. My colleagues at Oranjemund wonder what he finds to keep himself occupied.'

A small cloud of suspicion gathered in Keeler's mind over Gressitt.

They made their way through the dense fog.

'Here we are.'

Rill opened the door of her flat. Keeler knew in an intuitive flash that there was no devil in her, that her invitation was not a variation on the theme of come up and see my etchings.

There was a small pine desk with an angled light and a shelf full of books above it. A small electric drill – like a dentist's – a small hammer, and some pointed punches lay scattered about a fossil skull whose bones projected partly through the cleaned-up matrix.

She went to it. 'The modern okapi and giraffe descended from this creature. Herds of them once frequented the Orange River forests.' She shot a glance at Keeler and said, 'Sorry, I'm talking like a book. Help yourself to a drink – there's everything in that cabinet.

'It's not *my* liquor, John,' she said, misunderstanding him. 'CDM has a very charming custom of stocking up its guests' drink cabinets. One is expected to entertain. It's all on the house – like my entire stay here. CDM has been wonderful to me.'

'I'll skip this round,' replied Keeler. He gestured at the skull. 'Incredible to think that the surrounding sea of sand was once forest.'

'I'll show you tomorrow when you come to Arrisdrift,' she laughed. She added, 'I hope you didn't mind the way I threw the invitation at you. But you seemed uncomfortable with Major Rive.'

'Saved by the bell,' he answered lightly. Keeler sat on the arm of a chair and eyed her speculatively.

'You find this sort of life completely fulfilling, Rill?'

'Why shouldn't I be satisfied?' she asked. 'I am a free agent. I work for Cape Town university – on detached duties. I come and go as I wish. There are no deadlines or restrictions on what I may or may not excavate, and I love Oranjemund.' She went on quickly. 'Are you sure you won't have another drink? Twice tonight you looked as if you needed one and you've refused.'

'Do I look as if I need one now?'

'You do and you don't.'

Keeler laughed. 'You a psychologist as well as a palaeontologist and geologist?'

She leaned back against her desk and said quizzically, 'Most men I know would have made a pass at me, under the circumstances. A cosy *pied-à-terre*, a cabinet full of drinks.'

'There are ships that pass in the night – and others,' he answered quietly.

'That's the nicest compliment that has ever been paid me,' she said. 'I believe you mean it. But I think your mind is somewhere else, John.'

On that ship that is going to pass in the night, the *Rigel Star*, Keeler thought.

He deliberately steered the conversation off at a tangent. 'Tell me about the Richtersveld, Rill.'

'Is that a warning. I'm married, keep off the grass, woman?' she asked.

Keeler said in the same quiet voice, 'I'm not married. Never have been.'

'Women?' Rill's voice was level.

'Nearly made it once, but not quite,' he shrugged. 'That's the way it goes.'

'That's the way it goes,' she echoed. There was a short, taut silence. Then she said in a different tone, 'The Richtersveld frightens me. Those stark, vegetationless, aching ranges, one after another. They go on and on until the mind boggles. They rise up to about fourteen hundred metres at

59

their highest. The worst is named the Rosyntjiesberge, the Little Raisin Bush mountains. The peaks are red-hot by day and deadly cold by night and they change to all colours in the sunlight. The Richtersveld is largely unexplored because of the terrain. An old-time prospector named Fred Cornell was the first man really to venture into it round about World War I. Cornell was the man who was supposed in fact to have located the Orange River diamond fields long before their actual discovery. He was a great adventurer, geologist and explorer. There's a plaque right on top of one of the Richtersveld summits to his memory.'

'Where is Fannin's Mine situated?' asked Keeler.

'Where did you get to hear about Fannin's Mine?'

'Ross Gressitt. He had the story of the Copper Mountain at his fingertips.'

'I see.'

Keeler wondered what she saw, and if it was any different from his own undefined suspicions. 'Fannin's Mine lies close to the Little Raisin Bush mountains at the head of a great divide which splits the eastern side of the Richtersveld in half. It's called the Deurloop, or Throughway. The name's a misnomer. It is anything but a way through – it's a wild tangle of rocks and sand, completely unnegotiable by any vehicle. It's waterless, of course. It finally emerges on the Orange River opposite Aussenkehr. Fannin tried to use parts of the route – they're strewn with the bones of his transport oxen, I'm told.'

What she had told him about Ross Gressitt, Reutemann and the Richtersveld made Keeler more determined than ever to search the barge-train. Now he wanted to be up and away despite the fact that it was far too early; midnight was the time he had set himself to leave the party. Then there was Rill . . .

He held her eyes with his and said gently, 'I think you know Oranjemund doesn't contain your whole answer, Rill.'

60

She went behind his chair and slid her hands down to grasp his across his chest.

'I'm glad you told me that, John.'

Keeler reached up to kiss her lips. He knew from previous missions the sort of powerful stimulus he required for his keyed-up frame of mind. It wasn't a woman. Tonight it was Reutemann's ore-train.

8

The fog cloaked the riverside camp like shabby cerements. It wasn't a resort at the best of times. Now, as Keeler and Gressitt climbed down the river's sandy bank to the place, it was grim, unfriendly. They groped their way to the camp-fire. Runnels of heavy condensation coursed down the pup-tent's cheeks like tears. Herington's half-repaired kayak looked blue with cold.

On the half-kilometre walk from the ruined house to the camp, Keeler and Gressitt had concurred that the use of force against Herington for securing the use of his kayak would be easy but crude and in the long run not to their advantage; they preferred his co-operation and, with it, his skill. Particularly for the *Rigel Star* intercept in the wild seas off the coast.

The two men had decided that they would tell him the truth – part of it in any case, until they were sure of their man – as the best method with which to win his co-operation. In view of the approaching deadline, Keeler and Gressitt had also agreed that the *Rigel Star* must take priority over Aussenkehr. The importance of Fannin's Mine would be assessed on the strength of Rill's verdict on the nodule.

From the limited exchanges between Keeler and Gressitt on the fog-bound road, Keeler realized that Gressitt was as worried as he was about Herington. 'Don't get tough with Herington too soon,' Gressitt had warned him.

Herington emerged bare-footed from the pup-tent, wearing the kayaking clothes in which he slept. He had been awakened by the sound of the fire being banked. At the sight of the pistol in Keeler's belt and Gressitt's knife, with which he was splitting wood, sleep vanished from his eyes.

'What the hell goes on?' he demanded. 'What are you two up to? Where are you going?'

'We're not going – we've come back,' replied Keeler.

'From where?'

Herington's tough, angry tone surprised Keeler. Perhaps it was the sight of the weapons.

Gressitt answered. 'We just raided Reutemann's barge-train. Found some interesting stuff.'

'Such as?'

'Two sea-going kayaks, to start with,' Keeler interjected quickly.

Herington's face in the firelight looked as gaunt and fanatical and accusing as an Inquisitor's.

'So what?'

'Plus your kayak, that makes three.'

'Again, so what?'

'What do you know about them, Herington?'

'They belong to Reutemann and Trevenna. They are based at Aussenkehr.'

'Ah!' exclaimed Keeler.

'There is no "Ah!" about it,' snapped back Herington. 'Don't look for spooks where none exists.'

'Then why should Reutemann operate two sea-going kayaks complete with skegs on a river which has one of the gentlest down-gradients in Africa?'

'For God's sake!' flared Herington. 'I don't know what the hell this dawn interrogation about kayaks is all about. But I'll tell you, if it'll make you happy. They gave me details of Reutemann's kayaks at CDM's Canoe Club . . .'

'Canoe Club?' demanded Keeler. 'That is the first I've heard of it.'

'If you'd been here longer, it might well have come to your prying ears,' retorted Herington. 'There are canoeing enthusiasts among CDM's employees at Oranjemund and they established their own Canoe Club near the mouth of the river . . .'

'The lower reaches of the river towards the mouth are inside the Sperrgebiet and therefore out of bounds. You know that yourself only too well – everything seawards from the Oppenheimer bridge is banned. How is a Canoe Club allowed to function there?'

'What is this, an inquisition?' retorted Herington angrily. 'There *is* a Canoe Club, and it *does* operate inside the Sperrgebiet. But it is completely above-board and has the full permission of the mining company and Security. Members are only allowed to canoe where it is safe, away from the bar and the sea. They have no kayaks, only river-type canoes. In flood-time the out-of-bounds area is moved further upriver because of the danger. When the river's coming down and there's a gale, the sea on occasion builds up to eight-metre waves off the bar. Reutemann and Trevenna are members of the Canoe Club. They bring their kayaks from Aussenkehr to mess about in the lower reaches of the river on the occasions when their ore shipments come down by barge.'

'That still doesn't answer my question,' said Keeler.

'Blast it, I am answering it as well as I can!' blazed Herington. 'The reason why Reutemann has kayaks at the fort is that several kilometres below Aussenkehr there are a series of bad rapids. They are very tricky. An ordinary river canoe wouldn't be safe. So they have kayaks.' He faced Keeler and Gressitt truculently. There was an overkill somewhere, Keeler felt, as he added, as an afterthought almost, 'I should know. That's where I damaged my bow. Satisfied?'

Keeler felt that his accusation had been well met, but he added, 'Why should they have kayaks at all? There are plenty of other boats at the fort . . .'

'For crying out loud!' burst out Herington. 'Can't a man have a hobby?'

'You seem to know a hell of a lot about Reutemann and his kayaks.'

'Why shouldn't I? I'm a kayaker myself. Go and ask the CDM Canoe Club if you doubt what I say.'

Keeler realised he was up against a stone wall; the sort of tenacity that had carried Herington all the way across the sub-continent in his kayak.

Keeler tried a last long-shot question. 'So Reutemann and Trevenna use their kayaks to go out to sea beyond the mouth?'

'You're putting words into my mouth!' responded Herington. 'They do *not*! I've already made the position of the ban and the dangers clear!'

Herington rounded on Gressitt. 'I thought you were my friend the way you helped me at Blooddrift. It appears I was mistaken. You and Keeler can get stuffed.'

Gressitt decided to adopt a softer line. He said quietly, 'Peter, it is we, now, who need your help. John and I discovered tonight we had common interests. We'd like you to be on our side.'

'Who are you? What are you both up to?' demanded Herington.

Gressitt was diplomatic, suave where Herington's mood had made Keeler play it rough. Without mention of either SAMEX or FERRET by name, Gressitt outlined his role as an operative in the Resources War, his suspicions about Reutemann and his over-capitalized mining venture; the enigma of the security precautions round Aussenkehr. He explained Keeler's interest in the marine fraud racket operating off the Sperrgebiet coast as the reason for wanting the use of Herington's kayak. He emphasized the nearness of the *Rigel Star* deadline.

By the time he had finished, the coffee was boiling on the fire. Herington poured himself a cup of the scalding liquid as if it would help fuel his anger.

'I wish to heaven I had never clapped eyes on either of

you!' he burst out. 'What have I to do with all this? You've built up a fantasy! There is nothing here but a river and a desert! All the rest of this yarn is invented!'

Keeler noted that Gressitt had refrained from playing his trump card, the mystery nodule. If Herington would not go along with them, then the less he knew the better.

Keeler tried to emulate Gressitt's persuasive manner. 'Listen, Peter – you're entitled to your opinion. But you can soon prove whether or not what we're saying is a load of horse-shit. Let you and me take the kayak out to sea tomorrow night and see if we don't intercept the *Rigel Star*.'

'No!' he came back. 'I sail on the same date as Lüderitz – tomorrow. For the reasons you know, it will have to be after dark.'

'Tomorrow night.'

The way Keeler said it made Herington stare, and then his anger flared again. 'Are you trying to infer that I am in some way involved with your *Rigel Star* . . .?'

'I am not inferring anything,' replied Keeler. 'What I am asking is why your sailing date is so significant? It has no meaning for anyone but yourself. Who has ever heard of Lüderitz's abortive voyage? Who has ever even heard of Lüderitz?'

'I have – that's all that matters.'

Keeler went on in the same tone. 'It's not as if you are trying to match Lüderitz's achievement. He never arrived at his destination – you said so yourself. Also, there is no comparison in the types of craft – yours is a sophisticated product of modern technology, his was a wood-and-canvas job . . .'

Herington pitched the remains of his coffee into the fire with a hiss that doubled for his own. 'I sail as I said. Don't try and stop me, do you hear? Or I'll go to Major Rive and tell him what you are up to.'

Keeler interrupted sharply. 'Two can play at that game, Herington. I wouldn't try anything. I could wreck your

Lüderitz attempt by also going to Major Rive.'

Gressitt added quietly. 'That's the ace in the hole as far as John and I are concerned, Peter.'

Herington became slightly rattled. 'You seem remarkably chummy.'

'We share something which we view as being more important to either of us than our personal interests,' answered Gressitt.

'I don't like being bullied and threatened,' snapped Herington. 'Look at that gun in Keeler's belt!'

'I looked into its receiving end earlier tonight,' replied Gressitt grimly. 'John means what he says, I assure you. We're asking for your help. Your kayak.'

Keeler noted also that Gressitt hadn't brought Aussenkehr into his share of the argument; if Herington would not agree to the use of his kayak for the *Rigel Star*, he equally would not condone its use against the old fort at a still later date.

'No!' retorted Herington vehemently. 'I won't get involved with either of you!'

Daylight was starting to filter through the shroud of fog.

Herington went on, 'I suppose this means you won't help any further with repairs to the kayak?'

Keeler shook his head. A seaworthy craft, with or without Herington, was vital to his sortie.

'I'll see the kayak gets to sea – whatever,' he replied ambiguously. 'Once the patches have set, it is mainly a question of sanding and generally tidying up, isn't it?'

Herington seemed slightly mollified. 'Yes. But the sanding will have to be done by hand – that's where I need you. There aren't any machines at camp.'

'Ross and I are going off to Rill's dig at Arrisdrift this morning,' Keeler went on. 'You won't need my help until later today, as I see the situation.'

'It depends on how quickly the patches set. Blast this fog! The moisture plays hell with the quick setting of the resin.'

Beardogs and extinct antelope might enthral some visitors to Arrisdrift, but the mysterious heavy nodule was what was taking Keeler and Gressitt there.

And Rill.

9

Arrisdrift must have been a great place when the beardogs were around, fifteen million years ago. It was impossible to match the burning, pitiless white-grey sand which reached to the Orange River's edge with Rill's description of a forested area once inhabited by strange, long-extinct creatures. Arrisdrift lay at the eastern end of a gigantic, spectacular bend in the river ten kilometres across by the name of Grootderm, or Big Gut. Southward, the stupendous bastions of the Richtersveld ran back in serried ranks of unrelieved hell to heat-locked fastnesses where men had never been. The plant-bald ranges were shedding their early morning delicacy of colour in favour of tough, blast-off hues of browns, reds, blacks and unlikely greens.

It was about 9.30. Gressitt's Landrover headed towards a single sand-blasted prefab near a man-made pit a couple of hundred metres square and about ten deep. At the sound of the vehicle's engine Rill, wearing faded jeans, a blue tracksuit top, floppy blue hat and butternut-brown sneakers, scrambled up the side of the excavation.

Rill glanced from Keeler to Gressitt. 'You both seem uncommon solemn,' she remarked. 'No trouble with Security, I hope?'

There had not been. The X-ray screening inside the fenced-off diamond workings had, of course, picked up the nodule, but the checking officer had accepted Gressitt's word as a geologist that it was no more than an interesting little stone he had picked up. What worried Keeler more was

Major Rive's needling hint that there were plenty of agates at the diamond processing plant nearby waiting for his bid. Keeler had sidestepped that one by saying that Rill was awaiting the two of them. He knew, however that his game with Major Rive could not go on much longer.

Keeler looked about him. Arrisdrift seemed about as dreary a hole as he had seen anywhere.

'Give John a run-down on your Miocene showcase, honey, before I get started on dinosaurs,' said Gressitt.

Keeler felt uneasy at Gressitt's phony sales-talk and shabby himself in the face of Rill's genuineness and enthusiasm.

Rill said a little shyly, indicating the excavation pit and the river, turgid and brown, beyond, 'Arrisdrift is what we call a shoulder deposit. The total depth of the deposit is about forty metres – we're nowhere near that with our excavations. Massive quantities of gravels were brought downriver in the remote past by geological spasms. Further downstream, the mud deposit is even thicker – for the piers of the Oppenheimer bridge, engineers had to bore a hundred metres to reach bedrock.'

Keeler felt he had too much on his mind to care about what had happened fifteen million years ago. The present – in the form of the *Rigel Star* next day – was all that mattered.

'Before I show you the pit itself, come to the prefab and look at a few specimens,' said Rill.

On a couple of long trestle tables inside the prefab were a number of irregular-shaped lumps of rock, each numbered. A couple of locals, with the characteristic Tartar-shaped eyes and high cheek-bones of the Hottentot, were smoking and sorting. At the rate they were going, thought Keeler, they'd be occupied for the next fifteen million years.

Rill indicated a big chunk of rock. A piece of dirty white projected from it. 'Inside there is a proboscidean femur – part of the creature I mentioned to you last night from which evolved the elephant.' Rill was trying hard to re-establish the rapport with Keeler they had had the previous night.

'There are more of the same remains in the pit where we are working right now – like to see?'

Keeler felt glad of the excuse to move, although Gressitt took up Rill's palaeontological patter. The three of them went to the lip of the pit. Keeler's thoughts were on the vast panorama of the Richtersveld – what could that tiny nodule lead to in those forbidding mountains?

Rill mistook his summing-up glance. 'About seventy million years ago all the land you're looking at now beyond the escarpment rose and the currents in the rivers accelerated. The Orange broke through to the sea via the Richtersveld and brought down vast quantities of gravels from the interior . . .'

'Plus diamonds,' added Gressitt.

Keeler felt himself wanting to yell, shut up, for Pete's sake! All this prattle about millennia! My time-warp ends forty hours from now. Off the coast. *Rigel Star*.

Before they had time to start down into the pit, the men in drab overalls who had been busy with compressor-drills and shovels downed tools and began making their way to the surface.

'Tea break,' explained Rill. 'The men get pretty dehydrated down there. We seem to spend half our time drinking tea.' She looked keenly at Keeler trying to comprehend his abstraction. 'I brought along a tea basket for us. There are some sandwiches, if you want them.'

'You must have been up early to make them,' observed Keeler.

'I didn't sleep well, so I thought I might as well be useful.' Her eyes suggested the thoughts that had kept her awake. 'Did *you* sleep well?' She included Gressitt in her question.

Keeler saw the opening he had been looking for. 'As a matter of fact, neither Ross nor I had any sleep at all last night.'

Rill looked from one man to the other, and said thoughtfully, 'I guessed you both had something on your minds.'

'Yes. We have.' Keeler indicated the workers. 'Can we be private? We have something to ask you. Something to show you.'

'*Me?*'

'Yes. As a geologist.'

'But why me? Ross is also a geologist. What is all this about?'

Gressitt pulled the nodule from his pocket and held it out to her. 'We've got a lot going on this piece of rock, Rill.'

Rill took the nodule. 'Are you and John working together on something? You say you've both been up all night . . .'

'Part of the night was spent in finding it,' Keeler interjected. 'Ross and I started off independently on our own respective missions but finished up together.'

'You're talking in riddles.'

'You identify that for us, Rill, and then we'll tell you the rest,' said Gressitt.

'Where did you get it?' she asked. 'Why is it so important? What is it?'

'That is what we're asking you to find out. If it is nothing, then forget it. If it is something, there could be problems – dangerous problems.'

Rill's eyes held Keeler's for a while. 'You've said too much already for me to forget.'

'What *is* it, Rill?' Gressitt could not curb his impatience.

Rill held up the nodule to eye-level, turned it over and over, then balanced it in her hand like Justice weighing the evidence. In the intense sunlight, Keeler noticed for the first time that it had a slight yellowish overtone in its generally grey-white colour.

They waited. Keeler could feel the sweat trickling down inside his shirt.

Then Rill asked, 'Have either of you got a pocket-knife?'

Gressitt's hand went automatically to the sheath where he kept his commando knife. It was a reflex action; but he had left it behind at camp because of Security.

'Sorry, Rill – what for?'

'To see how hard it is. Then let's go to my prefab and check. I've got a magnifying lens there, too.'

Once inside, Rill gave the nodule a thorough examination. Then she gave a start, as if a sudden, unlikely, thought had struck her. She got up, rummaged in a drawer and came back to the bench where Keeler and Gressitt waited with an instrument which resembled a dentist's scaling tool. She scraped at the nodule with its fine steel point, then re-examined it under the glass.

She eyed the two men. 'You are still not prepared to tell me where you got this?'

'Not yet.'

'Have a look through the glass – do you see any scratches?'

Keeler tried, then Gressitt.

'Now,' said Rill. 'I'd like you both to try and mark it with this tool – it's a special one we use to clean fossils.'

To test the steel, Keeler first made a deep score on a nearby hard matrix. Then he scraped and jabbed at the nodule. When he had finished, he examined it. The surface remained unmarked.

Gressitt attempted the same thing. He was no more successful than Keeler.

'That narrows the field of identification considerably,' remarked Rill. 'What do you think of it, Ross?'

Gressitt hedged uncomfortably. 'You're the expert on the geology of this part of the world, Rill. I'd rather trust your judgment.'

Rill threw him an inquisitive, half-doubting glance, and then went on. 'Anything as hard as that has been specially fabricated or . . .' she left the sentence open-ended.

'Or what?'

'Whatever it is, it has been lying around for a long time,'

'How do you deduce that?' asked Gressitt.

'There is a tiny cavity. If you look hard, you'll see some

minute granules in it. I'd say at first glance that they were Namib or Richtersveld desert sand.'

A look of relief spread over Gressitt's sun-tanned face.

'Could be. In fact, we think it might be.'

'In that case, I'm completely flummoxed as to what to think this nodule might be,' replied Rill.

'Rill,' said Keeler cautiously. 'Would it help you to know that we believe this nodule came from upriver?'

She said impatiently. 'Don't you *know?*'

Keeler said slowly, 'We don't. Not for sure. You see, I removed this from its owner's possession without his knowledge.'

'You stole it? What are you trying to say, John?'

'First, it is vital to Ross and myself to know the significance of this. Then we'll tell you.'

Rill eyed them in a puzzled, half-hostile way. 'People who talk like that drive me round the bend!'

'Can't you tell us a little more?' Gressitt pressed her.

The way she responded made Keeler feel that she was not entirely unsuspicious of Gressitt's activities.

'Why don't you, Ross, with your geological background . . .'

Gressitt hedged again. 'If I could, we wouldn't be here, Rill.'

There was an uncomfortable silence. Then Rill said. 'Let's go back to Oranjemund – I'll have to test it in my lab.'

Gressitt said hastily. 'We wouldn't like anyone else to know about this nodule, Rill.'

'You ask me for secrecy, yet you are not prepared to trust me,' she replied off-handedly. 'Good. You have my word. I'll test it and give you an answer to the best of my ability. But there is a great deal of explaining to do on your part – robbery, refusal to disclose the nodule's place of origin, and your general cloak-and-dagger attitude.'

'All I can reveal at this stage, Rill, is that that object may or may not be of great significance. It all depends on what it turns out to be,' said Keeler. 'If it is nothing special, I may have to leave a great deal unsaid.'

And lose me, her eyes seemed to say. Just as we were getting into orbit. You and I.

'Let's get going,' she said abruptly.

It was a long, silent, strained thirty kilometre drive back along the river-bank track to Oranjemund. Although Rill sat close to Keeler on the Landrover seat, and he was acutely conscious of the warm, woman-smell of her body above the all-pervading dust which seeped into the cab, she was light years away from him compared to the previous night. To Keeler, Oranjemund also seemed hard and uninviting and utilitarian compared to his feeling of homecoming the previous evening.

They skirted the town to the south, missing the green streets and gardens, to follow an arrow-straight road which bored into the desert to the diamond workings five kilometres distant on the ocean. Here they went through the Security checks as Major Rive had stipulated. They returned to Oranjemund to a line of functional-looking buildings flanking the same road.

Rill seemed more remote when she slipped on a formal white lab coat and discarded her floppy hat; like a surgeon donning his operating gear. Gressitt and he stood to one side while Rill silently busied herself rigging up some apparatus on a bench, which was equipped with sink, gas burners and an array of bottles and flasks.

First, Rill examined the nodule under a powerful microscope. She seemed dissatisfied, and put the object into a glass flask. She pulled on a pair of rubber gloves and took a bottle of hydrochloric acid from a shelf. As she did so, a wisp of her lovely hair came loose. She removed her gloves slowly and deliberately tied it back into position. The way she did it, plus the fact that she kept her back to the two men, seemed to Keeler to be a tangible demonstration of her annoyance.

Then she put on her gloves again, fiddled with the apparatus, and finally poured acid over the nodule.

The two men waited, sweating inwardly and outwardly. Two – four minutes passed. Then, from the irregular globule there started to spread through the acid a rainbow of colours – blues, greens, reds, yellows.

Rill rounded on Keeler and Gressitt, incredulous.

'It is the metal of the legend!' she exclaimed. 'Unripe gold!'

10

'It can't be, but it is!' In her excitement Rill shook her head so that the hair which she had tied became detached again and tumbled over her face. 'But it is – it *is*!' She went on, peering into the flask. 'We mustn't let this dissolve any more!' She removed the nodule with a pair of forceps and washed it under a tap. Then she held it up to the two wordless but expectant men in a gesture half of triumph, half of disbelief.

'Iridium!' she exclaimed. 'That's what it is – iridium! Look at the characteristic rainbow the metal makes when it is dissolved in acid! That's what the name means – rainbow, iridium!'

'Iridium!' echoed Gressitt. 'Well, knock me for a row of tall red totem poles! Are you sure, Rill?'

Rill pointed to the flask with its spectrum of iridescent colours. 'No doubt. That is iridium's fingerprint!'

Gressitt went on in wonderment. 'You really mean to say, that is a pellet of pure iridium? It can't be! It is never found in the natural state!'

Keeler felt left behind. 'What is this all about? I'm only a dumb agate dealer. What do you mean by unripe gold? What's iridium?'

Rill hugged him spontaneously. 'Sorry, John, I was being dreadfully unscientific, but I was carried away when I realized what the nodule was. Correct me if I'm wrong, Ross: iridium is a sister to platinum and is known as one of the noble metals. It is the heaviest and most corrosion-resistant metal known. It can stand up to higher temperatures than any other element without breaking down. Right?' Gressitt nodded. 'It is also among the rarest of all metals.'

'Where does gold come in?' repeated Keeler. 'How can gold be ripe or unripe?'

Rill's voice vibrated with excitement. 'Crude platinum, which includes iridium and other metals of the same group, was first found in the river sands of Colombia in South America by the Spanish conquistadores. When they reported back to King Philip II he ordered that the metal – which is almost as dense as gold but whitish – should be thrown back into the rivers to ripen further into gold.'

'Rill,' went on Gressitt. 'You say that is *pure* iridium? The nodule doesn't contain the other metals of the group – palladium, rhodium, osmium or ruthenium?'

'That is what is so staggering,' she replied. 'Pure iridium – in that quantity! I didn't know it *existed*. Where did this nodule come from? It is unique!'

'I'm not with you,' said Keeler. 'This is way above my head.'

'I'm still trying to get my breath back, John,' Gressitt answered. 'Iridium is never found in its pure natural state but either in conjunction with platinum, or nickel, or cobalt and copper . . .'

'Copper!' exclaimed Keeler. 'Fannin's Mine!'

'You're jumping the gun,' replied Gressitt. 'The world's biggest source of platinum is from mines in the Western Transvaal. In conjunction with it, the other noble metals of the group I've just mentioned occur in trace quantities only – mere decimals of a part per million. Iridium also occurs as a by-product of nickel in Russia and Canada, but in nothing like the same quantities as in the Transvaal. A nodule of pure iridium, even if it weighs only a few grams, has never been seen before, anywhere.'

'There was a whole bagful aboard Reutemann's kayak,' Keeler remarked thoughtfully.

'I hadn't forgotten,' said Gressitt.

Keeler felt Rill's eyes upon him. Now that the first thrill of the discovery was over, he sensed in her the still unanswered questions about Gressitt and himself.

'Ross,' he said. 'This is the stage where we owe Rill an explanation, both about ourselves and the nodule. She has done her part – nobly. It is now our turn to take her into our confidence.'

'There is danger in the knowledge that the nodule is iridium,' he replied gravely. 'Are you willing to take the risk of knowing our involvement, Rill?'

Her eyes held Keeler's. 'Yes.'

'I'm not an agate salesman.' He outlined the true purpose of his mission to Oranjemund; the underworld marine fraud racket operating off the coast, the *Rigel Star* trap, and his need to get to sea the next night in order to intercept the ship and its tow.

Her eyes were alive, elated that she had trusted her woman's intuition in regard to the man. 'I'm glad, John.'

Then Gressitt explained about SAMEX and the Resources War, its focus of interest on Namibia's mineral wealth, the initial suspicions which had been aroused by Reutemann's mysterious operation of Fannin's Mine, and the discovery of the laser cutter in transit upriver.

When he had finished, Rill said quietly, 'You kept up the façade of a professor pretty well, Ross, except that once or twice you had me puzzled when you said things which didn't add up palaeontologically speaking.'

'*Touché,*' he grinned.

Rill addressed Keeler. 'What I don't understand is how you come to be working with Ross. Where do your respective interests merge?'

Keeler laughed. 'They merged unexpectedly, at the point of my pistol.' He went on to tell her about his raid on the barge-train and his subsequent encounter with Gressitt. 'I took that nodule from a waterproof bagful of them in one of the kayaks.'

'Reutemann can't be mining iridium nodules as a by-product of copper at Fannin's Mine!' exclaimed Rill. 'That nodule hasn't been cut by a laser cutter or anything else, and it would require a laser cutter to slice iridium – there is nothing harder.'

'My original hunch about Reutemann paid off,' said Gressitt. 'Still, I mean to find out what the hell is actually going on at Fannin's and Aussenkehr.'

'What was Reutemann doing with a bagful of nodules in his kayak?' went on Rill. 'Do you think he is transporting them out to sea, John?'

'If he is, that is not marine fraud.'

'It is a racket, whatever you name it,' said Gressitt grimly.

'A strike of pure iridium would be the most fabulous mineral find of the century,' said Rill.

'Not only that,' added Gressitt. 'In the context of the Resources War it could be devastating. Whoever owned the metal's source – the USA or Russia – would have a not inconsiderable lead on the other.'

'What is iridium's strategic significance, Ross?' asked Rill. 'I know only about its academic aspects.'

Gressitt looked puzzled. 'That's the kicker, Rill. Iridium is so rare and difficult to fabricate that its applications have always been restricted. We Americans use small quantities in our military and space programmes where high endurance is of paramount importance. Remember, it can stand up to temperatures of two thousand three hundred degrees Celsius without undergoing catastrophic failure. The Apollo II moonshot had platinum-iridium and platinum-palladium alloys in its engines. It has use in weaponry for growing laser crystals – iridium crucibles are a vital part of the process. Iridium also has a big place in aircraft spark plugs where high resistance to lead corrosion is of utmost importance. Generally speaking, though, pure iridium isn't often employed – it is usually in the form of an alloy with platinum, which it hardens. In this context it has a pretty wide application in electrical contacts where high reliability is involved. Platinum itself has a much wider field – in the petroleum, chemical, electrical and automotive industries. The snag about iridium has always been its extreme scarcity.'

'What is the annual output?' asked Keeler.

'You could measure it in terms of ounces,' answered Gressitt. 'The problem – even with SAMEX – is to get an accurate production figure. The platinum market – which includes iridium and the other noble metals of the group – is highly segmented and specialized. Also, the ultimate buyers are hard to trace. We in SAMEX know that only too well!'

'That makes it sound very sinister,' remarked Rill.

'It worries me like hell,' said Gressitt. 'Where is Reutemann's iridium bound for – Russia? It certainly is not coming SAMEX's way. If it is to the Reds, then what can they have up their sleeve in the weaponry line which can absorb hitherto unknown quantities of iridium?'

'Maybe it is not going their way at all,' said Keeler. 'Reutemann is a German. Maybe it is a purely commercial venture . . .'

Gressitt cut in. 'I can't give you the price per ounce of iridium but I'd say without fear of contradiction that that nodule is worth a king's ransom. Whoever is paying for it must have a helluva lot.'

'And to think I left the rest of the nodules behind,' Keeler remarked. 'I don't know how many.'

'Ross, would any sizeable find of iridium revolutionize strategic metallurgy?' asked Rill.

'I'll say.'

'You're saying that at this time iridium hasn't graduated weapon-wise because of its extreme rarity?' asked Keeler.

'Yeah. What we have here is only the tip of the iceberg,' went on Gressitt tersely. 'We have got to find out what Reutemann's masterplan is, and who's backing him.'

A convoy of massive dumper-trucks, bound for the coastal diamond workings, ground past the laboratory window, leaving each one with their own thoughts as the sound blanked out conversation. Like Reutemann's, it was equipment which cost plenty. In his case, however, he was mining copper. And copper isn't diamonds.

'We've got Reutemann in the hot seat,' said Gressitt when the noise had died away. 'But what about Herington and *his* kayak? It was in a kayak like his that we found iridium.'

'We approached Herington this morning about lending his kayak for the *Rigel Star*,' Keeler explained for Rill's benefit. 'We told him only part of the SAMEX–FERRET set-up – enough, we hoped, to convince him. We met with a point-blank refusal. He is determined to sail on the anniversary of Lüderitz's departure – tomorrow.'

'Is the Lüderitz date a cover or an excuse?' asked Rill.

'It's genuine – I had Cape Town check it out,' replied Keeler. 'My man thought I was mad. I couldn't explain the reasons for my request.'

'The deadline is too goddam close for comfort,' said Gressitt. 'I'll also be needing that kayak to get to Aussenkehr.'

'We may not have Herington's permission, but we will have his kayak,' Keeler added quietly.

Rill looked startled at his tone. 'Whatever you have in mind, take care of yourself, will you, John?'

'He knows how,' interjected Gressitt grimly. 'You should see him across a maggie sight.'

Keeler smiled. He said to Gressitt. 'As I see it, our schedule looks like this – first, tomorrow night, the interception of the *Rigel Star* in Herington's kayak; second, a river party up to Aussenkehr, also by kayak; third, a venture to the interior of the Richtersveld to have a look-see at Fannin's Mine.'

'Your order is reversed,' said Gressitt. 'I agree about the *Rigel Star*. But Fannin's Mine has top billing after that, with Aussenkehr next.'

'Fannin's Mine won't be easy,' said Rill. 'I know. I've been there.'

'*You've been there!*'

Gressitt took Rill by the shoulders as if he meant to shake or kiss her.

'Yes,' answered Rill. 'You two are not the only ones to be suspicious of Reutemann's activities. When I first arrived in Oranjemund about eighteen months ago, Major Rive and CDM were suspicious about the cloak-and-dagger atmosphere upriver. Of course, Reutemann justified his actions by his duty to protect the endangered elephant herd against poachers, but his guards took a very tough line, and their actions aroused a lot of talk and suspicion. Major Rive could not interfere, of course – both Aussenkehr and Fannin's Mine being outside his sphere of jurisdiction. Yet both are on his backyard, so to speak, and he couldn't remain impervious to what was going on. What worried Major Rive most was the sinister presence of Trevenna.'

'I guess he's still got a hangover from what John here gave him on the barge,' grinned Gressitt.

'Why Trevenna especially?' asked Keeler.

'For years Trevenna has been known to be the head of a gang of half-breed ruffians who are holed up somewhere deep in the Richtersveld,' explained Rill. 'Trevenna himself has a criminal record. When Major Rive heard that he had become Reutemann's right-hand man, he immediately became concerned at what might be going on.'

'Do you know how long ago Reutemann reopened Fannin's Mine?' asked Gressitt.

'Between three and four years back,' replied Rill. 'Reutemann brought with him a team of foreigners – Germans, it was believed. Some were technicians, Reutemann said, to service his machinery and aircraft, and others were game wardens. The game wardens are entitled to be armed – and they sure are, from what I hear. The Reutemann outfit kept very much to themselves. This naturally led to rumours in Oranjemund. Perhaps some of the stories came back to Reutemann himself, because he did a clever thing. He asked a party of VIPs from CDM to visit Fannin's Mine.'

'You're kidding!' exclaimed Gressitt. 'How then did you come to be included, Rill?'

'Reutemann said old bones had been found in a pit near the mine and that he would like an expert opinion on them. He obviously wanted to create the impression he had nothing to hide. As the only fossil expert in Oranjemund, I was included.'

'How did you get there?' Gressitt wanted to know.

'By helicopter – rather, two helicopters,' replied Rill. 'One was Reutemann's own, the one he uses to ferry copper ore from the mine to Aussenkehr, and the other was CDM's machine. The two helicopters flew upriver together to Aussenkehr . . .'

'Wait,' said Keeler. 'I need to get myself orientated. Both of you know the geography, I don't.'

'There are some maps next door in the projection room,' said Rill. 'For what they are worth. Come!'

'For what they are worth?' echoed Keeler as they left the laboratory and made their way into a spartan office which was obviously used for impromptu discussions. There was one long table, a number of hard chairs, a projection table, and some maps on the walls. Among them a big wall map of the Richtersveld showed the formidable terrain enclosed by a loop of the Orange about a hundred kilometres long. Range after range of mountains, some with names, some without, coalesced to form a picture which even cartographically looked daunting. The territory was shut off to the south by the Little Raisin Bush mountains. The names of the peaks were indicative of the hazards – Mount Terror, the Devil's Tooth, Gorgon's Head. Keeler wondered briefly what other outlandish names – Tswayis, Kwaap, Quaxous – meant. References at the foot of the map indicated that a partial aerial survey of the Richtersveld was carried out in 1964. There had never been a ground survey. The plane doing the aerial survey, loaded with geophysical instruments and mapping cameras, crashed. Some of the crew were killed and others died of thirst before the wreckage could be located – it went down somewhere among these mountains in the south-east. It was one of the horror stories of the time. Since then there had been a ban on overflying the Richtersveld.

'There are lots of uncharted white spaces on this map, as you can see.'

'Where is Fannin's Mine?' asked Gressitt.

Rill indicated a place marked Claim Peak, in the southern sector. 'It's not marked, of course, but it's near here. The mine is hard to find. The Throughway is really the road to it. The Throughway itself is a kind of great divide. It stretches all the way from the Orange at Aussenkehr past Claim Peak to the foot of the Little Raisin Bush mountains.'

'Is the Throughway a watershed?' asked Gressitt.

Rill smiled. 'If there were water, it would be. We flew along its course. It looks as if some giant had been playing marbles with enormous boulders down its whole length. And there is as much sand as in the Namib itself. It is really impossible to describe it.'

'Could a Landrover negotiate it?' asked Gressitt.

'Never.'

'About this helicopter trip of yours,' said Gressitt. 'To start with, have you any idea what kind of helicopter Reutemann uses?'

'One helicopter is the same as the next to me,' replied Rill. 'All I can say is that it looked squarer and bigger than CDM's machines – the ones Major Rive's men use for security patrols.'

'What's on your mind, Ross?' enquired Keeler. 'Know anything about 'copters?'

The big American grinned. 'I fly 'em, fellah. I graduated in the Green Berets. And they are no candy-assed outfit.' Then he went on thoughtfully. 'The make of helicopter would maybe give us a lead as to who is backing Reutemann.'

'Surely the make of hovercraft would give us the answer just as easily?' asked Keeler.

Gressitt shrugged. 'It tells us nothing – it's British. Standard SRN6, export model. You can see 'em anyplace.' He addressed Rill. 'Okay, let's get on. The two choppers take off from Oranjemund, fly upriver – right?'

'Right. It was fascinating. The higher upstream you get, the grander and wilder the scenery becomes. Near Aussenkehr you could be flying over the surface of the moon. Approaching the old fort, we passed the Lorelei mountains on the Namib side though I can't imagine anything less like the Rhine. The river cuts through the mountains in a series of twists and turns – it must be a magnificent sight in flood. The desert mountains come right down to the bank – there is only a narrow fringe of vegetation. Then suddenly we came upon Aussenkehr.'

'I've also seen it – from two thousand metres up,' said Gressitt grimly. 'Tell me what Aussenkehr looks like from ground-level.'

'We didn't land,' continued Rill. 'There stood the old fort in front of our eyes. The setting is colossal – it sits on top of a cliff about five hundred metres above the river, at the junction of the Fish, which flows in at the far side. And then, running southwards into the Richtersveld, is the great gash of the Throughway.'

'Tell me everything you can remember about Aussenkehr itself,' demanded Gressitt.

'At that time Reutemann was busy restoring the place

still,' she answered. 'There was a helipad close to the fort itself . . .'

'Yeah, yeah, I saw it too,' broke in Gressitt impatiently.

'We circled the fort. Nothing could be more out of place in that rugged setting than its architecture – all towers and battlements – that sort of thing.'

'Did you see any activity?' Gressitt pressed her.

'Nothing that I could see. There was a jetty with a string of barges at the foot of the cliff and a number of lorries which I suppose they used for the copper ore.'

'That doesn't carry us much further,' remarked Gressitt.

'It was the setting of Aussenkehr I concentrated on, it was so stunning,' went on Rill. 'I wasn't on the look-out for any suspicious activity.'

'Okay. You circled Aussenkehr. What then?'

'We crossed the river and headed into the Throughway – its local name is Gonakouriep. The way the mountains tangle into one vast incredible complex has to be seen to be believed,' she said. 'One range with its valleys looks exactly the same as the next, and the next, and.the next. I am not surprised the search planes could not locate the wreck of that aerial survey aircraft. The Throughway provides a kind of geographical highway to fly by. Otherwise I am sure we would have got lost.'

'Is there no landmark at Fannin's Mine itself apart from Claim Peak you spoke of before?' asked Gressitt.

'There is – a very distinctive one,' replied Rill. 'We flew for about forty kilometres up the Throughway – I checked the distance by map later – and then very soon after passing Claim Peak I spotted a kind of pillar of white quartz jutting out from a whale-back shaped peak – quite unlike the surrounding terrain. The main shaft of the mine has been driven into this whale-back.'

'It sounds mighty impressive, the way you describe it,' said Gressitt.

'The setting is, but the mine itself is far from impressive,' answered Rill. 'The workings lie in a kind of lop-sided crater which is blocked by the whale-back. We landed on a helipad in this crater, right alongside the mine proper. There were modern prefab hutments, some old ruined buildings which I suppose date from Fannin's days, and a narrow-gauge railway track which ran from the mine shaft to the helipad.'

'Did you go in?' asked Gressitt.

'Our party was allowed only a short way into the shaft itself – there was danger of subsidence, we were told. There was some copper ore in the rail trucks, which I examined. There was no doubt – the ore was very rich indeed in copper.'

'Did Reutemann seem as if he were trying to hide something?' asked Gressitt.

'No. The visit was formal and stiff. Both sides had an air of constraint as if the real underlying reason for it was known. We had light refreshments at the miners' mess – Reutemann explained that the men were flown in daily from Aussenkehr, where they were accommodated. The expedition turned out to be rather a damp squib after all the rumours that had been circulating. Even Major Rive seemed satisfied.'

'What about the bones you were invited to pronounce upon?' asked Keeler.

'Also a damp squib – they weren't fossils at all but merely old bones, maybe some of the oxen Fannin drove to death in trying to haul his ore across the mountains.'

'What then?' asked Gressitt.

'We all flew back down the Throughway to Aussenkehr. Again, we didn't land. We circled and proceeded downriver to Oranjemund. The trip ended on a formal, polite note. Handshakes and goodwill all round – as a token of it, Major Rive gave Reutemann permission to kayak on the lower reaches of the river near the mouth if he joined the CDM Canoe Club.'

'Did Reutemann specifically ask for permission?' demanded Keeler.

'I suppose he must have,' replied Rill. 'I don't really

remember the details of the request. It's a long time ago and I found – find – Reutemann off-putting as a man.'

'With that all-male set-up at Aussenkehr, you'd think he'd be polite to any female he met,' quipped Gressitt.

'It's not an all-male set-up,' replied Rill warmly. 'There are women – the Trevenna gang women. As I said, the gang has a bad reputation. They are said to inhabit an island in the river near the fort.

'The rumours about Fannin's Mine and Aussenkehr died down after our visit,' added Rill. 'Now the barge-trains have come to be taken for granted as part of the scenery.'

'Perhaps that was the object of the exercise,' remarked Keeler.

'After you've finished with *Rigel Star* tomorrow night, you and I have a job to do, fellah. Fannin's Mine and Aussenkehr are my top priority targets.'

Rill's chin came up. 'I'm coming also.'

12

'You must be nuts!' exclaimed Keeler. 'It's no place for a woman!'

'I *am* a little crazy.' The ambiguous words were directed to Keeler alone; there was a slight smile at the corners of her generous mouth. 'It is every place for this woman.'

Gressitt looked as taken aback as Keeler. 'Fannin's – and Aussenkehr – are no-go areas, honey. You can't . . .'

'I was good enough to identify your bloody iridium nodule,' went on Rill, her anger rising. 'That makes me good enough to tag along to Fannin's and Aussenkehr.'

Her warm defiance sparked an excitement in Keeler which had nothing to do with the thought of the adventures ahead; it sprang from Rill's identification with him.

'I am not asking to take part in the *Rigel Star* business,' she went on heatedly. 'But Fannin's and Aussenkehr – yes!'

Keeler regarded her, half in admiration, half in awe. 'Listen, Rill, at this stage we haven't really come into close contact with Reutemann, Trevenna, and whoever else is involved. The mere fact that iridium is involved is enough to make the opposition highly dangerous. Can you understand that?'

'I understand perfectly. You went to the barge-train in the frame of mind that is taking you out to sea tomorrow night. What happened? You tangled with one of the toughest characters in these parts and half-killed him in the process.'

'I only hit him – once.'

'With what?' she blazed in reply. 'I'm coming – whatever! Don't treat me like a little old lady to be tucked away with a hot water bottle.' Rill went on. 'That I am not!'

No, Rill, you're a beautiful young woman and you're falling in love, and I am too, thought Keeler.

'Who is going to identify whatever you might discover at Fannin's Mine?' she went on. 'The geologist from the Smithsonian? I'm not coming as a tourist – you *need* me!'

'Jeez,' exclaimed Gressitt. 'I hadn't really thought of that.'

Rill went on, 'Both of you are talking very glibly as if you had already arrived at Fannin's Mine. How do you intend getting there, in the first place?' She banged the big wall map with the back of her hand. 'Show me your route.'

'It will have to be by land, of course,' said Gressitt.

Rill laughed derisively and indicated the map again. 'Show me. If it had been as easy as all that, do you think the Richtersveld would have remained virtually unexplored all these years?'

'Let's take a flash at the possibilities,' said Gressitt. 'What about the Throughway?'

'Out,' said Keeler. 'Reutemann's helicopter uses it daily. Its take-off point is just across the river from Aussenkehr anyway. Our vehicle – I presume we'll use your Landrover, Ross – would be spotted for certain.'

Rill laughed again. 'You talk as if the Throughway were a four-lane highway. I've seen it. It is one vast channel of enormous boulders and sand. Even without the threat of certain detection from the air, you'd never make it.'

Keeler surveyed the big map. 'The Throughway is the key because it leads to Fannin's,' he said. 'What about trying to intercept it fairly close to the mine by approaching by land from the west – the quarter where we are now?'

About forty-five kilometres upriver from Oranjemund, the map showed a winding jeep track leading from the river through the foothills to the western rim of the escarpment. The track ran dead at a point named Hell's Heights. Beyond, the range had the name Paradise mountains. Maybe because no one ever went there.

'This track starts near my dinosaur site at Blooddrift,' said Gressitt. 'I've tried it – for a distance. I never got as far as Hell's Heights. It seems the only way in.'

'Once we're on top of the escarpment, we could head east and intersect the Throughway near Claim Peak – from there it is only a step to Fannin's according to Rill,' said Keeler enthusiastically.

'What you see on the map and what you will see in front of your eyes are two totally different propositions,' replied Rill seriously. 'I agree that the Hell's Heights route seems the only possibility. There do not seem to be any other options. If we get as far as Claim Peak, I can guide you to Fannin's.'

'We'll work on it more closely once we have disposed of the *Rigel Star*,' said Keeler. 'That's my immediate problem – and Herington.'

'You haven't agreed yet that I am coming,' objected Rill.

Keeler took her by the elbows. 'We need you and we want you, Rill – if you really want to come, thanks.'

Gressitt broke the moment between them. 'John, have you any idea of what action you intend to take off the coast, or do you simply intend to ass around in the darkness looking for a ship which might or might not show up?'

'I reckon Socos is the place,' he answered.

'Where in hell is that?' exclaimed Gressitt. 'I've never heard of it.'

'It's Oranjemund's offshore tanker anchorage,' explained Rill.

Keeler indicated the spot on the map ten kilometres upcoast from the Orange River mouth, directly opposite the shoreline diamond workings and about three kilometres out to sea. Here tankers discharge oil at a series of fixed moorings, which is then conveyed by undersea pipeline to the shore, and then onward to Oranjemund itself.

Keeler then outlined his theory, that the *Rigel Star* would rely on the system of navigation lights which tankers use to moor at Socos in order to determine its position.

There are no lights or navigation aids off the mouth of the Orange itself, or, in fact, anywhere between Socos and Lüderitz, which is a good three hundred kilometres to the north. He was betting that Socos would be the place where the *Rigel Star* would rendezvous and subsequently disappear.

'What do you hope to find out at Socos, John?' asked Rill.

'It could be anything. I'll have to play the situation by ear. That is why I want Herington's kayak so badly, so that I can observe without being seen.'

'Herington has a special brand of obstinacy,' said Gressitt thoughtfully. 'He's got this bug about leaving on Lüderitz's own departure date. We must try and talk him out of it.'

'It's a fixation,' Keeler agreed, 'and it makes me suspicious.'

'He could simply be a hard-headed romantic,' said Rill.

'I believe the best way to approach Herington is to put all our cards on the table,' went on Keeler. 'We've tried a part revelation, and it didn't work. Now is the time to come clean with him.'

'Including the iridium?' asked Gressitt.

'Including the iridium.' Keeler was emphatic.

'I'll keep my fingers crossed,' said Rill.

The meeting was a disaster. Herington, with his disproportionately powerful shoulders, wiry body, long face and wispy beard, looked like a guru denied his one-way ticket to Nirvana when Keeler and Gressitt asked him to delay his upcoast trip to Lüderitz. He was wearing shorts and a T-shirt and was sweating from the exertion of sanding by hand the patched fibreglass hull.

'You will not get my kayak!' he burst out angrily. 'Bull – that's what I think of your story about the world's rarest metal – bullshit!'

Keeler kept his cool. 'Listen, Peter. Enormous issues are involved. You – and your kayak – have a key role.'

'We could blow the chances on something of major importance to the West if we don't have your kayak,' added Gressitt.

Herington displayed nothing but his stubborn mulishness. He gestured at the kayak. 'I need your help to get the kayak ready in time, Keeler. Instead, you and Gressitt go off and waste a morning hatching up this fantastic plot . . .'

Gressitt held out the nodule to him. 'We told you, we spent the time with Rill identifying this.'

Herington shrugged. 'It could be anything you say. I don't know. You could be using it simply to pressure me. My objective is absolutely plain – to get away to sea tomorrow night bound for Lüderitz once the fog is down.'

'You'll need our help both to get the kayak ready and transport it to wherever your starting-point might be.'

'That is what I have been saying!' he retorted angrily. 'Now you're backing out . . .'

'We're not backing out. You will still get my full cooperation to make the hull shipshape.'

Keeler's offer seemed to mollify him slightly. 'You must also realize that I have to test the kayak tomorrow before I venture out to sea,' he said off-handedly. 'For years I have planned and schemed to make my trip starting on the same day as Lüderitz. Nothing is going to stop me.'

Only a Browning barrel in the base of your neck, Herington, thought Keeler.

Herington now addressed Gressitt. 'You promised your Landrover to transport the kayak to the beach. I intend setting off from a point just south of the mouth – outside the Sperrgebiet, of course. There's a marsh, and no habitations. I need you also.'

'I won't renege on it,' replied Gressitt.

Herington eyed the other two angrily still. Keeler realized he had something like thirty hours in which to persuade Herington.

He pulled off his shirt. 'Let's get on with the job,' he said.

94

Herington accepted with the same measure of gratitude as would a mule when you stop kicking it.

Gressitt went off to make his daily radio report to SAMEX's next-in-command in Namibia, Ron Walker. On their way to the camp, Gressitt had wanted to pass on full details of the iridium identification to SAMEX's Fort Meade headquarters. After a long argument, Keeler had dissuaded him on the grounds that their freedom of movement might be restricted in handling the situation as they saw fit, instead of by someone sitting thousands of kilometres away. Keeler had stressed that in FERRET he had always played a loner's game. Gressitt had finally been persuaded not to inform SAMEX of the iridium nodule until at least after the *Rigel Star* intercept, when the position might become clearer. In the meanwhile, however, Gressitt was adamant that he would order Ron Walker to Lüderitz to wait on the sidelines, so to speak, and to be ready for any eventuality.

Keeler and Herington worked all afternoon in a state of armed neutrality. They finally finished the kayak by the light of the fire after the fog had come down, sweating on the side where the flames were, freezing on the other.

Gressitt reappeared with the arrival of the fog. He brought an unfavourable offshore weather report for the following day. A warm berg wind – a typical wind which sweeps down from the inland plateau across the desert and heats itself in the process – was forecast for the early part of the next day, switching characteristically later to a southwesterly gale. It seemed that the kayak would be in for a rough ride up the coast.

The three men went to bed early. Keeler fell into an overtired, uneasy sleep. Thoughts of the *Rigel Star* scrambled through his mind, on the borderline between consciousness and sleep.

Suddenly, as if warned by some deep-down primitive instinct, Keeler jerked up fully awake.

Danger!

13

Keeler did not make the mistake of a giveaway movement. He lay motionless in his nylon sleeping-bag, every nerve alert and tingling. He was on a small sand bank, with the fire well beyond his feet. Further on, the river was blotted out by fog. On one side of the fire was Herington's pup-tent, and on the other Gressitt's Landrover, in which he slept.

Keeler found the Browning's muzzle, warm and comforting under his pillow.

He lay still.

A slight sound from the direction of the fire; a low bird-call – a signal – from the river; the sight of a fragmentary silhouette moving swiftly towards the kayak; his own rapid wriggle to rid himself of the sleeping-bag's folds; his ducking full-length into the soft sand – all were telescoped into a second or two.

The outline of a man was revealed crouching by the kayak. He had something in his hand, but the fog obscured it.

Keeler lifted the Browning, aimed the sight at the man, but his unwillingness to shoot him in the back lost him his target, as a swirl of fog reached out to envelop him.

Keeler edged forward in the sand silently, but the capricious fog eased aside.

Keeler now saw the man's face. He was an Oriental!

It wasn't a knife in his hand. Keeler knew the cricket-ball lump could only be a limpet plastic explosive!

The hand reached out to clap the lump against the kayak's side. At that moment the fog intervened again. The picture faded.

Keeler fired.

In the intense silence the sound crashed out like a battleship's broadside.

Keeler saw a movement like turbulence in the fog. The figure catapulted in the direction of the river.

There was a splash. Keeler risked another shot. There was an answering thrash of water as the swimmer used every ounce of muscle he could muster. Again, from further out, came that low bird-call signal. Its location was as dicy as pinpointing a ventriloquist's voice.

Keeler sprinted to the water's edge, but saw nothing. He was not going to blaze away merely in the hope of hitting something under impossible conditions. There was the sound of a paddle stroke. The murk was thicker over the water than the land, as it always is.

Keeler first realized that Gressitt was next to him when he heard the clunk of the UZI as he rammed over the selector to rapid fire.

'Hold it!' Keeler snapped. 'They're probably safe behind the sandbank by now. A burst from the UZI will bring the whole of Security about our ears!'

Herington appeared alongside the two men. 'For God's sake, what's happening . . .?'

'Quick – if you want to save the kayak!' Keeler went on. 'He was fixing a limpet bomb to it when I spotted him!'

'Where?' demanded Gressitt.

'Know anything about them?'

'Yeah, sure.'

Herington started to spring towards the kayak.

'Leave it, Peter!' yelled Keeler. 'You'll only get yourself killed!'

Gressitt dropped the UZI and he, too, raced for the kayak.

When Keeler and he reached the craft, Herington was about to pluck at a lump which stood out from the smooth curve of the hull like breast cancer.

'For Chrissake – they caught us all asleep at the switch!' exclaimed Gressitt in disgust. 'Leave that goddam thing for me, Peter!'

'Get it off!' yelled Herington. 'Get it off my boat!'

'Peter, get me a flashlight! John, the UZI! Shoot the hell out of anyone or anything that moves while I work on this! This is my baby! Keep well away! I don't know whether that sonofabitch had time to set it!'

Herington passed Gressitt a flashlight; he and Keeler retreated to the water's edge. All they could see from there was Gressitt hunched over a tiny pool of light.

Three minutes.

Herington burst out. 'I'm going back!'

'Hold it!' retorted Keeler. 'Ross knows what he is doing. You'll only be in the way.'

Herington's reply was shaky. 'He's risking his life for me – for my trip.'

Keeler said nothing.

Herington went on. 'If it hadn't been for you also, the kayak would have gone up in smoke – and with it my Lüderitz trip.'

Five minutes.

Keeler gestured with the automatic. 'It may still go off. Perhaps the fuse has Ross licked.'

'Call him off, John!' Herington exclaimed. 'The kayak can go!'

Six minutes.

Herington said. 'I shouldn't have refused you the kayak. Now I know you two weren't conning me.'

Gressitt was now on his feet. He walked across to where the two men stood. His face seemed tougher, the mouth harder than before. He held out his hand. In the palm was a tiny cylindrical object, like a cheap ballpoint pen top.

'Safe?' burst out Herington.

'Yeah. It wasn't too complicated.'

'How long to zero?' asked Keeler.

'Hard to say,' replied the big American. 'Ask the guy who planted it!'

'You saved my Lüderitz trip. And my kayak,' said Herington.

Gressitt seemed embarrassed at the intensity of his gratitude.

'Forget it,' he replied. 'I would have been quicker, but this is a new type of detonator!'

'Russian?'

'Standard Soviet stuff.'

'That doesn't tell us who's behind it,' said Keeler.

'It's the sort of explosive you'd find anywhere in the world where there are terrorists.'

'The guy that planted it wasn't Russian,' said Keeler. 'He was either Chinese or Jap.'

'You must be kidding,' exclaimed Gressitt incredulously.

'I got a bead on him when the fog cleared for a moment – I saw his face,' said Keeler.

'The only ones to fit your description,' went on Gressitt, 'are the VIP Japs, CDM's guests. I don't see one of them soft-shoeing around in the middle of the night trying to blow up someone's kayak he's never heard of.'

'With all that fog you could have been mistaken,' added Herington.

'Of course, it could have been one of Reutemann's men from upriver,' said Gressitt. 'A lot of Hottentots look oriental.'

Keeler shook his head, not convinced.

'Okay – we'll leave that file open for the moment,' said Gressitt.

'Let's get back to the fire and I'll tell you what I think,' said Herington, as if he had just made up his mind about something.

They threw some wood on the embers and fanned them up. Keeler and Gressitt kept their guns within reach.

Herington said, as he kneeled over the fire preparing coffee, 'I've come to a decision. After what has happened tonight, the kayak and myself are at your disposal.'

'Well, I'll be damned!' exclaimed Gressitt.

Keeler clapped Herington on the shoulder. 'Good man, Peter! Good man!'

Gressitt was grinning. 'John and I have been going round with our asses in a sling wondering how to work things out. Thanks, fellah!'

'What about your Lüderitz trip?' asked Keeler.

'The bomb has changed my way of thinking,' he said, half embarrassed that he should have to reveal his inner feelings. 'If I have to wait a few days, even a week or two, it's too bad. The deadline is entirely my own. It can wait.'

'This calls for a celebration!' grinned Gressitt. 'If it weren't that I intend sitting guard all night with the UZI, I'd open my bottle of tiger sweat!'

Herington swept aside their appreciation and went on hesitatingly. 'There is something else you should know. The damage to my kayak wasn't an accident. I was escaping from Reutemann's men.'

Keeler and Gressitt stared. Keeler said, 'Go on.'

'I think you should know this because it may throw some light on what happened tonight. When I came downriver, I intended pulling into the jetty at Aussenkehr. It was dusk. As I started to do so, one of the guards started firing at me with his automatic. I beat it – fast. But I wasn't fast enough. Before I could get clear of the fort, I spotted two kayaks racing after me. They were catching up when we entered the rapids, which are a couple of kilometres away. Trying to dodge another burst of fire I collided with a submerged rock. I thought I was a goner. However, I lost them in the dark and rough water – I think they were scared to press on, or they lacked experience.'

'It would have helped us a lot if we'd known this before,' said Keeler.

Herington's embarrassment grew. He said rapidly, as if to put the incident finally behind him. 'John, with the sort of weather that is building up, it is going to take us all our time to intercept the *Rigel Star*.' Discussion of the logistics of the venture seemed to enable him to conceal his feelings. 'When is that ship of yours due?'

'I'll check again with my man in Cape Town – he'll have the latest from Lüderitz,' said Keeler. 'Originally I expected the tow about nightfall. However, a southwesterly bluster will slow it down. There'll be no such thing as exact timing.'

'We'll use the kayak for the job, of course,' said Herington. 'For Aussenkehr we'll need a second boat also. There'll be three of us. I'll borrow a canoe from the Canoe Club.'

'Four of us,' Keeler corrected him. 'Rill's coming too.' He explained briefly how she had refused to be left out.

Herington shook his head, and added. 'We'll have to keep a sharp watch for Reutemann and Trevenna's kayaks.'

'How can you be sure they'll be out?' asked Gressitt.

'The explosive business spotlights their purpose – I think the inference is clear – they were trying to destroy our kayak so that their own could operate freely,' said Herington.

Keeler repeated his conviction that the *Rigel Star* and her tug, the *Sumarai Maru*, would home in on the tanker terminal lights at the Socos anchorage. It was there, he believed that Reutemann and Trevenna would rendezvous with the ship.

Herington agreed, and Gressitt added, 'I'd feel happier if you would take the UZI along, John. You never know what might happen.'

'I'd rather rely on this baby – and the fog,' he replied waving his Browning.

'It'll be as thick as hell at Socos at night,' said Herington. 'It could even scupper our sighting of the *Rigel Star*.'

'Hold it!' interrupted Gressitt. 'I've got something which will give you the edge.'

He slipped away to the Landrover and came back carrying a small leather case. He unclipped it and pulled out what seemed to be a foreshortened telescope.

'You don't know what this is,' he said. 'Starscope – to see in the dark.' He fiddled with the adjusting mechanism. 'To see without being seen. This little baby will illuminate the target with infra-red rays, which is then viewed through this combination telescope sight and fluorescent screen. *Voilà!*'

'Where did you get it?' asked Keeler.

'Top-secret issue to SAMEX operatives,' he replied. 'You'll spot Reutemann and Trevenna at Socos long before they can sight you.'

'What sort of range has it got?' asked Herington.

'About a hundred metres,' replied Gressitt. 'The Starscope will give you a good advantage over Reutemann and Trevenna in the dark.'

'That's great, Ross – we'll take it,' said Keeler. 'Let's now hope we can manage to make our way to sea and don't run into a gale.'

'I've worked it out,' replied Herington quickly, now fully attentive to the task that lay ahead. 'I'll approach Security tomorrow and ask permission to try out my kayak on the lower reaches towards the mouth during the afternoon. We'll then be inside the Sperrgebiet – and we'll stay there.'

'Security isn't that naïve,' said Keeler. 'They'll check.'

'Of course they'll check,' answered Herington. 'We'll recce the mouth and select the best spot to break out once the fog descends. The river is starting to come down and the turbulence where it meets the sea is going to be bad, especially with the oncoming swells. There is a mass of little reed-covered islands near the mouth – they're at their most luxuriant at this time of year. We'll keep deliberately in sight of the Security patrol helicopter and then hole up in one of the islands. When darkness comes, we'll hightail it out to sea – and to Socos.'

After a moment of reflection, Gressitt, fiddling with his coffee mug, asked abruptly, 'What if you guys don't come back from Socos?'

'You contact SAMEX immediately and tell 'em to get a hot line to FERRET in Hong Kong,' replied Keeler. 'Tell FERRET to pick up the *Rigel Star* before she succeeds in losing herself.'

'And Reutemann and Trevenna?'

'I'm quite certain you are capable of rounding them up by yourself.'

Gressitt blew into the UZI's muzzle. 'I sure will.'

14

Next night, the fog was down on the Orange River mouth and it was pitch dark. The gale was howling as if for vengeance. Keeler and Herington were on their way to Socos. They expected the *Rigel Star* to arrive at the offshore tanker anchorage at eight p.m. It was now a little past six.

The first breaker the kayak encountered as it broke clear of the sandbar blocking the mouth to the open sea tried to stand the frail craft on its stern skeg and shake Keeler and Herington out of the double cockpit into the icy, cappuccino-coloured water. They were in a no-man's-land of sea where the confrontation between two opposing bodies of water produced a maelstrom. On the one hand there were the giant swells, accelerated by the gale across a drag-strip of seven thousand kilometres of ocean from Antarctica, and on the other the counter-punching power of a river starting to rise with the force of a season's inland rains. The drum-beat of the breakers on the iron bar, which sealed all but a hundred and fifty metres of the river mouth, added to the chaos.

Herington rose in his seat like an off-road rider and threw his weight forward to bring the kayak's bow down.

'Don't let her broach!' he yelled. 'For Chrissake, hold her!'

Keeler's paddle went deep. He knew that if they were once caught in the trough of the breakers, the kayak would be rolled over and back across the bar. He gave the stroke everything he had. The yaw went on, the kayak's bow went down as if looking for diamonds on the seabed. Then Herington's stroke took and the craft steadied while the water foamed by at cockpit-level.

'Steady as she goes!' The words scarcely penetrated the earflaps of Keeler's blue nylon cap. 'Keep course – don't lose it!'

Another wave came at the kayak and it stabbed through it, taking the run of the sea on its port quarter. Both men knew that they had to fight clear of the surf-line before they could attempt to head parallel with the coast in the direction of Socos. The prevailing sea, coupled with the rollers that were being kicked up as the swells gained speed on striking the offshore land shelf, produced a torque effect which screwed the light hull landwards – towards the concrete-hard bar.

That bar across the river mouth and the problem of navigating the narrow gap on its southern end, had anxiously preoccupied the two men throughout the afternoon. Testing the kayak for water-tightness, they had described the operation when they had approached Major Rive for permission to use the lower reaches of the river in the out-of-bounds area. Major Rive had made no objection. The uncomfortable moment in the meeting had come when Major Rive had tossed an apparently casual question – had either of them heard a shot in the night from the vicinity of their camp? Keeler had realized that it would be futile to deny it, and admitted that he had heard the shot. It had woken him, he had said. Major Rive's eyes seemed to become more steely. The report, he had said, had claimed two shots, yet Keeler had heard only one, Keeler had stuck to his story; the undertow of doubt remained.

The extent of Major Rive's acceptance of the rest of their story had shown itself later in the afternoon as Keeler and Herington had cruised among the innumerable small reedy islands, sandbars and shallows near the river mouth. A Security helicopter had appeared above the kayak and given them a long scrutiny. Later, when it had safely disappeared, the two men had holed up in a mass of reeds and shallows about two kilometres from the mouth to await the night – and Socos. They had completed their reconnaissance of the bar and had decided to break out through the southern gap.

Other eyes besides Major Rive's had been interested in the kayak's activities. Keeler and Herington had been obliged to pass by Reutemann's barge-train on their way downriver. They deliberately hid their warm-weather gear and water-proofing out of sight and appeared in their shirt-sleeves, as if they were off for an afternoon of fun. One of the crew of the hovercraft reported it to Reutemann, and he and Trevenna rushed out on deck to watch it pass.

During the preparations for the kayak's departure that morning, Rill had made her surprising arrival, baggage and all. Keeler, with Herington, had earlier gone to her flat in Oranjemund after their interview with Major Rive, wishing to inform her of Herington's change of heart and their planned Socos sortie. Rill had been out. Presumably she had gone to the Arrisdrift dig. He had left her an affectionate note and the two men had gone to collect a canoe from the Canoe Club. Major Rive had made no mention of Rill. When Rill had told them earlier that she had informed Major Rive that she was profiting from a unique opportunity to go fossil-hunting in the Richtersveld with the men, it occurred to Keeler that Major Rive had cleverly kept silent about her visit. A contradiction between what he might have said and Rill's story would have given them away. That's how the Security chief's mind worked.

It was not, however, the thought of Major Rive which had given Rill cause for concern. It was the sight of the kayak surrounded by all that special warm waterproof clothing, the Starscope, Gressitt's UZI and Keeler's Browning cleaned and stripped, as well as a couple of grenades which Gressitt had tried to persuade Keeler to take.

Rill's tension had increased progressively as the kayak's departure time had neared. Especially when Keeler had added an extra fifty rounds to the Browning's armoury.

When they had finally pushed off from the camp, she had not said goodbye; when Keeler had raised his paddle in farewell salute she had simply stood and stared as if engraving the picture on her mind. The last sight he had had of her was of her lovely hair being blown all over her face as if to mask her feelings.

Keeler deliberately blotted the picture of Rill from his mind and concentrated on getting the kayak clear of the breakers. Another breaker, and another – two more softening-up punches for the final knockdown. The kayak gave a bump and a crash which made Keeler fear for a moment that it had bottomed. Then it leaped as if it had been stung and tried again to screw sideways. Two paddles held the movement. Next – the waves dramatically lost their streaming plumes, and changed to a deep, charging swell.

The kayak had broken clear of the surf-line!

'Turn!' shouted Herington.

They paddled in tight synchronization to follow the line of the coast. The kayak's motion became different. The waves' punches were slower and looping, unlike the previous deadly steep, chopping blows. Conversation remained impossible. With the unspoken rapport of two experts, they fell into a long stroke for the ten-kilometre haul to Socos.

They had nothing to guide them but a small compass – and their own instincts. Fog and night made it impossible to see more than a few metres ahead – except with the Starscope. Off the coast, also, there is a local current which dodges at its own whim between the offshore reefs and shoals. It takes direction from the wind and the river. It is uncharted, unchartable. Their target was a small area a few hundred metres square with three permanent marker buoys, a massive tanker mooring buoy, and another marker buoy demarcating the submerged end of the oil pipeline to the shore. The key to Socos was the presence ashore of two flashing lights. One, in front, stood twenty-seven metres high. It emitted a quick flashing light. Behind it was sited a second light, sixty-nine metres high, which gave off a white flash. When put in a line bearing of forty-three and a half degrees, the two lights pointed directly at Socos. They were the tankerman's guardian angels.

Dip, lift, switch – dip, lift, switch – the treadmill paddling pattern went on and on as Keeler and Herington continued in rhythmic tandem. Nothing mattered but the sweep of their muscles. The exertion seemed to iron out from Keeler's mind the imponderables and dangers of the rendezvous.

Herington's paddle went up. 'Stop!'

'Socos?' shouted Keeler. 'See the buoys?'

'Too soon for them yet – I guess Socos is still about three kilometres away. Take a look over there.' He pointed right with his paddle – landwards.

From the crest of the next roller Keeler spotted what looked like an amorphous pink ghost of a UFO above the land. It was the reflected lights of Oranjemund town against the fog ceiling. That was their datum point for Socos, where they bore off. Keeler marvelled at Herington's uncanny sense of direction and place. The kayak now struck off seawards at an angle from the coast. The beam-on sea rolled the craft sickeningly.

'Keep a sharp look-out – we must be getting near the line of the leading lights for Socos,' Herington shouted after they had pursued their new course for a while.

A new pinkness appeared in the direction of the land, but in a different quarter from Oranjemund.

'Foreshore diamond workings,' exclaimed Herington. 'Hold while I get my bearings.'

'Peter!' burst out Keeler urgently. 'Listen! Breakers!'

'Can't be . . .'

'It is!' he retorted. *'Listen!'*

'Could be machinery ashore . . .' Herington began, and then rapped out. 'Get her round, John! We're among them! That bitch of a current!'

They shoved the kayak's bow round, stroked as hard as

they could. The choppy motion eased. The long swells – the seaward waves began again.

'We were right inshore!' exclaimed Herington breathlessly.

They rested on their paddles and Keeler said, 'We could go on all night like this and never locate Socos. Have you any idea where we are?'

'I thought I did. I'll try the Starscope.'

Keeler steadied the kayak while Herington used the instrument.

'Spot anything?'

'The bloody angle of sight of this thing is so narrow, it's difficult to hold an image,' he replied. 'No . . . nothing.'

'Let me try.'

Keeler focused. On the tiny screen, a succession of waves, green like sci-fi monsters – all the instrument's pictures were in the colour green – hurtled at him. It was better, he decided, not to see them coming. Certainly, there was not a solid object within the Starscope's hundred-metre range.

Keeler put the Starscope away; he preferred the fog-ridden blackness. His watch showed the time -- seven thirty. In half an hour the *Rigel Star* was due – if she made good time. The gale seemed more intermittent than steady now. It had, however, kicked up enough sea to last for the next two days.

'We have *got* to locate those lights ashore!' exclaimed Herington. 'What we have to achieve is an intersection of the imaginary line they make to Socos from the land. If we miss them, we miss Socos.'

'So does the *Rigel Star*,' said Keeler. 'Her problem is the same as ours.'

'I'd say the leading lights have a visible angle out to sea of about twenty-five degrees,' Herington went on. 'That gives us a bit of elbow room in which to pick them up.'

'The fog and God willing.'

'The lights are pretty high up,' Herington answered. 'They may even show above the fog ceiling.'

'What course now, Peter?' demanded Keeler. 'Our timing's getting short.'

'We'll work on the assumption that we haven't overshot the lights,' said Herington. 'Five minutes' paddling, then stop. We'll try and steer by the sea on our beam – okay?'

Dip, lift, dip. Dip, lift, dip. Four minutes.

The kayak soared to a crest. Shorewards, something caught Keeler's eye. And there it was – a white flash.

High on its sixty-nine metre tower in the desert, the light – probably fog-penetrating, they came to reckon later – pointed the way to Socos.

'There'll be a red flash next from the lower tower in front!' went on Herington. 'We must have arrived on the southern fringe of the light range – they're not in line yet . . .'

'Don't lose it, whatever you do!' exclaimed Keeler.

They didn't. Soon, they had aligned the red with the white flash astern.

They steered the kayak towards Socos.

15

The fog played strange tricks. One moment it was thick and impenetrable, the next thin enough to sight and keep check on the homing lights.

Herington signalled another halt while he probed the murk with the Starscope.

'Anything in sight?'

'No. But we're on the beam now.'

Although the Starscope was a splendid extension of the human eye, it still had disadvantages. First, there was its narrow angle of sight – only fourteen degrees – and, second, the strange varying shades of green which the screen threw up for all objects. Its range was a hundred metres, while the Socos mooring area from end to end was over five hundred. This meant that even from mid-point, where a marker indicated the undersea pipeline, the big mooring buoys at either end – bow and stern for a discharging tanker – were out of its vision. They decided to keep their voices down from now on, not wishing to alert Reutemann and Trevenna, who might be there already.

The words were scarcely spoken when Herington hissed. 'Something right ahead!'

Whatever it was, he had sighted it without the Starscope. Now he groped for the instrument. Keeler slipped the Kapitän into his gloved right hand and readied it against the edge of the cockpit.

'Big – it's big, John! It's one of the buoys!'

Keeler craned to see through the fog but could distinguish nothing.

'One – only one?' he asked in a whisper.

'Yes. Must be the tanker-bow mooring buoy.'

'How far away?'

'Close, that's all I know. This instrument isn't calibrated.'

'Check round for Reutemann and Trevenna,' Keeler said.

Herington got himself into a crouch in the forward cockpit, steadying himself against the kayak's roll.

'Nothing,' he reported. 'But they could be at the stern group of three buoys. They're out of our range.'

Keeler did a quick calculation. The *Rigel Star* would be coming from the north and therefore she would encounter the stern-anchoring buoys first. There was still ten minutes to go to eight o'clock – the minimum ETA time possible.

'We're safer here,' he told Herington in a low voice. 'We'll make fast – for the moment.'

The kayak homed on the red-painted metal of the buoy. It was slimy with sea-things and rode at the end of its massive chain grinding against the shackle.

'It would be a miracle if the *Rigel Star* were on time in this weather,' said Herington.

Unless – Keeler thought grimly, the whole idea of the rendezvous might only be a figment of his imagination.

After half an hour there was still no sign of the ship. Keeler began to psych himself into believing he had been wrong. He eyed Herington's yellow anorak in the cockpit ahead and began to blame himself for needlessly depriving him of his dream – the trip to Lüderitz.

The night became colder. The great columns of murk which swept by were less dense – some even had the wispiness of Herington's own beard. At times the flashing lights ashore became relatively clear. The other buoys of Socos, however, remained invisible.

Keeler felt the cold starting to penetrate his shoulder muscles. Finally he said, 'Peter, let's explore the other buoys. You keep the Starscope going – I'll paddle.'

It was now possible for one man to navigate the craft; the

wind had dropped to a fresh breeze, although the swells remained formidable.

Herington nodded in silent agreement. His disenchantment spread like the fog on the surface of the sea.

They first came upon a smaller, orange-painted buoy, the mid-point marker indicating the pipeline terminal. Herington probed myopically with the Starscope's narrow sight-angle. The triangle of stern buoys they were aiming for, lay another couple of hundred metres ahead. Herington concentrated on this sector. Then suddenly both men froze.

'Trevenna!'

Reutemann's voice seemed to come from right alongside their kayak. Instinctively, Keeler and Herington crouched low in their cockpits. They held their paddles and their breath.

'See the ship?' called Reutemann. He made no attempt to keep his voice down. He could not suspect their presence, the message flashed through Keeler's brain in relief. 'She must be somewhere around.'

A voice answered from a different place in the murk.

'Not a bloody thing, Kurt.'

Keeler tapped Herington on the back as a signal to locate Reutemann by Starscope. He took a firm grip on the Kapitän, hardly daring to breathe. Any moment the uncertain fog could part and reveal them.

Herington indicated a direction to Keeler in silent mime and passed him the Starscope.

'She's close! I smell her Kurt!'

Reutemann's reply was abrasive. 'Sure you're not smelling your own stink, man?'

'She's near – listen!' The pitch of Trevenna's voice rose.

Without waiting to use the Starscope, Keeler took the enemy's advice.

There was a curious long swish, and a thump-thump-thump.

Tow-rope! Tug's engines! *Rigel Star! Sumarai Maru!*

Keeler leant forward to make Herington a hand signal. At that moment, the fog was torn aside by a brilliant red burst.

Simultaneously, a volley of automatic fire crashed out, seemingly almost alongside them.

Both men ducked.

The flare – one of those Keeler had noted amongst Reutemann's kayak's equipment – rose high, and the fog curtain lightened slightly ahead and to the right of Keeler and Herington.

A ship, riding high in ballast, bore down almost on top of them.

A second burst of automatic fire clattered from her upperworks.

Flare – signal – answer!

The pyrotechnics and the automatic fire, Keeler and Herington realized, had not been directed at them. The curious sound which Trevenna's keen ears had picked up had been the tautening and slackening of the tow-rope to the *Sumarai Maru*, which was still not visible to Keeler and Herington.

It seemed to Keeler that they could not but be spotted, even with the fog's protective screen.

But how right he had been in his assessment of a kayak's low-profile virtues came when Reutemann, unnoticing, shouted, '*Jawohl*, Trevenna! Ready! Paddle! Take us to the ship!'

Although he could not risk raising his head, Keeler guessed that Reutemann and Trevenna's kayaks had been linked in tandem by a tow-rope as a means of keeping together in the fog.

Now the thud of the tug's engines stopped. The *Rigel Star*'s outline became less distinct in a thicker swirl of fog. She had, in fact, been further away than Keeler had judged when she had first showed up out of the murk.

Keeler said softly to Herington. 'Follow 'em! Keep close – but not too close.'

Herington turned and gave the thumbs-up sign. Muffling their paddle-strokes, they sneaked after the other craft. They did not have to use the Starscope to keep track of them – Reutemann's Teutonic-sounding words and Trevenna's answers were enough. The fog, thicker now again, played tricks with the sound, however.

Keeler thought he had misheard when a yell from Reutemann came through the darkness. '*Rainbow*!'

The password floated back from the *Rigel Star*. 'Rainbow!'

Rainbow – iridium! The Socos rendezvous was concerned with iridium.

'Get closer!' whispered Keeler urgently to Herington. 'We must see what is happening!'

In a clearer patch, the *Rigel Star* stood out like a high-rise building. Lights were everywhere. A brace of spotlights was focused on a scrambling-net rigged over the ship's side. Ready to climb up were Reutemann and Trevenna, crouching in the cockpits of their respective kayaks.

Now the thud-thud of the tug's engines started again and the tow-rope gave its long swishing sound as it took up the strain. The tug was taking no chances in the heavy swells. It began to ease along with power enough only to give steerage way.

Fog blew across Keeler's line of vision. Keeler aimed the Starscope at Reutemann as he started up the scrambling-net. He had something small in his hand. The greenish vision of the Starscope was not enough to define it. They were, Keeler thought rapidly, farther away from the ship than he had judged.

'Closer!' he whispered.

'It's risky, John!'

Keeler and Herington edged their kayak to the extreme limit of their concealing patch of fog. Then they both saw it. Reutemann was carrying the small waterproof bag containing iridium nodules!

Keeler barely had time to be sure before Reutemann

reached the top and swung a leg over the rail, followed by Trevenna, who carried nothing.

Reutemann didn't waste time on ceremony. He gave a perfunctory hand-shake to a man who greeted him, handed over the little bag, and received in return from him a bulky load, partly wrapped in yellow waterproofed oilskin.

It was an elongated package from the bottom of which projected what seemed like the skeleton butts of a gaggle of sub-machine guns.

Reutemann went back down the net with his package, Trevenna followed with another. They carefully eased the loads into the kayaks' empty cockpits and returned to the ship's deck.

The next parcels they received had no tell-tale identification but they were evidently fairly weighty.

In their eagerness to observe the operation, Keeler and Herington's craft had strayed closer to the *Rigel Star*, or perhaps the ship had edged nearer to them.

There was a sudden yell of alarm from the ship.

They had been spotted!

16

Before Keeler and Herington had time even to dip their paddles there was a rattle of fire from the ship.

The chop-chop of the sweeping burst was lost in the surge of the swells. Fortunately, the kayak presented a difficult target; yet one bullet would have been enough to finish it. The kayak wheeled on its skeg like a rearing horse. As it spun round, Keeler had a glimpse of Reutemann and Trevenna hanging at the top of the scrambling-net, as if pinned there by shock.

They forged ahead into shelter of thick fog. Both men threw everything they had into their strokes.

'Where are we going?' Herington managed to utter.

'Anywhere!' Keeler gasped in reply. 'No, damn it, coastwards.'

'There are two of them – and they mean business!'

One, two – six paddle thrusts.

The kayak rose on a swell. Keeler grabbed the Starscope, but his attention was only half on the instrument. From somewhere astern he thought he heard the splash of a paddle.

'Hold it!' he rasped imperatively to Herington. 'Three buoys – right ahead! We're among the stern anchorages!'

Their momentum threw the kayak almost into a big buoy, gaudy with lateral red stripes, which loomed out of the fog like a fat ghost in pyjamas.

Keeler swivelled the Starscope this way and that. 'The buoys are in triangle – this one is the farthest back. We turn now at right angles and we're set to go down the coast . . .'

If the two men in their haste had not already started on the turn as Keeler ordered it, Keëler probably would not have spotted Reutemann. One moment there seemed to be a blank wall of fog; the next, Reutemann's face appeared framed in a black balaclava.

He spotted them simultaneously. He dropped his paddle and made a grab for a gun.

Keeler yelled a warning, stroked, and swung the kayak all in one movement. He realized three things at lightning speed – that in reaching for his automatic and dropping his paddle, Reutemann would lose speed; that in the rough sea his kayak would be a highly unstable firing platform; and that he would have to give himself time to steady his aim to have any hope of accurate fire.

Keeler thrust the kayak behind the big steel buoy, and blocked Reutemann from view.

Herington – for reasons unknown – blew their advantage. He stood up, grabbed the big shackle which secured the buoy to its chain, as if he meant to make the kayak fast. He exposed himself as the perfect target, Reutemann might miss the kayak low down in the water, but he would not miss a standing man. Keeler hooked the blade of his paddle across Herington's neck and shoulder, pulled him down.

As he flopped down, the air was filled with flying lead and noise. Ricochets screamed and bounced off the buoy. The slugs went whooping away into the fog.

'Trevenna!' Reutemann, who plainly thought he had nailed Keeler's kayak, yelled 'Here! Here! Cut them off!' But Trevenna's answer came from further away.

Keeler admired the way Herington made up for his initial blunder. For a moment, while he oriented himself, he remained immobile. Then he said quietly and coolly, 'This is our way! Down the coast!' And the two men threw all their strength and skill into their getaway strokes.

From behind came the sound of a single shot followed by a metallic whang, as either Reutemann or Trevenna, mistaking one of the buoys for the kayak had taken a shot at it.

There followed shouts and savage oaths from astern, as Reutemann and Trevenna's craft probably narrowly missed each other.

Herington's kayak now surged forward with gathering speed, despite the run of the sea. But speed was nearly their undoing when the single, final, bow mooring buoy loomed unexpectedly before them. Herington gave a masterly twitch of his paddle without slowing down and the danger slid by within touching distance.

From behind came a long, heavy burst of fire. This time it was from two automatics, not one. Clearly Reutemann and Trevenna had joined forces and were machine-gunning blindly round the compass in the hope of picking off Keeler and Herington.

The racket gave Keeler a momentary opportunity to talk without giving himself away. 'If they reach the river mouth first, we're done for!'

'We won't give them that chance!' retorted Herington. 'Their kayaks are weighed down with all that hardware. Let's get the hell out – now! Get going!'

They did so. Then the fog gave one of its fickle sceneshifts. To starboard, as big as the Empire State Building, the *Rigel Star* suddenly materialized, still burning all her lights. The fog, by the same sleight-of-hand it had displayed in revealing the ship, concealed the tug. The *Sumarai Maru* was invisible but not inaudible. The powerful thud-thud of its engines seemed to match Keeler's own heart-beats. It seemed impossible that they would not be spotted, yet they were not.

Suddenly the whole scene shut out again as dramatically as it had shown up.

Herington and Keeler dug their paddles hard. Wind and the run of the sea were on the starboard bow. The kayak, rolling a full fifteen degrees, sliced into the waves. Every time its sharp bow lifted to a crest, it threw icy spray over the two crouched men. Keeler's ungloved hand was half-frozen. If they thought the upcoast slog had been a battle, their new course promised to be sheer hell.

'We're still safe!' said Herington briefly as the *Rigel Star* vanished. 'Save all your breath for the work!'

They needed it. By the time two of the ten kilometres to their objective had passed, Keeler was gasping in lungfuls of the ozone-laden air to keep pace with Herington's full-stretch, powerful stroke. All sight and sound of pursuit had disappeared.

By the halfway mark, Keeler's mind was preoccupied with the thought that Reutemann might have left orders with the *Rigel Star* to radio ahead for someone to intercept them as they came upriver by the Oppenheimer bridge.

Their treadmill resolved itself into a muscle-cracking haul, up yet one more roller, followed by a surfboard-like descent into yet one more trough. The pattern repeated itself relentlessly until the muscles across Keeler's chest were cracking like angina pains. Herington stroked on in apparently tireless rhythm. And then they were there. But neither of them slowed his stroke. From their left came the sound of the heavy thud of breakers. Herington kept the paddling going while Keeler probed the darkness. The Starscope allowed him to see a confused mass of moving green with the lighter crests of white spray. The instrument was of no help in trying to determine their position – the shoreline on either side of the river-mouth being flat and featureless. It was the narrow entrance gap they had to find.

Herington, thanks to mysterious instinct Keeler could not fathom, seemed confident. 'We're further out than we should be,' he called. 'We'll head shorewards for a while. When the breakers change their pitch, it means we're facing the gap in the bar.'

They swung landwards. A beam sea rolled the kayak until their elbows were awash. Keeler lost all sense of time or place. All that mattered was to keep the stroke going.

At some undefined spot in the blackness – the fog was

thicker here over the river water than at Socos – Herington called a halt, if change in the roller-coaster motion could be called a halt. He had overshot on purpose, so as to have the run of the sea to help them through the entrance.

The kayak bumped and banged in the short sharp seas like a Scotch cart on a corrugated road. Herington feathered his paddle, dipped a hand overside, and tasted the water. Fresh for river, salt for sea, Keeler's tired mind registered.

'On! we're going in!'

Keeler felt Herington's power come in. The kayak lurched forward into the breakers. Would it beat the collision of two great forces – the sea striking landwards, the river striking seawards? For a moment Keeler had a fantasy of their paddling until the end of time, in and out the mouth, like the Flying Dutchman off the Cape.

Then the sound of the breakers drowned everything. The kayak yawed and leaped like a wild thing. Keeler heard Herington shout above the racket.

'Now – together! Give it everything!'

In a flash, the surface under the kayak became quiet, noiseless. The silence of a river.

They were safe inside the sandbar!

17

---❖---

The two men lay slumped forward, gasping in lungfuls of air for a couple of minutes, until Keeler felt the kayak starting to swing on the seaward-going current.

He pulled himself upright. They had to move on, just in case Reutemann had managed to alert some of his men!

Herington maintained that the fog on the river was now thick enough to hide them from anyone.

'It's not us I'm worried about, it's Rill and Gressitt at the camp,' retorted Keeler.

'You okay? Let's go then.'

The distance from the mouth to the camp was about fifteen kilometres, not one of which was without its invisible sandbar islands, or shallows. In the fog they fumbled like blind men. And they had not gone more than fifty metres up river when they were thrown forward in their seats as the kayak grounded on a sandbar. They lost valuable minutes while easing the craft free.

Their next obstacle was of the reedy kind. Before they knew where they were, the kayak went slap into an island of reeds. More minutes were wasted, more breath expended on futile oaths.

The stretch of nine kilometres to the Oppenheimer bridge was an agony of frustration, stretched nerves from an endless succession of groundings, precious time lost, and growing anxiety for the safety of the other two at the camp. Finally, when the great piers of the bridge appeared, they were as welcome to the two men as a vision of the Pearly Gates. Here they switched from one bank to another to avoid the barge-train jetty. In doing so, they had to abandon the deep-water channel which follows the southern side. The result was a fresh series of keel-jarring groundings. The cold was as intense as the fog. Their protective clothing had become soaked through by their frequent plunges overside to free the kayak.

Herington, with his sixth sense of direction, headed across the river towards the spot where he said the camp lay on the opposite bank.

Herington held up his hand for silence.

Keeler peered into the darkness. There was no sound from the direction of the camp, no sign of a fire. The stillness of death – the words kept repeating themselves in Keeler's mind like a persistent musical tune.

Had Reutemann's men from the barge-train descended on the sleeping camp, shot or taken Rill and Gressitt captive, and were they now waiting in ambush for Keeler and Herington to return?

Keeler tapped Herington's shoulder to wait while he found the Kapitän, which he laid in front of him.

The kayak went in – swiftly, silently. The bow touched bank. Herington jumped out into the water to secure the craft, making a faint splash.

A yellow foglight stabbed out, and a voice ordered, 'Stand!'

It was Gressitt's voice. He had positioned the Landrover strategically among the underbrush by the landing-place to cover an attack. Behind the vehicle's foglight, the UZI was trained on them.

'Let me see you in the light, because there's a tight-ass behind this gun.'

'Ross! It's us,' and Keeler displayed himself in full view, with Herington alongside him.

Satisfied, Gressitt said with evident relief, 'Jeez, fellahs – you been in the rhubarb? You look all beat up!'

Rill sprinted down the shaft of yellow light into Keeler's

arms. 'Ross. It *is* John! It's them! They've come back!

'God! I thought you were never coming.' Keeler could feel her half-hysterical sobs mixed with laughter running through her body hard against his own. 'I've been praying for you both.'

She held his mud-stained face. 'Look at you! You're a mess – you're soaking wet . . .'

Gressitt tried to pumphandle Keeler, thump Herington on the shoulder, and prevent the UZI from banging against everyone, all at once.

'It's been a long wait!' he exclaimed. 'What the hell happened? It's after two!'

Rill said with relief, 'Anyway, you're not hurt. I'll get some hot coffee.'

But Keeler brushed all the effusion away. 'There's no time for coffee – or anything else. We have got to get out of here before Reutemann or Trevenna show up.'

'What the hell happened?' Gressitt wanted to know.

'John was right about the rendezvous at Socos,' Herington replied. 'The *Rigel Star* showed up, just as he thought she would. Reutemann and Trevenna were waiting. They went aboard . . .'

'What about the iridium?' Gressitt asked impatiently.

'I'll give you a rundown as we pack,' said Keeler tersely. 'We've no time.'

'Is it as bad as that?' Gressitt asked.

'We've been dodging their bullets half the night,' replied Herington grimly. 'Thanks to John we're still here!'

'You can't go without something hot!' exclaimed Rill. 'You're frozen, both of you.'

'Some rum will do,' said Keeler.

Gressitt went off at the double. Keeler felt the reaction starting to hit him. He knew that until they had broken clear of the camp and the river, none of them was safe. He was now worried about Rill. She looked very lovely and vulnerable in her dark blue track suit and woollen cap in the muted yellow light. The strain of the night's vigil showed itself clearly, and not for the first time he was worried that they had agreed to take her along.

'Here's your sheep-dip.' Gressitt was back, grinning, with two mugs and a bottle.

'Thanks, but keep an eye and an ear on the river while I tell you quickly what happened. Shoot first and ask questions afterwards.'

Keeler felt the powerful spirit start to pump new life into his veins. Aided by Herington, he outlined the events that had taken place at the Socos anchorage.

When he had finished, Gressitt ventured, 'You don't resort to kayaks if you're seriously engaged in arms smuggling. The amount of stuff a kayak could carry is very limited, even if it were a shuttle operation. Nor do you re-open a derelict mine, ferry copper by helicopter and hovercraft barge-train – unless you're involved in something very lucrative. And *not* smuggling a few small arms. It doesn't add up, John.'

'If Reutemann were indeed smuggling weapons into the Richtersveld, what were they for? The territory is practically uninhabited. Moreover, he could find easier and better ways than by bringing them in from the sea in a couple of kayaks.'

'You're overlooking the iridium,' said Herington.

'Not me,' replied Gressitt. 'For my money, iridium is what it's all about. My guess is that what you saw at Socos was just part of something really big. Reutemann – or someone connected with him, needs weapons. For what purpose, we don't know yet.'

'There's only one way of finding out. Investigate Fannin's Mine and Aussenkehr,' said Herington.

'We're wasting time talking. Let's get moving!' broke in Keeler.

'Where to?' demanded Gressitt.

'Fannin's Mine, of course,' replied Keeler. 'We're all dead ducks if we hang around here any longer. We disappear – this very night – into the Richtersveld. There must not be a trace of us left at this camp by morning.'

'The Richtersveld isn't a Sunday afternoon jaunt, John,' said Rill. 'Also, we need supplies and fuel. We can't get them tonight at the drop of a hat.'

'I've got everything we need at Blooddrift,' cut in Gressitt. 'We'll head straight for there, load up, and then make for the mountains.'

'How far is Blooddrift from here?' demanded Keeler.

'About forty kilometres. The road to it follows the southern bank of the river. For most of the way it is good and hard – not a track.'

'We'll load my kayak and the CDM canoe on the Landrover's roof,' said Herington. 'We'll need them later to take a good look at Aussenkehr.'

Keeler asked Rill. 'You've got maps?'

'Yes – in my car. I brought some along which I thought might be helpful though no maps of the Richtersveld are reliable. But they'll serve as a rough guide. What concerns me still is how we are to find enough fuel for two Landrovers.'

'We don't,' said Keeler shortly. 'One is enough.'

'We can't just abandon mine,' said Rill. 'It belongs to Cape Town university.'

'I've got an idea,' said Keeler. 'We'll hide it in the old ruined house up the road where Ross and I went after our barge encounter. Even if Reutemann and Trevenna come this way looking for us, they won't spot it holed up there.'

They struck the pup-tent in less than a minute and hastily threw together their scanty possessions. Keeler and Gressitt alternately stood guard with the UZI in case of an attack. Finally, they lashed the kayak and canoe onto Gressitt's Landrover's roof. The racket of the two vehicles starting up and charging up the sandy bank to reach the road from the camp sounded to Keeler like an invitation to Reutemann's men downstream.

Keeler joined Gressitt in the cab with the UZI at the ready. They followed in Rill's dust to the ruin. In the short distance, dust and fog combined to form an impenetrable screen.

Rill sprinted from the ruin after parking the vehicle and jumped in alongside Keeler. It was four-thirty a.m.

The drive along the Orange River to Arrisdrift was a blur to Keeler. Drunk with fatigue, his eyes saw all sorts of shadow-images reflecting from the fog curtain. He felt he was more a menace than an asset with the loaded automatic across his knees. Gressitt drove beyond the limits of visibility, hard and fast, while Rill called out instructions from her own knowledge of the shrouded landmarks, like a rally navigator. Once Gressitt missed a corner and the top-heavy vehicle slid off into thick sand, canting over. Gressitt gunned the engine savagely until they pulled clear again.

On they raced. Keeler thought he must have fallen asleep, but he was jerked wide awake by Gressitt's call – 'Arrisdrift!'

That was where the fog lifted, as if it had been programmed.

If the hovercraft was waiting, Arrisdrift was where it would be. They'd be able to see the headlights now that the fog had cleared. From the top of an incline nothing looked more peaceful than the great tranquil sweep of the river towards Arrisdrift. It was narrower and with fewer islands here than downstream. The water reflected the Landrover's headlights and a swathe of stars above.

Keeler tensed and gripped the UZI while he searched the water's surface for the hovercraft. There was nothing.

Gressitt put on speed. Arrisdrift vanished behind in the dust. The road still hugged the river. While it did, the danger lurked. About seven kilometres beyond Arrisdrift, a hill seemed to block their onward road, the surface of which had deteriorated progressively since leaving Arrisdrift.

Gressitt swung the heavy vehicle into a tight right-hander so that they faced away from the river. 'We made it!' he exclaimed. 'That's Koeskop – Duck-and-Dodge Hill. From here we head inland!'

The Landrover now left the river behind to make a big triangular detour in order to avoid an impossible sea of soft sand which flanked the river between Duck-and-Dodge Hill and his camp at Blooddrift.

Straight ahead of them, blocking out the horizon and the dawn, lay the mighty battlements of the Richtersveld. The peaks left only a segment of stars and sky clear above the southern horizon. The day was still an indeterminate thing when the Landrover jolted down to the river again along a dry riverbed track to Gressitt's camp at Blooddrift.

Keeler and Herington helped pack like zombies. Like automatons, too, they lashed the kayak and canoe afresh to the Landrover's roof with a length of strong nylon mountaineering rope which Gressitt had obviously accumulated – together with a number of other useful things such as canvas rubber-soled climbing bootees and pitons – for a possible ascent of Aussenkehr's cliff following his abortive reconnaissance flight over the old fort. Gressitt as it turned out, was well schooled in rock climbing. He had graduated from the tough Green Berets' survival training course at Camp Mackall in North Carolina, where sixty-five per cent of candidates fail. When the loading was done, Keeler and Herington threw themselves exhausted into the vehicle's rear along with a tumble of gear and jerry cans of fuel.

The mountains began to take form in the new light; wave after wave of ranges as uncharted and unchartable as a storm-tossed sea.

They headed into the Richtersveld.

18

The crash and the Landrover's sideways roll clouted Keeler and Herington back into consciousness.

The first thing Keeler's sleep-filled eyes fixed upon looked like a giant distorted spider clinging to the vegetationless slope. It was, in fact, a type of euphorbia plant which can withstand the kiln-dry slopes. The oddity was in keeping with the goblin-land, unreality on every side.

Keeler and Herington lay sprawled in the rear of the Landrover. Cans of food and packets of stores showered down as the vehicle went over on its side against a huge boulder.

Gressitt's voice reached them from the driver's seat. 'Grab a handful of air, Rill, for Chrissake! Else we'll roll all the way back down the pass!'

'Handbrake is holding, Ross.' Rill's voice was tense, controlled.

Gressitt gunned the engine to its maximum. The interior was filled with the stink of hot oil and burning rubber. 'I've barrel-assed this bucket of bolts as far as I can!' he yelled above the din. 'All out – it's push from now on!'

The Landrover sat perched near the summit of the pass, appropriately called Hell's Heights. It towered some six hundred metres above the river – twenty kilometres behind them now – on the edge of the Richtersveld escarpment. Its surface consisted of boulders varying in size from a head to a house. Behind them the pass fell away in a staggering series of jagged loops and gut-shaking S-bends. The peak above them looked ready to fall apart at the seams.

Keeler and Herington tumbled out the rear door. The

Landrover lay canted leftwards at a drunken angle, its dented side jammed against a huge rock. Herington rushed to check the kayak and the canoe on the roofrack, which were undamaged. The intense heat bounced off rocks as grey and old as a dinosaur's hide.

The four of them jammed some stones behind the wheels. Keeler pointed to the way they had come. The river was visible, dominated on its farther bank by a huge strip of pale brown sand – perhaps ten kilometres by fifty. Its colour contrasted with the whiteness of the rest of the desert, and it looked like a monstrous tongue laid out for drying. It was known as the Obib Dunes.

'I can't believe it!' he exclaimed.

'If you can't believe that, take a look ahead!' snorted Gressitt. 'That's where I aim to drive this crate.'

At the top of the pass the route vanished into thin air.

'We'll have to unload everything and carry it to the top on foot – including the canoes,' said Gressitt. 'Let's just hope that after that the Landy will make it.'

'How long have we been travelling?' asked Keeler.

'Five – six hours. It's the best progress I could make on this great big turnpike!'

'Any pursuit?'

'We spotted the hovercraft belting upriver about an hour ago,' answered Rill.

Keeler instinctively turned towards the river. Rightwards, to the east, its course faded from sight into an amorphous, lunar backdrop of a horizon.

'We must have left a dust trail like a comet,' he remarked.

'Hope not, not at the speed we were travelling,' Gressitt reassured him.

'The hovercraft went on its way without a pause.'

'Could be sending the helicopter to come and search us out.'

'Right now we're a target nailed against the wall for a gunship,' replied Gressitt.

Stripped to the waist, Herington and Keeler hefted the kayak and canoe from the roof to portage them separately to the top. The two men had to pick their every step and try to work in tandem. A wrong move might mean a strained or broken ankle. It took them two hours to cover a little over a kilometre from the immobilized vehicle to the top.

They had arrived on the outer rim of the Paradise mountains. Southwards, they were confronted by a staggering panorama. It seemed impossible that any wheel could roll through the fearful array of ranges. Ahead stretched a double, higher range divided by a flat plateau about three kilometres wide. Its westerly spine, towering over a thousand metres, was known as the Kuboos, its easterly counterpart was the Tswayis. The plateau, in reality a sand valley about five hundred metres high and fifteen kilometres long, helioed an intensity of light which hurt the eyes. Further to the southeast, majestic and unapproachable, soared the seared and serried peaks of the Richtersveld's inner citadel, the Little Raisin Bush mountains.

Herington turned his back on the sight – it was the only thing to do.

'Let's go back for the canoe,' was all he said.

They made a foursome with Rill and Gressitt to return to the summit with the canoe and stores. A thermometer in the Landrover's cab showed the temperature to be forty-three degrees Celsius. The footslog to the top would have to be repeated until everything was transported. The spectacle of the great ranges was a compensation to Rill and Gressitt the first time. In the strong sun, the peaks had shed the softer colours of early day, and were turning to brilliant greens, flaming reds, savage blacks. One summit was striped like a zebra's flank. The terrain reflected its total desolation as if it had been scorched by fire.

While Gressitt and Herington returned to the Landrover, Rill and Keeler remained admiring the sight.

Suddenly, Rill said to Keeler, 'For the first time in my life

I am really frightened. Don't leave me! I have an awful feeling that we are never going to come out of the Richtersveld alive.'

Keeler kissed her. Her skin tasted salty and dusty. 'We know all the options – and the risks.'

'I'm not backing down,' she broke in. 'I'll go anywhere you go, please understand that. But it doesn't make me less afraid.'

Hand-in-hand, they went further to get a better view where the pass turned in an S-bend round the water-melon coloured peak.

Keeler saw the man, then.

He stood absolutely motionless. Had it not been for the slight forward inclination of his upper body and head, he would have missed him.

Keeler clapped a hand over Rill's mouth, dragged her out of sight behind a rock.

'There's someone ahead! Quiet!'

From where she was, Rill had a wider arc of vision than Keeler. She squirmed sideways in the dust to see.

Then she sat up, put her head between her knees, and started to laugh a little hysterically.

'Rill! Shut up! For Pete's sake!'

She gestured in the direction of the man. 'Look! He's just standing there still!'

'Rill! It's one of Reutemann's men . . .!'

'It's only half a man – look!' She went on, 'He hasn't moved – he'll never move!'

The figure, in fact, remained as Keeler had sighted him first, his head forward in a listening pose.

Rill jumped to her feet. 'That's the Richtersveld Half-Man,' she said. 'Its resemblance to a human is uncanny. You're not the first to be deceived. It's a unique kind of aloe. It's found nowhere else but here and it always inclines its head towards the north.'

Keeler said, his voice shot with relief, 'I'm glad Ross

wasn't here with his UZI – he would have blasted your Half-Man to bits.'

They went on for a couple of hundred metres beyond the aloe until the view opened up to its full extent. There were no words for them to describe it. They simply stood and stared.

Then Rill exclaimed. 'John – isn't that a gap in the mountains? If it is, it would take us in the general direction of the Throughway.'

About halfway along the eastern rim of the sand valley, between the two nearby ranges, the Kuboos and Tswayis, the aching continuity of peaks seemed broken. A river of sand appeared to plunge through the gap; they could see its broad, continuing sweep on the Throughway side of the Tswayis range. Without binoculars, however, it was impossible to distinguish whether or not the gap was negotiable.

Rill and Keeler hurried back and met Gressitt hauling himself, two jerry cans of petrol and the UZI up the slope.

'Rill has spotted a possible route to the Throughway!'

Gressitt dumped his load. 'No kidding?'

'We'll check against the map, but I don't remember seeing such a place marked,' said Rill. 'We've named it Half-Man Gap.'

Gressitt shared the joke when they explained. They let him go on while they went for the American's powerful binoculars in the Landrover. With the help of these, a careful study of the gap and the route beyond made it seem feasible, although the heat haze made it difficult to make out much in the direction of the Throughway. From their position, however, Half-Man Gap seemed the only possible way out of their present predicament.

With Keeler, Gressitt and Herington carrying the heavy gear and Rill the lighter, the four of them spent the next two hours in lung- and muscle-straining toil hefting the stranded Landrover's load to the summit of the pass. By the time the last package was safe, they were slogging past one another on the steep slope like sleep-walkers, unspeaking, saving their strength and breath for the next load.

Eventually, by dint of shoving, pushing and driving, they miraculously flogged the Landrover to the top and then repacked. They pushed on throughout the blazing afternoon. There was an awful gut-tearing monotony about the bogging-down in the soft sand, the off-loading, the reloading, the pushing, the sweating, the futile oaths thrown at the unresponsive cliffs and cloying patches of sand. Rill took the wheel. She kept her cool while the three men searched their vocabularies for fresh oaths. When the time finally came to halt, the Landrover had covered less than half the distance between the top of the pass and Half-Man Gap.

Sunset flash-ranged all the stupendous galaxy of peaks to their view from their camping-place deep in the shadow of a huge rock. The Richtersveld assumed a terrible splendour of total desolation as the free-flowing colours once again changed through a spectrum of reds, oranges, yellows and blues to a final purple and mauve. The place seemed to possess a life of its own like the sea – secret, excluding man, and destined to sterility and silence. Another day had contributed its minute share of red-hot heat to the vast degeneration of the peaks, heat to herald the equally destructive processes of darkness.

Night rode into the sand valley like one of the Horsemen of the Apocalypse. The iron peaks of the Little Raisin Bush mountains blacked out the Southern Cross to the south, and those of the Kuboos range, Orion to the west. The only sound in that immense and intrusive solitude was the harsh cry of the Richtersveld gecko, a reptile survivor of millions of years. It was all as remote and unreal as the moon's Sea of Darkness. The only reality was the guns that might be awaiting them at Fannin's Mine.

19

The shock came out of the rocks at dawn.

They had decided that the most effective way of reaching Half-Man Gap was to make use of the cold of pre-sunrise hours so as to conserve their strength for the inevitable packing and pushing.

Their overnight camp was in the lee of big rocks, a kind of crumbling circular Stonehenge of a place though, unlike Stonehenge, it held no mystery. The origins of the boulders was plain – they had fallen from nearby summits.

The cold was intense. They had no fire because there was no wood. The blue flame of a gas burner on the ground was complemented in the heavens by great bursts of white stars. Rill was busy preparing coffee and rusks; the men were huddled in sleep-short silence round the minute flame.

Rill lifted her head. Her body went rigid.

'Rill!' exclaimed Keeler. 'What is it?'

Her eyes remained transfixed at something in the darkness over Keeler's shoulder.

'Rill!'

'Something moved back there!'

Gressitt started running for the Landrover and his UZI.

Keeler wheeled round. The butane light was too small to pick up definition; it picked up only colour – yellow. What looked like a flow of yellow goo was advancing towards the gas burner.

Before any of them could move, the first newcomers were immolating themselves on the flame.

Tarantulas!

The slope descending to the camp was a solid mass of tarantulas.

'Run!' yelled Keeler. 'Get inside the truck!'

They may have been in the course of a mass migration, the sort which occurs in Africa for which there is no known explanation.

Keeler plucked furry bodies from his face and hands, grabbed Rill's hand and pulled her towards the Landrover. Hundreds of the beasts piled on to the flame. Smoke rose like a votive offering.

They all jumped into the Landrover, and slammed tight all windows and doors. Gressitt wanted to use the headlights, but Keeler prevented him, lest the light attract the obscene creatures to the vehicle.

At the fire, tarantulas were heaped a foot high, the outermost fighting their way to the flame, now almost swamped by charred bodies. It looked like a swarm of bees, wriggling, writhing, burrowing. The centre sizzled and smoked. And then the flame died. The blackened remains seemed to freeze.

'The moral of that is, wait till daylight for your coffee in the Richtersveld,' Keeler said.

After clearing up the mess they pushed on in the same manner as the previous day – the interminable bogging-down, the unloading and reloading, the pushing, the oaths.

There was general relief as the Landrover reached Half-Man Gap. A second attempt at breakfast was a light-hearted affair. They all behaved as if they had already reached Fannin's Mine. Gressitt went as far as to venture that they were within striking distance of it.

But it did not feel like striking distance once the Landrover had ground its way for a couple of kilometres beyond the Gap. The sand river now led northeast instead of due east, where the Throughway lay. They decided that an isolated peak sticking up from a flank of the Tswayis range would provide a good look-out point. Keeler and Rill set off with the binoculars, while Herington and Gressitt checked the kayak and canoe.

The sand burned underfoot. Heat reflected like fire off the rocks, revealing green stripes which, according to Rill, was a sign of copper.

When they reached their look-out, which had a steep face, they both saw what looked like a beacon. It was a cairn of stones about a metre high, clearly man-made. Who would put that beacon up here, and for what reason, neither knew.

'Some dead-and-gone prospector's mark, maybe,' ventured Rill as they examined the pile. 'That's all I can think it might be.'

But then they saw another beacon at the top of this hill.

Keeler focused the glasses on it. 'Just like this one – and pretty ancient too, I'd reckon.'

Keeler's binoculars started to scan the slope of the cliff-face. What appeared to be wooden pegs projected at intervals from holes in the rock. They continued downwards in the direction of the cairn at its base.

'They look like climbers' pitons!' exclaimed Rill, when she, in turn took a look. Nearer the base, Keeler could make out only fragmentary remains, but higher up the pitons were better preserved. He concentrated on these.

And then something else higher up caught his eye. Bees were swarming in and out a small cavity. The pitons led to it.

'I've got it!' exclaimed Rill. 'I know what it is! The Bushmen in these mountains used to love honey-beer. That's where they got the honey. They used hardened sticks to climb up and get to the bees' nest.'

'And the beacon?' asked Keeler.

'Probably to distinguish this particular one from the hundreds of other similar hills,' she said quickly. 'This was a honey peak, and therefore special. That's what the cairn is for.'

'You're top of the class,' said Keeler. 'Now see if you can

reach the nearest stick this way.'

He swung her up on his shoulders so that she could almost touch the first dried-out piton. But it wasn't on the piton that her eyes were riveted. Her voice was urgent.

'Hand me the glasses – quick!'

Keeler handed them to her.

'There it is! There it is!' she burst out. 'I see it! The Throughway! There is Claim Peak!'

She slid down, gave the glasses to Keeler, pointing. But it was no good. The extra little height she had had on his shoulder had enabled her to catch a glimpse of the landmark which was their gateway to the Throughway. To double-check, she tried again from Keeler's shoulders.

'Are you sure?' asked Keeler.

'There's no mistaking it. Let's find a higher vantage-point for you to see also.'

'If those pitons were still safe, I'd try them,' said Keeler. 'Let's get back and tell the others.'

They retraced their path to the Landrover, running and slipping, and told the others what they had seen.

But they soon realized they would not be able to risk the Landrover close to the mine itself. Close to the Throughway, there would be the danger of its being spotted from the air. Near the mine, its engine would be heard.

'We'll hole up as close as we can to our objective and make the final stage on foot,' said Gressitt.

'Holing up with the kayak and canoe won't be easy,' said Herington. 'They'll be very conspicuous from the air on the Landrover's roof, even if the vehicle itself isn't.'

'What do you suggest?' asked Keeler.

'Bury them in the sand once we've located a suitable hideout – it won't harm them,' answered Herington.

The prospect – even distant prospect of their objective acted as a shot in the arm for the party.

Before they started, however, Gressitt reminded Keeler that Fannin's Mine was his baby. 'You and Peter had your turn at Socos.' What they might discover here was vital to SAMEX.

Keeler grinned. 'Okay, skipper. We're under your orders from now on.'

Rill smiled too. 'I drive, with or without orders. You men can keep your eyes skinned on the horizon.'

Gressitt eyed the blistering way ahead, where the lower ranges led to the Throughway. It was only their certainty that their target was close that kept them unloading, shoving, reloading, digging out the bogged-down wheels.

In the late afternoon, even while the going was still good, Rill braked to a standstill and pointed south.

'There! Look – it's like a lighthouse!'

In the far distance, the sun's elongated light helioed off an obelisk of white quartz projecting from a whale-backed mountain, wholly different in colour from the surrounding grey-brown peaks. It rose, timeless as the legend of the Copper Mountain whose site it signposted.

'Fannin's Mine!' she exclaimed.

20

That night, that quartz pillar resembling a lighthouse steered Keeler, Gressitt and Rill to Fannin's Mine.

Now, however, it was not the sun which reflected from it but electric light from the mine itself, which lay hidden from direct view in a crater-like depression. Lights streamed upward, illuminating the pillar and nearby high points. Elsewhere, there was only starlight to soften the total blackness.

The three worked their way on foot. They stumbled over unseen obstacles in the darkness, but dared not risk using a flashlight in spite of being still about four kilometres from the mine. Rill carried the Starscope plus Gressitt's conventional binoculars, Keeler his Browning Kapitän, and Gressitt the UZI. The Starscope proved itself again in picking out otherwise invisible hazards on the way ahead.

They had left Herington behind at a rock overhang they had discovered that afternoon about five kilometres from the mine after an interminable and nerve-racking journey. As they had neared the Throughway, there was the danger of their dust trail being spotted; there was as little they could do about it as the sound of the Landrover's revs as it hopscotched from one sand trap to the next. Herington had finally spotted the hide-out – an ideal place whose rock roof would conceal the vehicle from view from the air, and whose sand was soft enough in which to bury the kayak and canoe. Herington's job was to home the other three back to the hide-out after the sortie, which they might well miss without his flashlight signal. The password was 'kayak'.

'Stop!'

Rill raised her arms and held back both men.

A noise. They all paused, holding their breath. Their approach to the mine was side-on, from the west, keeping clear of the Throughway itself, which ran north–south. They knew that the workings were in the crater-like depression and would therefore be concealed until the last moment.

'Diesel generator,' said Keeler. The sound was unmistakable. It had probably served to dampen the sound of the Landrover that afternoon.

They picked their way, helped by the growing half-light which was being thrown upwards from the crater.

Finally, they were confronted by a moat-like hill. Mechanical noises, in addition to the thud of the generator, came from the other side.

'This is it!' Gressitt said. 'Crawl! We don't want to be spotted against the skyline!'

Gressitt led the way on hands and knees. Near the top, he went down on his stomach and motioned Keeler and Rill to do likewise. On their bellies, they squirmed alongside him.

'Get an eyeful of that!' Gressitt whispered.

The big crater was filled with light. Strings of mine lights made bright circles everywhere. Groups of old, renovated buildings and modern prefabs clustered to one side. It was on the centrepiece, however, that Keeler's eyes remained riveted. A battery of powerful floodlights was trained on a concrete slab. On the slab stood a square-looking, powerful helicopter. A narrow-gauge rail track ran from the helipad to the mine shaft. More lights gleamed inside the entrance to the shaft tunnel like wolves' teeth. Half a dozen armed men stood guard round the helipad.

'That's a Kamov Ka-25!' whispered Gressitt knowingly.

'It's the same machine they used for our trip,' said Rill.

'Russian!' Keeler stated flatly.

'Sure is,' replied Gressitt. 'Could be a line on who is backing Reutemann.'

'Not necessarily,' replied Keeler.

'The Ka-25 is special – it's got a NATO classification name, the Hormone,' Gressitt replied in a low voice. 'It's one of the best machines in the world for lifting heavy loads. That gondola underneath is specially designed to take a special pilot for visual loading. We've already got part of our answer: the Reds are in here, boots and all.'

'Recognize the guards' weapons?' asked Keeler.

Gressitt took the Starscope from Rill and snorted when he obtained his image. 'AK-47s. Mining copper – a lot of crap!'

With a burst of noise, the Ka-25's turbines fired and the rotors began to revolve slowly. 'Goddam it! – we've come too late!' exclaimed Gressitt. 'What did it take aboard before we arrived?'

The rotors picked up speed. The machine lifted, then hovered a few metres above the concrete strip. Then out of the shaft emerged a light truck or cocopan, pushed by two men. Flanking it were two more. Even at the distance, the red hair of one of them was unmistakable.

'Trevenna!' rasped Gressitt. He put the Starscope on the other. Reutemann! There was a pause, and then he went on in stunned disbelief. 'I don't believe it! It can't be true! Rill – look at that rock in the cocopan!' He passed her the Starscope.

With his naked eye, Keeler could make out a big boulder. The helipad's powerful lights gave it a kind of grey–white sheen.

Rill put aside the Starscope and said to Gressitt, 'This colours everything green – give me the ordinary glasses.'

She focused the binoculars on the cocopan, now almost on the helipad in position under the hovering Ka-25.

'*It can't be – Ross, it can't be!*' she burst out.

'Iridium?' Gressitt sounded shaken still.

'There's no piece of iridium that size anywhere in the whole world!' she went on incredulously. 'But it is – look at that sheen – there's absolutely no doubt about it! *Iridium!*'

'There must be four or five tons of the stuff,' Gressitt marvelled.

'They brought it out from the mine – solid iridium! It's been cut. That's what the special laser cutter was for! That means there must be more of it!'

A cargo sling dropped from the Ka-25. There was a movement in the perspex gondola below the belly. The second pilot Gressitt had mentioned was obviously in action.

'They'll have to sling-load a lump that size – even for a Kamov, it's too big to get inside,' said Gressitt.

The sling was attached to the lump while Reutemann and Trevenna stood by, braving the rotors' slipstream. Keeler focused on Reutemann's face. The light made him look triumphant as he shouted something to the helicopter above his head.

'Watch the chopper take the strain!' exclaimed Gressitt. 'Rill – that rock must be worth millions!'

'Priceless,' she replied. 'It would be impossible to put a figure on it.'

The boulder rose out of the cocopan, swung loose for a few moments while the pilot winched it up. There seemed to be a battle going on between the lifting power of the Kamov and the tons gyrating at the end of the steel cable. Then finally it was snugged against the aircraft's belly.

'Give her the gun!' exclaimed Gressitt. 'You'll never get over the rim of the crater if you don't, fellah! That must be about the Kamov's near-maximum load!'

The helicopter's engines rose to a crescendo of sound. Reutemann stood with his hair blowing in the slipstream as he raised his arm shoulder-high with a fist clenched as if to give the machine an extra take-off shove, like a golfer urging in a vital putt.

The Ka-25 painfully gained height.

'Keep low!' Gressitt warned the other two.

They ducked. The machine rose sluggishly above the rim of the crater where it was shallower on the Throughway side, cut its lights, and disappeared northwards in the direction of the Orange River.

'Aussenkehr!' exclaimed Gressitt. 'That's where we go now.'

21

'*Kayak!*'
  '*Kayak!*'
There was an urgent, tense exchange of passwords in the blackness.

Then Herington's relieved voice came from out of the rocky overhang.

'What the hell happened? The helicopter passed by here hours ago. I was thinking of coming to look for you.'

'You'd have never found us,' replied Keeler. 'Only the Starscope enabled us to find this place again.'

It was almost midnight. Guided by the Starscope ahead and the lights of Fannin's Mine at the rear, Keeler, Gressitt and Rill had threaded their way past otherwise invisible obstacles such as huge eroded blocks of rock and sand hillocks. It was the instrument, too, which had finally picked up the outline of the Landrover inside the rock overhang; they could have passed it by half a dozen times and not seen it.

'First, coffee!' ordered Gressitt. 'It's goddam cold.'

'It's been waiting for the past hour,' replied Herington.

The small, intense blue flame of the gas burner heated the back of the overhang no more than does a candle an Eskimo's igloo. Herington with his wispy beard looked like an old-time cave hermit.

Gressitt outlined the course and results of their reconnaissance. He could still scarcely credit it could be a lump of iridium.

'The helicopter seemed pretty low – I couldn't see it, of

course,' said Herington. 'It made a hell of a racket approaching and disappearing. I heard it miles away.'

'By now I guess it has landed at Aussenkehr,' said Gressitt. 'We have *got* to find out what is going on there!'

'What do the Reds want iridium on that scale for?' went on Herington.

'That's what we have to find out,' replied Gressitt. 'There must be more to all this than the metal's conventional uses.'

But Herington still wasn't satisfied. 'What I can't understand is why, even if they discovered a source of supply of such a rare metal, the Russians should require this elaborate charade – of barge-trains apparently conveying copper, the hovercraft, and all the rest of it. They could have exploited it in the ordinary commercial way.'

'My nose also tells me something stinks around here,' answered Gressitt. 'Aussenkehr's where we'll find out what it is.'

'What's your plan now?' asked Herington.

'I'll play it by ear once we get there, the same way as we did at Fannin's,' replied the American. 'We had a lucky break at the mine. Maybe we'll have another at Aussenkehr. We must not blow our chances.'

'Okay, but where do we go from here?' persisted Herington.

Before Gressitt could reply, Keeler, who had been studying a map of Rill's with a flashlight, broke in.

'We take the shortest route to the river – here!' He stabbed the map with a finger. 'It's only about twenty kilometres as the crow flies. We leave – now.'

The other three of them stared at him in astonishment. Gressitt put down his coffee mug and said slowly.

'And I thought *I* was keen to get moving!'

Keeler explained rapidly, again indicating the map. 'We strike due east. We'll then pick up the Orange at a point about forty kilometres above Aussenkehr. Peter knows the river route already, but I'd guess it was an easy ride. No rapids according to the map. The gradient is easy. Reute-mann would never expect anyone to approach Aussenkehr from *inland* because there is nothing inland. At the river we leave the Landrover and continue by kayak and canoe. Once we're clear of the Throughway, we're clear of the mountain ranges in this sector. The escarpment falls away to a great belt of flat land called the Springbok Flats. That's the way for us.'

They crowded round the map.

Rill said, 'It looks like a piece of cake – on the map. What is it actually like? Why, if the river is only twenty kilometres away, didn't Reutemann establish his copper ore loading point there instead of at Aussenkehr, which is twice the distance away in a different direction? Why didn't he simply build a road across the Springbok Flats and transport his ore by truck?'

'If the operation were genuine copper mining, I'd go along with you,' answered Gressitt. 'We know that he chose Aussenkehr because of the iridium.'

'Then the sooner we get cracking the better,' said Gressitt. 'If we leave now, this moment, we can be at the river by morning and Aussenkehr by nightfall.'

Keeler waved at the blackness at the overhang entrance. 'It's night, fellah. They'd spot our headlights from Fannin's before we got as far as the Throughway.'

'Either we go now – or we lose at least another twenty-four hours – twenty-four hours during which we could be sighted by either the helicopter on ferry duty or by men from the mine,' he replied.

'Now is the time to safely negotiate the Throughway, while the helicopter is away at Aussenkehr,' went on Keeler quickly. 'We don't use headlights. We use the Starscope. One of us will drive while another navigates with it. The rest of the party use their own eyes.'

'That's it, then!' exclaimed Gressitt excitedly.

While the lights at Fannin's Mine still burned, the sound

of the Landrover's engine was not likely to be heard, and they would be safe. That diesel generator hammering away was enough to drown out any sound. But if the mine lights went off, they would stop. It would mean that the generator had been cut and their safety screen was gone. But the mine seemed in fact to be working round the clock. Everything pointed to this being the safest moment to depart.

They dug up the kayak and canoe from their hiding-place, lashed them to the Landrover's roof once again, and set off, Rill driving. Keeler sat next to her operating the Starscope, with Gressitt making a third in the front seat.

'What we need is a man with a red flag walking on ahead,' observed Gressit as the vehicle headed into the blackness.

'Illuminated, preferably,' added Rill.

Without the Starscope, they could never have made progress. Even with it, the ride was a nightmare. The instrument's narrow angle of vision made it possible to pick out objects only directly ahead; the vehicle's fenders were unsighted. Their first crash into an unseen rock took place after only several hundred metres of painful going. They knew that the Throughway was not more than a couple of kilometres distant but the only beacon of their snail-like progress was the changing angle of the reflected mine lights to their right. Every so often Rill had to halt while the others went ahead on foot to reconnoitre the way.

Then – the Landrover's nose started to incline downwards.

Gressitt, who was at that stage operating the Starscope, gave the order to stop and cut the engine.

Rill halted and switched off the engine in one swift movement.

There was a dead silence. Gressitt aimed the Starscope. Something like a human form seemed to be standing still, ahead of them.

They waited, hardly breathing.

'Seems to have horns,' said Gressitt softly.

He passed the Starscope to Keeler.

'It's a tree!' he exclaimed. 'A tree! That's what it is!'

'A tree in the Richtersveld – you gotta be joking!' said Gressitt.

'It is and I'll also tell you what it means,' went on Keeler excitedly. 'It means we're almost in the bed of the Throughway. At some stage or another a ravine of this size must carry stormwater, however little, enough to give life to the odd tree or bush.'

Keeler's assumption was right. They double-checked their whereabouts against the lights of Fannin's Mine.

The Landrover edged on.

Twice, in the half-kilometre width of the Throughway, the vehicle became bogged down in the heavy sand – river sand. They were at their most vulnerable. Fear of being exposed spurred them on. The recurring effort of unloading, digging out wheels, pushing, reloading, proved no different in river sand than in mountains. Finally, when the vehicle started to pull out of the far – or eastern side of the Throughway, it was two-thirty a.m.

They swapped drivers. Unidentifiable ghosts in the Starscope's vision slipped by. There were more forced halts. The Landrover picked up height all the time now, getting more into the type of ravine-mountain terrain they had encountered on their way to Fannin's Mine.

Dawn came in a great sweep in the sky ahead. They put away the Starscope; they could see. For the first time in days – years, it seemed to them – the horizon was unobstructed by peaks and ranges. They were perched on the summit of a south-trending range about seven hundred metres high. Ahead and below stretched a vast concourse of flat land which must reach all the way to the Orange River, they speculated, although at that distance they could not make out the actual waterway. This was the Springbok Flats, a corridor ten kilometres wide and twenty long leading to the river.

'Only a couple of hours to the river now!' exclaimed Herington.

They were not. They understood, once they had descended to the plain, why Reutemann had chosen the rugged Throughway route in preference to the flats.

It was solid sand – soft, cloying, talcum-powder, wheel-bogging sand. It drew the Landrover into its soft texture like one of those carnivorous flowers which lure insects to their death in their gentle folds. The gracious scene of the dawn-light evaporated like the sweat on their bodies as they fought to manoeuvre the recalcitrant hunk of metal onward through the unending sand bog. Fuel was running low; soon, they knew, they had reached the point of no return. They had to push on to the river – or else . . .

By mid-afternoon they had given up talking about the river in case it, like everything else on the horizon, turned out to be a mirage. As a result they never saw it before they came upon it.

One moment the Landrover was grinding through a sand-filled ravine encased on both sides by two hundred metre high escarpments; the next, as they headed into the gully's mouth, a great band of turgid, brown–green water spread in front of them.

They stopped, gazing in silence with seared and burning eyes upon the willows, the reeds and bankside greenery, and the wide river.

'Jeez!' said Gressitt with a kind of stunned wonder, 'That's a sight for sore eyes!'

They unlashed the kayak and the canoe, fingering the soft surface of the water unbelievingly; it would turn their onward journey to Aussenkehr from the bruising brutality of the land route to a feather-bed journey.

When night came, they had the satisfaction of a brush-wood fire without fear of detection from either land or sky. They drank the last of Gressitt's whisky, adulterated with muddy river water. The great stars and immensity of the mountains at their back brought them a strange detached kind of euphoria. Danger seemed to be distant.

Yet it lay only a hundred and fifty kilometres away, at the mouth of the river which flowed before them. It was already reaching out its claws and would shortly focus the attention of the world upon this remote, unknown part of the globe.

22

Those claws had first unsheathed themselves and begun their nefarious work five years before, when a gold-and-white Boeing of the Libyan Arab Airline had touched down at Tripoli airport in Libya after a flight from East Berlin.

The plane carried a party of beer-swilling German tourists styling themselves the Froth-Sniffers in search of sun and fun in Colonel Mu'ammar al-Gaddafi's radical leftist militant Arab state. The Libyan pilot, a Muslim, viewed his passengers with the distaste his religion bestowed upon alcohol; he despised equally the short leather pants and braces some of them sported, along with their drinking songs. He swallowed his disgust as he put the Boeing down, remembering (as his leader had stressed) the importance of good relations with the East German communists.

Had the pilot been able to view the passenger cabin, he would, nevertheless, have approved of the behaviour of one of the East Germans. The man, though casually dressed, seemed to be making a great effort to appear as one of them, though he barely sipped his beer, and his smile was as forced as his bonhomie. For him, the flight could not end quickly enough.

He was Dr Kurt Reutemann, whose passport gave his occupation as physicist, employed by the State Laboratories for the Advancement of People's Knowledge in East Berlin, and his age as thirty-six. He was of medium height, with stocky shoulders and hands, and a sallow skin whose dark pigmentation made him less conspicuous than the winter-whiteness of his beery companions. The bump of the wheels on the runway seemed to return his facial muscles to their normal contours and his eyes under heavy brows from their play-acting to their customary brooding, penetrating manner.

Reutemann made no attempt to reciprocate the Froth-Sniffers' camaraderie as the plane taxied to a standstill. He had too much on his mind for frivolity, even if his top honours in metallurgy and physics ever permitted him frivolity. He intended to avoid the hotel's tourist bus, although nominally he was booked in with the group. He was to be met. That was all the intermediary who had arranged this undercover meeting could, or would, say. A password had been arranged – 'Rainbow'. Reutemann agonized now whether anything could be read into the word that would give away his secret if the meeting proved unsuccessful. It *had* to succeed.

The Froth-Sniffers moved through the formalities; Reutemann became more concerned at the absence of anyone to meet him. Then, as he was finally collecting his luggage and debating whether he should go on with the German group, a voice at his elbow said, 'Rainbow taxi?'

It was his man; it was no taxi which was waiting but one of the plush American cars which seemed to be in the possession of every Libyan under thirty. They represented a small reverse flow of the billions the United States had once spent on Gaddafi's oil. Nor was the driver a taximan – he was one of Colonel Gaddafi's dreaded secret police.

Reutemann was taken to a villa, where he dropped his suit-case and changed into sombre clothes – he always had a liking for dark browns and blacks. They drove quickly through the city – Tripoli was still garish and tawdry, before the city's extensive facelift in anticipation of the summit meeting in 1982 of the Organization of African Unity, which then planned to elect Colonel Gaddafi as its chairman.

Reutemann's destination was the presidential palace. His interview was with Colonel Gaddafi.

Reutemann lit his corncob pipe. If he did not succeed in selling his idea to Colonel Gaddafi – he could not even contemplate the thought – there was the prospect that the Libyan leader would pass on his secret to the East German authorities. There was only one outcome to that eventuality – a labour camp for life. How should he introduce the subject? He had pondered over this for weeks, ever since the intermediary between himself and the Libyan leader had notified him that the interview had been set in train. That was a debt which would have to be paid – out of the deal with Gaddafi, he hoped.

Should he try and impress Colonel Gaddafi by starting with abstract concepts and then work up to the particular? To point out that the Germans as a race had always had a talent for two things, namely, advanced technology and submarines, and that in the U-boat these national attributes had found their highest fulfilment? It would be no surprise that even in the 1980s the Germans felt they had to be ahead in this field. Nor would it be overstating the case that in himself, as a German, the two national characteristics had crystallized and enabled him to create the deadly machine he, in fact, had designed.

He could also stress to Gaddafi that nuclear power was noisy, and therefore vulnerable to sonic detection. The giant new thirty thousand ton Soviet nuclear submarine would be a good example to quote – its hull was of titanium, but it was wide open to the Achilles heel of that type of propulsion. It would be appropriate at that stage to tell Gaddafi how he, Reutemann, had invented silent underwater propulsion . . .

Reutemann was so lost in his thoughts that he came to with a start when the car was challenged by sentries at the gates of the presidential palace. He did not have time even to catch more than a glimpse of the building before the car drove quickly through a gateway into a courtyard. Reutemann was escorted, wordlessly, to an office where he was searched by the man who had driven him, assisted by two other secret police. The search was quick, professional, thorough. They removed Reutemann's cufflinks after frisking the insides of his sleeves for a hidden connection to a possible mini-recorder under his armpit. The cufflink, presumably, acted as the microphone for such devices. They confiscated Reutemann's stainless steel ballpoint pen after carefully examining it to see whether it doubled as a single-shot gun. The corncob pipe was dismantled, its hot ash checked, and also denied to the German for the interview, as well as his watch, which could – in spy terms – convert to a recorder or transmitter.

Satisfied, the taximan led Reutemann through to Colonel Gaddafi's office. The passageway to it and reception area was guarded by armed soldiers. As he walked into the Libyan leader's private office – almost spartanly furnished – the words of Sudan's leader General Nemery kept going through Reutemann's mind, 'If you have to choose between a poisonous snake and Gaddafi, welcome the snake.'

Reutemann, who had read up everything he could find from both sides of the Iron Curtain on the Libyan leader, was unprepared for the handsome young man with a warm, welcoming smile who came forward and held out his hand. Gaddafi was relaxed and polite; he put Reutemann at his ease with a small-talk query about how he had enjoyed his flight to Tripoli. Reutemann immediately found himself unable to equate the figure in front of him with the image he had gained from American studies of the most dangerous man in the world who had sponsored more than fifty acts of international terrorism, and had bought twelve billion dollars' worth of Soviet weapons out of oil revenues with which to arm Libya and any trouble-seeking bunch of terrorists anywhere – in North Africa from Chad to Egypt, from Somalia to Ghana, and elsewhere in the world from the Philippines to Bangladesh.

This was the paymaster of Carlos the Jackal, international terrorist supreme. This was the man the Americans stated was mad because he had claimed that the Red Indians were, in truth, Libyans, and had offered his support to the IRA in Ireland if they converted to the Muslim faith.

Public Enemy Number One, the Americans called him. Reutemann, under the immediate influence of Gaddafi's charisma, opted rather for what Africa called him – 'Mr Africa', designate-head of the Organization of African Unity, champion of the downtrodden millions of Africa, the only leader actually willing to *do* something positive, both militarily and economically. Reutemann found himself inclined to dismiss as American propaganda, media reports that Gaddafi had once tried to buy an atom bomb from China and was involved in a deal with Pakistan to produce the 'Islamic Bomb'.

The preliminary exchanges had been through an interpreter as the two men sat down in easy chairs; Reutemann's pompous rehearsed speech about German national character evaporated in the face of the sincere attitude of the Libyan leader. The German saw him as so many in Africa viewed Gaddafi – purposeful, firm, gracious, dedicated. When Gaddafi switched into rather formal English (he had learned the language in order to read for himself what the Americans said about him, he remarked with a smile), and asked Reutemann if he spoke it also, the Libyan's coup was complete. Reutemann, who spoke English with a degree of fluency, responded in the same tongue, but had to remind himself before getting down to business that Gaddafi was desert-born and had the cunning of a Bedouin.

There was a faint flicker of amusement in Gaddafi's eyes when Reutemann asked that the room should be cleared before he revealed his business. That told him that the conversation was being taped anyway; the two secret police withdrew only as far as the door. Reutemann knew that they were continuing to watch him like hawks.

It was now or never. Reutemann told his story.

After taking top university honours in physics, Reutemann was given a job in the State Laboratories for the

Advancement of People's Knowledge in East Berlin. He was involved in experiments to reduce the risk involved in nuclear power stations, air pollution by conventional power stations, and environmental air pollution by vehicles. Naturally his attention had been directed to the value of platinum since it was used in catalytic converters in motor-car exhausts to ensure non-poisonous emission fumes apart from the metal's wide-spread use in the electrical, chemical and petroleum industries.

Reutemann had also taken a close look – from published material – at the way the Americans had employed platinum in a fuel cell which had powered the Apollo space vehicle. The fuel cell had proved fairly reliable, but its application had been limited. At that stage the fuel cell had been regarded as a moderately interesting laboratory experiment which showed that chemical energy *could* be converted into electrical energy, and that platinum had shown itself to be a useful catalytic agent for promoting various chemical reactions.

Reutemann pointed out, however, that the American electronics industry preferred metals such as palladium and silver in films and pastes since that was far cheaper than platinum; but where endurance was required – in weaponry and space vehicles – platinum was still Number One. Further, the Americans also had a black mark against platinum because there was no domestic source of supply. The metal had to come from two countries which were politically *'non grata'* – namely South Africa and the Soviet Union.

In a nutshell, Reutemann explained, the platinum fuel cells had been a slow starter, if not a non-starter, in certain quarters. The American version was clumsy and primitive and would continue to be – for abstruse scientific reasons – while it continued to use platinum. Some research had also been done in France, Canada, Japan and Sweden and, for unknown reasons, the British had dropped promising experiments after a good start about a dozen years before.

Gaddafi listened to Reutemann's recital with the polite patience of a Bedouin drinking coffee in his desert tent with a guest while debating in his own mind whether to slit his throat or not. The Libyan leader's face remained inscrutable. Interest flowed back when Reutemann began the account of his breakthrough. Reutemann had asked himself what would result if he stuck to the platinum group but tested in the same role the other rare metals of the group – ruthenium, rhodium, palladium, osmium, and iridium.

Reutemann had Gaddafi's full attention now. Perhaps because of the new note in his voice; perhaps it was Gaddafi's attribute of being a good listener; a characteristic which had gained his support for the hopeless causes of way-out terrorist groups.

It had been a long, and at times, a heart-breaking road, Reutemann told Gaddafi. Last of all, he had tested iridium as a catalyst for the fuel cell after all the other metals had yielded negative results. Iridium had been very, very scarce in East Germany. He had obtained only a minute quantity from an associate institute of the State Laboratories which was employing it in anti-cancer experiments. Iridium, he explained to Colonel Gaddafi, was produced along with platinum and other metals of the group by only three countries in the world – South Africa, Russia and Canada. Both the latter two produced iridium only as a by-product of nickel, not as a primary product, like South Africa.

Gaddafi's eyes became slightly hooded with impatience at Reutemann's emphasis on the scarcity of the noble metal. Now, however, he sat upright in his chair.

Iridium had worked. Reutemann had invented the first fuel cell which used iridium as a catalyst – with a feedstock of naphtha, distilled from coal tar, of exceptional purity. The Reutemann fuel cell was designed for submarine propulsion. It was light years ahead of what any other nation had produced. A submarine powered by it became the ultimate –

the true silent killer, undetectable by modern sonic listening devices. By comparison, nuclear propulsion was as out-of-date as the steam locomotive. Reutemann added that in his invention the two leading German national characteristics (those he had mulled over in the taxi coming to the interview) of technology and submarines met.

Further, Reutemann had explained to Colonel Gaddafi, he had designed the fuel cell to have an almost unlimited potential since it consisted of a series of interlinked modules which could be tailored to individual output requirements. This dispensed completely with the problems of minimum viable size which were such bugbears in conventional nuclear power plants.

Despite his jubilation at his invention, Reutemann's central problem remained – where to obtain enough iridium to make his fuel cell a practical proposition instead of a mere laboratory experiment? The usual sources of iridium (even if they could supply enough via a complex and highly segmented marketing system) were closed to him; South Africa being politically out of bounds to East Germany; Canada because its output was minimal; the Soviets because to show an interest in its iridium (whose output and marketing were both controlled by Moscow) would be to play Russian roulette of a new kind.

Gaddafi eyed Reutemann speculatively. It seemed, he observed, that there was something lacking in his loyalty to the state not to reveal his discovery. Not at all, Reutemann replied with a touch of latent megalomania. He was not one to hand over his genius on a plate to some on-the-make politician in Moscow or Berlin. He was too big to be contained by any political system, either communism or capitalism.

The iridium fuel cell had, Reutemann went on, reached an impasse. It meant little that he had proved it could work: it was not a practical proposition.

What would follow, Reutemann continued, could only be

described as fated, predestined. It was his use of the phrase – he had deprecatingly preceded it by stating that he was an atheist and that science was his god – sparked something in the Libyan leader. Gaddafi's militant love of Islam was well known and he had used his great wealth to implement it practically. He, like another religious fanatic, the Mahdi, who in Victorian times had killed General Gordon in the Sudan and had finally been routed by Kitchener, had sprung from the same desert origins. Perhaps Gaddafi, like the Mahdi, at that moment had an illusion-of-grandeur vision of world power. Reutemann was putting the tool to achieve it into his hands. Whatever it was, the meeting from then on was one between kindred souls. Reutemann had Gaddafi's unqualified attention.

By chance, Reutemann went on, he happened to be visiting the *Institut für Deutsche Geschichte*, a museum in East Berlin which housed relics of the German occupation of Namibia in colonial times. One of its exhibits was the equipment of an old-time German prospector named Hans Schneider – his geologist's rock hammer, rucksack, washing-pan, and some samples he had collected.

One of the stones interested Reutemann. It was about the size of a peach stone. It had a distinctive grey–white sheen which made him suspect that it could be only one thing – iridium.

Nothing would have stopped him then, said Reutemann. He was not prepared to say how he obtained possession of the pebble, but he did. Tests showed that it was as he had thought, pure iridium.

If that were so, asked Colonel Gaddafi, why hadn't someone woken up to the fact long before?

Because it had really only been since World War II that the technology of the platinum group metals had come into their own, replied Reutemann. In Hans Schneider's day, three quarters of a century before, the group had been a closed book, known only to a handful of advanced scientists.

Where had Schneider found the iridium pebble? demanded Gaddafi.

There had been no specific indication amongst his gear at the Institute, replied Reutemann. He had fine-combed the records for information. The only indication that he had was that in his travels Schneider had crossed the formidable mountain area adjoining Namibia which was known as the Richtersveld.

Reutemann stopped. He gave his narrative a dramatic ending. He took from his pocket a small heavy stone and held it out to the Libyan leader. With enough of that to power a fleet of submarines, the nation who owned it could dominate the world's oceans and thumb its nose at today's superpowers.

23

Gaddafi got slowly to his feet, reached out and took the pebble from Reutemann. He addressed himself more to it than to the German. He did not look like a power-drunk visionary cut in the Mahdi's mould; the form-fitting black sweater-shirt and brown pants gave his body rather a twentieth century athlete's appearance.

He would, he said quietly, teach the Americans to call him names such as the madman of Tripoli, Public Enemy Number One, power-crazy lunatic, the patron of terrorism, the maverick who used murder and petrodollars to stir up trouble wherever trouble could be stirred up. He would realize his dream of proclaiming the Mediterranean, a Libyan Sea of Peace where imperialist warships, and especially those of the US Sixth Fleet, would be prohibited – under pain of immediate sinking. Already, he said, he had taken the first steps towards the ideal by extending Libya's territorial waters by three hundred kilometres. The Gulf of Sirte – that great bite out of Libya's central coastline – would be reserved exclusively for Libyan ships and aircraft.

Gaddafi eyed Reutemann. In a flash, it seemed, the power-crazy dictator had vanished. In his place was the shrewd, calculating Bedouin. What did Reutemann hope to get from him? he demanded.

Sponsorship – for him to go to the Richtersveld and find the source of the iridium Schneider had happened upon.

To bankroll him for what might turn out to be a never-never search, countered Gaddafi.

That was the stake involved, replied Reutemann. It would require a lot of money – and a lot of faith. He had no idea how long it might take. The Richtersveld, he had established, was still largely unexplored, a formidable, mountainous desert.

The project sounded nebulous and unsatisfactory, answered Gaddafi. Reutemann realized that he was bargaining as only an Arab in the market-place can.

Reutemann produced his own bargaining counter. The type of submarine he envisaged – he had already made sketch plans – was of about two thousand tons, the size of the Soviet Foxtrots already in service with the Libyan Navy. This was the optimum size for a small ocean like the Mediterranean. He had his own contribution to make to the submarines in the form of high-tensile, non-magnetic hulls to help beat underwater detection. The iridium cell propulsion system had only to be scaled up from his laboratory prototype to make it a valid proposition.

Gaddafi regarded Reutemann with increased interest, but still refused to be outbidden. Assuming that Reutemann were to locate adequate supplies of iridium for such a type of submarine . . .

Rainbow class, Reutemann interjected with a smile. It was the first time he had relaxed during the interview. Rainbow – iridium.

There was no one outside the United States or Soviet Union who had the expertise to construct an iridium fuel cell submarine, Gaddafi argued further.

Reutemann shook his head and Gaddafi's respect grew for the swarthy German.

He had also explored that problem, Reutemann answered. Two Yugoslav shipbuilding yards, the S. & D.E. Yard at Split and the Uljanik Shipyard at Pola, both had the know-how. A telling factor was that Yugoslavia was friendly towards Libya, unlike other Mediterranean shipbuilding countries.

Suddenly Gaddafi laughed, took Reutemann by the hand and shook it warmly. The deal was on. Reutemann would get all the money he needed to search the Richtersveld for iridium. He would receive a blank cheque. There were no strings – except total secrecy. Reutemann shivered inwardly and remembered President Nemery's words about the snake when Gaddafi fixed him with a long look and said that if one word were ever revealed of what had transpired between them, one of his special hit squads – men who had murdered Gaddafi's Libyan opponents abroad after he had warned them that they were doomed – would hunt him down to the ends of the earth.

It was a long, hard, and at the start disheartening search. Once in Southern Africa, Reutemann realized that he had seriously under-estimated the physical and administrative difficulties of getting into the Richtersveld. Even his attempt at a preliminary reconnaissance by air over the territory had aborted due to the overflying ban. There were no surviving records of Hans Schneider or his route. He made his way to the Orange River mouth under guise of a free-lance geologist. While there, the news had come through of the exciting fossil discoveries at Arrisdrift. Reutemann had managed to obtain permission to visit the site in a party of other interested experts.

Arrisdrift proved to be the breakthrough. Soil samples he took secretly from the dig – then in its early stages – proved on analysis to contain an unusually high concentration of iridium. It is accepted scientifically that the earth's major source of iridium, occurring as it does in minute traces only, is meteoric dust from the stratosphere. The amount at Arrisdrift could not be rated as a viable proposition, but it did seem to Reutemann to point a way in the context of Schneider's discovery.

Next, Reutemann visited the dinosaur site at Blooddrift under the same pretext of scientific interest. An analysis of the soil from there revealed a much heavier concentration of iridium – a hundred and sixty times the normal. Reutemann became very excited. He believed that such a high concentration, coupled with the fact that Blooddrift was a dinosaur graveyard, could be accounted for by an asteroid colliding with the earth. This was in line with the accepted scientific theory that the dinosaurs vanished from the world about sixty-five million years ago due to an asteroid crashing into the earth and throwing up a colossal dust cloud which shut off the sun's light and stopped photosynthesis – the very process of life – for several years. All food chains broke down. Hardest hit were the large flesh-eaters which included the dinosaurs. They disappeared as a species.

Looking at the formidable jumble of vegetationless mountains in the background of Blooddrift's dinosaur graveyard, Reutemann speculated whether the geological shambles which was the Richtersveld had, in fact, resulted from such a natural cataclysm – that an asteroid had indeed landed there in pre-historic times. The territory still looked fire-blasted; the sterility of the adjoining Namib desert was further backing for this theory.

Reutemann, with Teutonic thoroughness, thereupon began a grid search from Blooddrift in the direction of the Richtersveld mountains. He claimed to be operating as a free-lance geologist. Since the area was outside the Sperrgebiet, he could not be denied entry once he had gone through the necessary red tape to obtain a prospecting permit.

Then came Reutemann's moment of truth. Between Blooddrift and the Richtersveld escarpment he found a nodule of iridium! It weighed only a few grams, but he would not have exchanged it for all the diamonds in the Sperrgebiet. He was now firmly on the trail. Near the ascent into the mountains at Hell's Heights, Reutemann located several more nodules. After months of tedious searching, his total haul now weighed only a few grams whereas each module of the Rainbow iridium cell required several kilograms – and in addition a number of modules were required for the total propulsion system. At that stage, Reutemann estimated that, given enough time, he himself could collect enough nodules to build only one fuel cell for one Rainbow submarine.

Reutemann pushed on into the mountains. His solitary and mysterious activities aroused the suspicion of Trevenna, leader of a band of ruffians, who regarded him as a police spy. He was seized and taken to Trevenna himself. Reutemann had to buy his way out, but the meeting gave him the opportunity to do a deal with Trevenna. At a price of ten thousand gold Krugerrands (which Trevenna later stashed away in a secret hiding-place), Trevenna agreed that his gang should collect iridium nodules for Reutemann.

The men – and women – of the gang proved adept. Soon Reutemann had several handfuls of nodules – almost enough for the first fuel cell.

The success of the venture made it imperative that no one – least of all Consolidated Diamond Mines – should suspect the activities of the Trevenna gang. As a front, Reutemann decided to re-activate the ancient Fannin copper mine, whose location had been lost sight of for more than a century, but was known to Trevenna. Colonel Gaddafi, with proof of the iridium nodules in front of him, agreed; he also fell in with Reutemann's suggestion that in order to beat the almost insuperable problem of transporting copper ore across the mountains, a helicopter ferry should be employed. For the rest of Reutemann's imaginative masterplan – the restoration of Aussenkehr fort, a barge-train towed down the Orange River by hovercraft – the Libyan leader gave Reutemann carte blanche. The building of four Rainbow-class submarine hulls was commissioned in Yugoslav yards. Engines would be installed as soon as enough iridium became available. Gaddafi assured Reutemann that he was prepared to wait years, if necessary.

In the event, Gaddafi's patience was not put on trial.

Reutemann made a further startling discovery – the deeper Trevenna's collecting gangs pushed into the mountains and the closer they got to Fannin's Mine, the higher grew the concentration of nodules.

In the meantime, Reutemann had had to drive the old main shaft of the mine deeper into the mountainside in order to keep up the pretence of mining copper ore. Suddenly, the miners could go no further.

The rockface proved too hard for any known tool. Reutemann sent urgently for a laser cutter.

The miners worked round the obstacle, exposing a massive boulder of about twenty tons' weight. It was solid iridium.

It was the core of the asteroid which had destroyed life on earth sixty-five million years before.

Now, as Keeler's party reached the Orange River after negotiating the Springbok Flats sea of sand, two freighters, the *Beryte* and the *Bachir*, each of twelve thousand tons were making their way down the coast of northern Namibia. To an outsider, there was nothing strange in the fact that two sister-ships, both flying the flag of Ghana (their home port was shown on their sterns as Accra) were sailing in close company along what was recognized to be a dangerous coast. Their destination was a joint one – the port of Maputo, the former Lourenço Marques in Mozambique. There was nothing odd in that either – it seemed natural that one West-African state should be trading with another.

It was early morning. The fog had just cleared. On the bridge of the *Beryte* Vice-Admiral Heykal of the Libyan Navy decided to rehearse the drill for the last time. Nearer Walvis Bay or the Orange River mouth there was always the danger of being spotted by one of the long-range maritime reconnaissance aircraft with which he had heard the South Africans were accustomed to patrol this unfrequented coast.

Vice-Admiral Heykal eyed the *Bachir* out to starboard. Even anyone sharing the secret would have found it hard to guess that the ship was not the freighter she appeared to be. The same applied to the vessel under his feet. No one – a probing search plane, for example – would spot anything beyond a couple of men lounging on the bridge in typical merchant marine uniform; his operational staff was safely tucked away out of sight in what once had been the *Beryte*'s navigational centre. His eye went for'ard along the *Beryte*'s deck. There were no tell-tale signs of the missile screens or the large crew – over three hundred of them – who would man her armament at the drop of a hat.

Vice-Admiral Heykal gave an order to alert the *Bachir* for the exercise. It applied to the *Beryte* as well. He waited until a radar scan gave a clear sea and sky. He watched the second hand on his watch – now!

The camouflage screens which had appeared to be deck-houses fell away and revealed six SS-N-2 missiles in triple launchers, four 130mm and eight 57mm guns mounted in twin, and a brace of Oerlikons. Aft, what a moment before seemed to be rather a high freighter's poop, showed square holes as the lifts went down to bring into sight two naval Ka-25 helicopters, each with its characteristic double three-bladed co-axial contra-rotating rotors, the multi-fin tail unit, and the four-wheel landing gear. The Glushenkov turbos were already firing as the lifts levelled on what was, in fact, a helipad. *Bachir*'s helicopters were a trifle slower. Heykal frowned and noted that *Bachir* must not lag behind *Beryte* when it came to the operation itself.

The flag officer glanced at his watch. Forty-seven seconds. Not bad, although he had heard that the German armed merchant raiders of World War II – wolves in sheep's clothing like his own pair of ships – could drop their screens and have their guns firing in twenty seconds. But then, he consoled himself, in those days they didn't have the complicated process of helicopters to cope with.

168

Not bad. Heykal ordered the screens back into position and the helicopters below. He set course for the Orange River mouth.

24

The place where Keeler, Gressitt, Herington and Rill had finally struck the Orange River by way of the Springbok Flats was a vast open space of land embracing both sides of the river. Ahead of the kayak and canoe the turgid stream dived into a dark portal of mountain rocks. To their left, or the western flank, there rose a formidable array of peaks and ravines which on the map were named Nabas, and to their right was an equally sinister, but unnamed, agglomeration. The whole area looked as if the river had been dammed by this barrier of mountains aeons ago, and had formed a lake where the flats were now situated, and had finally probed a narrow passage through the gap toward which they were now headed a few kilometres ahead.

There should have been a holiday spirit about their venture, but there was not. It was not yet six o'clock, and the early light served only to increase the gloom and starkness of the ravines which flanked the river. Herington and Gressitt were leading in the kayak, followed by Keeler and Rill in the canoe. Rill had been in a strange, withdrawn mood ever since their hasty breakfast over a driftwood fire.

Rill leaned forward in the rear cockpit of the canoe and, placing her hands gently on the base of Keeler's neck, started to massage the muscles straining with the effort of paddling and keeping up with the swifter kayak ahead.

'What's the matter, Rill?' he said after a while. He would have liked to look into her eyes, but he didn't dare stop paddling for fear of falling too far behind.

Rill's reply startled him. 'Aussenkehr is haunted,' she said.

'That's ridiculous,' he retorted.

Her fingers dug into his neck. 'Listen to me, John,' she said almost fiercely. 'Don't let us go on with this; let's turn back – now. We still can. Something terrible is going to happen – I feel it.'

'To do with Aussenkehr being haunted?' said Keeler speculatively.

'Please don't make fun of me,' she pleaded.

'I'm not making fun of you. I'm only trying to find out what's been bugging you since we got up this morning,' Keeler replied, trying to keep his voice as matter-of-fact as possible. Then he stopped paddling and looked back at her and saw that her face was drawn and pale and that her eyes were beseeching him. She stopped her massage and said, 'Last night I had a nightmare. I saw that terrible place Aussenkehr, like some old castle out of a Grimm fairytale. It was all distorted and horrible. The old ghosts were there, too.'

'What old ghosts, for Pete's sake, Rill?'

'There is this old legend. Everyone in Oranjemund knows it. That's where I heard about it. In colonial times the Germans used Aussenkehr to guard the frontier against intruders. The officer in command had an affair with a Hottentot woman who was supposed to be his housekeeper. His daughter came from Germany to visit him and found out about the set-up – her mother was still back home. So when her father was out on patrol, she shot the woman with his service pistol and then turned it on herself. When the father returned with his patrol he found the bodies and shot himself with the same pistol. And they say that when something terrible is about to happen, the patrol is seen riding up the path to the old fort, headed by the dead German officer. That's what the legend says . . .'

'And you saw the patrol trotting in your dream last night, is that it?'

'You're still trying to make fun of me, John, I can see it. Anyway, it wasn't a dream, it was a nightmare. Everything was distorted, and yes, I did see this patrol as if I were looking down on it from a helicopter hovering above the fort with its quaint towers. I saw the girl and the dead woman lying in a pool of blood. And there was the clop-clop of the troop's hooves, and then I saw them in their old-fashioned German uniforms with swords and carbines and at the head was the officer . . . and then the picture vanished and I woke up in a sweat. It was horrifying. I couldn't wait for you and Ross to wake up . . .'

'Now, now, Rill dear, this place is enough to give anyone the creeps,' Keeler said soothingly. He resumed his paddling with a quicker stroke and said nothing more. He reckoned they would be within striking distance of Aussenkehr by mid-afternoon.

After a time, Rill went on. 'The nightmare left me with this overwhelming feeling of impending doom.'

'Because of the ghosts or because of Reutemann and his iridium?' asked Keeler. 'And you think we four are in danger because of this bad dream and that local legend?'

Rill had a very stronge urge to come out with the truth: that she loved him, and that she was frightened she might lose him. That she was not just being a hysterical female who believed in ghosts. But she had a genuine presentiment of some coming catastrophe which she could not explain rationally. Yet she wished with all her heart that she could find a way of getting these men to abandon their crazy venture.

Keeler felt that he had to calm her down, so he reminded her that Gressitt had sent a message to Ron Walker, his SAMEX back-up operative, who was now on his way to Oranjemund. 'If he's anything like Ross, we don't have to worry about a thing,' he said. 'He knows we are on the trail of something very important, and he knows where we are.'

In fact, they had contacted Walker the previous night by radio, using the Landrover's powerful transmitter. Gressitt had not told him the whole story – the iridium set-up at Fannin's Mine – because Keeler had felt it better not to. Walker had previously moved to Lüderitz to await further developments. They had agreed that important though their discovery at Fannin's Mine had been, they did not want to jeopardize the secret of their final destination by bringing a team of SAMEX operatives to the Orange River, which could hardly have escaped the notice of Reutemann and his gang. And so Walker had been told to get himself to Oranjemund as soon as possible; that iridium was involved; that they were on their way to Aussenkehr.

To keep in touch with Walker further, Gressitt produced a tiny but extremely powerful sophisticated transmitter-receiver in the form of a Lucky Strike cigarette pack – it was special to SAMEX, he grinned, and based on the sort of instrument used in space vehicles. Inside the pack, he showed his astonished audience a pair of earplugs – like a hearing-aid – for silent reception, as well as a mini-speaker fitting the Lucky Strike emblem on the pack. Walker had also been told that if he failed to hear from them within four days, he was to go to Major Rive at CDM Security, tell him what he knew, and mount a search for them, concentrating on Aussenkehr.

Rill and Keeler paddled in silence; later, he could tell how her mood cleared by the way her paddling improved. It was strange to be travelling north for the first few hours when his every instinct told him that the river headed east to the sea; it is only after Aussenkehr that it makes a great bend for its final run-in to the Atlantic. Great mountain ranges – barbarically named Kwaap, Gamkab, Stormberg, Richtersberg, Rooiberg – slid by comfortably. The two craft made excellent time. The river broadened and still continued north in a general direction with the exception of one big easterly sweep in the vicinity of Kwaap.

At about three o'clock Herington raised his paddle high above his head – the signal for the canoe with Keeler and Rill to close up.

They drew alongside. 'We're almost there!' Herington said.

There was nothing to show in the awesome monotony of the peaks that they were anyplace else than they had been hours before.

'We're about five kilometres upriver from Aussenkehr,' Herington explained. 'See that big peak there on the left? It's called Rooilepel – Red Spoon. The river starts its big bend to the east there. At that point also the Fish River comes in from the north-east and meets the Orange at Aussenkehr.'

'*Verboten*. Elephant game reserve,' said Gressitt ironically.

'About two kilometres further on there's a notice to that effect in English, German and Afrikaans,' said Herington. 'It warns that trespassers will be strictly dealt with.'

Remembering Reutemann's remarks at the party, 'I bet they will,' said Keeler.

'That includes us,' added Rill.

'Don't fret, honey,' said Gressitt. 'We aren't risking our necks in day-light. Aussenkehr may be a no-place but it's got a ferocious guard dog in Reutemann. Peter reckons there's a small island close under Red Spoon peak where we can hole up while we give the onward situation one hell of a scrub-down.'

'Is it inside the game reserve area?' asked Rill.

'No,' replied Herington. 'The game reserve is quite clearly marked by a fence which comes right down to the water's edge.'

'Let's get on to the hide-out – I feel naked sitting here knowing Reutemann is only five kilometres away,' said Rill.

'Plenty of places to hide,' Herington reassured her. 'Reeds, greenery, even some trees.'

It was all of that when they came upon it about a kilometre further. Wild willows appeared on one bank, and a tonsure of waterside greenery was like a glimpse of paradise to their sun-struck eyes. As they pulled in to the island, Red Spoon peak was already starting to shut off the sun from the river. In a dozen strokes from the main waterway they were safe, camouflaged from sight on the river, and from above from the god-like eye-in-the-sky of Reutemann's helicopter.

But not from the ghosts of Aussenkehr.

25

The council of war – scrubdown, as Gressitt continued to insist – was dominated by Herington's stubborn insistence that he alone should make a preliminary recce against the fort in order to formulate a subsequent full-scale attempt to get in. Except for two things the discussion might have been a picnic with the four of them seated on the warm sand of the island – the reeds and willow-wands had been carefully laced by Gressitt into a camouflage screen, and ready to hand lay Gressitt's UZI, a brace of grenades, his commando knife and Keeler's Browning. Herington reinforced his argument by pointing out that, of all of them, only he knew the river layout in the fort area; he felt it would be crazy for two craft to blunder about when he himself could spy out the area using the canoe.

'You're talking as if the place were guarded night and day,' said Rill. 'You may be able to cruise about without interference.'

'That wasn't flukum the Kamov airlifted out of Fannin's, honey – it was iridium. Worth starting a war for. The fort will have rollers, for sure,' said Gressitt.

'Rollers?' asked Rill.

'Guards, sentries, whatever you like to call 'em – and they'll be armed. You can lay a silver dollar against a plugged nickel that every game warden is in reality a trained killer,' he replied. 'We gotta find out where they are stationed so that we can get past – pick 'em out, if necessary.'

Gressitt was all for attempting to sally that same night; Herington refused to budge from his determination.

Suddenly Rill, who had become very quiet, said. 'You three have forgotten something.'

'What?' asked Gressitt.

'Me!' she exploded. 'You talk as if I don't exist! What do you expect me to do while all this cloak-and-dagger business is going on – sit here and wait until your all-male shooting party returns? It was I who identified your blasted iridium in the first place! It was I who told you about Fannin's Mine! Now you calmly propose to ditch me on the home stretch! Not likely! I sweated it out and bit my nails waiting over the Socos venture, but I'm not doing it again – do you all get that?'

'There is no question of ditching you, Rill,' Keeler reassured her. 'Tonight is a preliminary reconnaissance only, not the real thing, in which you, of course, are included . . .'

That settled it in Herington's favour. They agreed that Keeler and Gressitt should escort Herington in the canoe as far as another small island Herington knew of just out of sight of the fort, short of the big bend, and rendezvous with him there on his return. The time was fixed for midnight.

'You'll need a gun,' addèd Gressitt. 'What do you prefer – my UZI or John's Browning?'

'Neither,' Herington replied. 'I don't hold with guns. I prefer my hands.'

'I don't like it,' Gressitt answered. 'If you're spotted, you're out in left field anyway. Reutemann's goons aren't Sunday school teachers, fellah.'

'I know that already from my own experience,' Herington replied tersely.

'What happens after midnight?' asked Rill.

'It depends on what Peter finds,' said Keeler. 'We'll play it by ear from then on.'

As it turned out, the game played itself. At about seven o'clock, when it was completely dark, the four of them emerged from their shelter like the nocturnal Richtersveld geckos do from their rocks. They carried the kayak and canoe to the water. As they came into the open, Rill pointed downriver and exclaimed, 'What's that light?'

Behind the bulk of Red Spoon there was a sky-glow in the direction of Aussenkehr.

They lowered the two craft to the ground and stared. 'It can't be a star,' said Keeler.

'If it were moving, I'd say it was the Ka-25 using a spotlight,' said Gressitt. 'What in hell can it be?'

'The only possibility is the fort's helipad – but it looks much brighter than the one at the mine,' said Keeler.

Herington's determination manifested itself in his words. He said curtly, 'The best way to find out is to get on.'

'Could be searchlights,' Gressitt pondered further. 'Peter, you're going in at the deep end tonight. If the river's all lit up, take care, fellah. They mean business.'

They left Rill standing disconsolate on the bank while Herington led the way downriver in the canoe. At the anti-trespassers sign and the game reserve fence, Keeler laid the Browning on the cockpit coaming and Gressitt did likewise with the UZI. This was where the shooting could begin.

The two craft ranged within close distance of the bend which led to Aussenkehr's front door. The land between the river and the fort grew lower; the glow in the sky grew brighter. They were still puzzled as to its source.

'Here! Stop!' Herington's sense of place was remarkable. To the others, there was nothing to show that the trailing willows and underbrush were any different than before. 'This is where we meet at midnight,' he went on. 'A good way to spot it is to use that hump against the light as your landmark – it looks like a woman's breast. It's called Kabies.'

'At midnight, if you don't spot us, flash your torch once or twice in an upriver direction – away from the fort,' said Gressitt.

'It's my skin too,' he replied.

'Good luck, Peter,' said Keeler as the canoe merged with

the shadows and vanished from sight. Keeler and Gressitt hung around for a while in the hope of spotting him rounding the bend towards the fort, but they did not.

They returned to Rill and spent the next couple of hours in an anxious, silent vigil on the tiny island. Finally, they went back to the rendezvous point, searching the darkness for Herington's flashlight signal when midnight came.

It was Keeler who spotted what seemed to be a slight glow at the down-river end of the rendezvous-island, They made for it.

The bottom of the canoe seemed awash with blood and water. The waterproof flashlight was shining through it. Herington sat in the stern seat with an AK-47 bayonet projecting from the right side of his chest. Slumped in front of him in the forward seat was the body of a man. A hideous head wound contributed its share of blood to the mess on the bottom-boards. Both men were dead.

Keeler and Gressitt sat frozen and shocked at the spectacle. Each knew what the other must be feeling about Herington. Keeler was the first to recover. 'Get that light out – we could be spotted any minute!'

Gressitt reached forward, pulled the body in front aside to get at the pinkish submerged light.

'Take a load of this stuff!' he exclaimed, showing Keeler the dead man's face.

It wasn't one of Trevenna's mountain Hottentots with their high Tartar cheekbones and copper-coloured skins. This man's skin was dark and his nose aquiline. To both Gressitt and Keeler who knew something of North Africa, he looked like an Arab.

There was no identification when they searched his dark green para-military uniform. All they found was a spare twenty-shot magazine for an AK-47, a half-empty packet of Lexington cigarettes, and a cheap lighter. It was clear that his identity had been deliberately brushed out.

'What in hell goes on at the fort? Here's what looks like an

Arab with Soviet weapons . . .' Gressitt said in a low, tense voice.

They put the light out after the search. Keeler was glad that Herington's face – determined even in death but showing its agony in drawn lips and dilated nostrils – was obscured.

'We'll come to that in a moment,' replied Keeler, almost whispering. 'First, there is the fact that Peter somehow managed to get himself back here to warn us. Moreover, he brought his assailant with him so that the body wouldn't start a hue-and-cry when they found it. In the army he'd get a Victoria Cross.'

'It sure beats any act of courage I've ever known,' added Gressitt sombrely.

They were about to try and remove the bodies from the canoe when they drew back at the sound of a helicopter's rotors from the direction of the fort. Their only thought was that the guard's absence had indeed been discovered and that the Ka-25 had begun to comb the river with its searchlight. They drew their kayak deep inside the reeds and hid the canoe as best they could alongside it. They saw the machine's navigational lights as it rose above Aussenkehr.

They waited. The sound of the machine's rotors could be heard clearly but when they took a quick look, there was no sign of it. They could not believe that it would not soon be overhead. Then, when the noise of the rotors started throwing back long echoes, they realized that the Ka-25 was not, in fact, searching the river but flying down the Throughway which at that point was parallel with the river about five kilometres distant. Relieved, they sat for several minutes before getting down to the task of burying the bodies in the soft sand and clearing up the canoe. They used paddles as spades and smoothed over the impromptu graves as best they could to make them invisible from the air. Then, towing the canoe, they returned to Rill at their original hide-out under Red Spoon peak.

Keeler spotted Rill's silhouette first, called to her, and jumped into the shallows.

Rill raced to him. 'God!' she burst out, half-crying, half-laughing. 'I thought you were never coming back! I don't think I can handle this sort of waiting ever again!'

Keeler took her in his arms and tasted her tears on his lips.

'Rill . . .' he said gently, 'you weren't so far wrong about the ghosts of Aussenkehr . . .' and he told her about Herington.

'Peter? Dead! No! It can't be!' she exclaimed. Keeler could feel the involuntary muscular spasms running through her body as he tried to comfort her.

Gressitt, who had joined them, said, 'I think he was the bravest guy I knew, Rill. I can't say more.'

'With . . . with that sort of wound, how could he have managed to paddle back to the rendezvous?' she asked.

'No one will ever know,' replied Gressitt sombrely. 'But he warned us, and he brought us the evidence.'

'If he's an Arab?' she wanted to know. 'What does an Arab mean in this part of Africa, Ross?'

'Anywhere in Africa up to now the presence of Arabs has meant trouble,' replied Gressitt. 'But this is the first time I've known of any so far south.'

'What's your guess, Ross?' she went on.

'There is one country mainly, which exports Arabs in conjunction with Soviet weapons – Libya,' he replied.

'What possible interest has Libya in Southern Africa . . .?' exclaimed Keeler.

'That's one thing we may find out at Aussenkehr,' he answered grimly. 'It makes it more important than ever to find out what is going on there.'

'You and John will both get yourselves killed – like Peter! That's all,' Rill hurled at them.

'Libya or no Libya, it means trouble – big trouble. If we don't find out, a lot of innocent people might get hurt. It's big, Rill. I have my duty.'

'What about you, John?'

'I go along with Ross,' he replied. 'What we've unearthed so far is only the tip of the iceberg.'

Rill drew in her breath sharply, and followed it with a quick double sigh. Then she ran her hands up Keeler's forearms to the elbows in a caress as if she had never touched him before. When she next spoke, her voice was level, matter-of-fact. 'Yes, I know we must all go and find out. When? Tonight?'

'It's too late – we've lost too much time. It will have to be tomorrow, after dark,' answered Gressitt.

Rill nodded. 'How are we going to handle both boats? John is now the only expert canoeist. Ross and I are still greenhorns.'

'We'll have the current behind us,' said Gressitt. 'John and you can lead in the kayak towing the canoe containing me. Okay, John?' He laughed without humour. 'That will leave my hands free for the UZI if we run into trouble.'

'Not if, but when,' Rill corrected him.

26

That was the way they went to Aussenkehr next night.

After a day which proved to be a mixture of boredom and tension, the kayak and canoe, roped together, edged into the final bend about three kilometres from the fort. It was seven o'clock.

Gressitt manned the canoe alone, with the UZI at the ready; it also contained the climber's rope and pitons they had loaded at Blooddrift. Gressitt wore his special climbing bootees, of which he had a spare pair that fitted Keeler, a big man like himself. If any climbing became necessary, Rill would manage in her sneakers.

The helicopter's daytime search of the river islands which they feared did not materialize. They kept their fingers crossed that the dead Arab had been at an outlying sentry-post rather than at the fort proper and therefore might not have been missed immediately. Or that the Ka-25 was on more urgent duties ferrying another load of iridium from the mine than to divert to search for a missing man.

The river was dark as they floated downriver; the area where the fort lay – still hidden from direct view – was strongly illuminated. How, they still had to discover.

Then – the river turned sharply. Leftwards, the land which obstructed the view receded. The stars gave way to man-made lights.

Suddenly, dramatically, Aussenkehr stood out.

The exterior of the fort was floodlit. It looked like a cross between a Disneyland fantasy and a homesick German's dream of a Rhine castle. It was perched atop a five hundred metre cliff. High candle-snuffer towers jockeyed for place with crenellated battlements and bartizans. That part which had not been rebuilt sagged in ruins. There were look-out points dominating the Orange River. To one side was the winding road from the river to the summit up which the German patrol had ridden so long ago. On the cliff-edge, where the road levelled out on reaching the fort, was a helipad whose brilliant floodlights threw hard shadows into the deep gullies which scored the cliff-face.

The cliff itself showed no signs of having been tamed by man. It was a strongpoint in its own natural right. It stood athwart the junction of the Orange with its tributary, the Fish, which flowed in from one side through a series of spectacular S-bends. At the foot of the cliff, where the rivers met, was a huge sandspit shaped like a viper's head. Almost directly across the river on the Richtersveld side the Throughway debouched via a boulder-strewn, waterless ravine. The old Germans had chosen well; who held Aussenkehr held the key to the Richtersveld.

Also at the base of the cliff, where the winding road ascended, a jetty projected into the turgid brown water. Five barges lay moored in mid-stream in line-ahead formation; their tug, the hovercraft, snuggled against the jetty like a giant turtle.

Men with automatic weapons guarded the jettyhead and the winding roadway; the main concentration, however, was in the helipad area. Floodlights glinted off their weapons.

To avoid detection in the lighted riverfront, the kayak and canoe switched from one bank to another where one big island and a scattering of smaller ones offered the protection of dense reeds. This took them onto the side where the Fish River flowed into the Orange, on the right. At this point the Orange was about five hundred metres wide.

As they started to sneak along a channel between the big island and the bank, they spotted the glow of a fire on the island and heard the sound of loud voices.

Keeler back-stroked, allowing the canoe with Gressitt to draw alongside.

'What do you make of that?' asked Keeler in a whisper.

Gressitt, cradling his UZI, said after listening a little longer, 'That bunch is shikkered! It's a party – women, too!'

A burst of raucous laughter underscored his remark.

'That, I think, must be Big Belly Island – the Trevenna gang's hideout,' said Rill under her breath. 'It's marked on the map, but I didn't realize we were so close to it.'

Before either man could reply, something in the water clunked against Keeler's paddle. He grabbed the floating object from the water.

'An empty beer container, the best home brew!' he exclaimed.

'Jeez! . . . Some rotgut!' remarked Gressitt softly. 'It smells like puke.'

'Made from honey, I'd say,' went on Keeler. He restored the gourd gently to the water to avoid a splash.

While Keeler held the two craft steady with his paddle, they discussed their ongoing strategy. They agreed that a frontal approach to Aussenkehr would be suicide in view of the powerful lights everywhere. This also applied to a side-on attack from the Fish River side since they would have to run the gauntlet of an illuminated stretch of water where the two rivers met. Generally, however, the Fish River side of the fort seemed to offer the most promising possibilities. It appeared as if most of the guards were concentrated on the Orange frontage, while the dilapidated, less accessible – and therefore less guarded – side faced towards the Fish. Their problem, nevertheless, was to gain access without being spotted.

The racket from the booze-up offered a solution. Keeler pointed out that if Big Belly Island had been the Trevenna gang's home since long before Reutemann had appeared on the scene, it was reasonable to assume that they had access to the shore across the narrow channel, especially when the river was low enough for wading. That meant in turn footpaths which, he felt sure, must lead to Aussenkehr. If this assumption were correct, the only way to reach the fort would be across the Fish. If they could locate such a path, they could reach unseen the base of the cliff on which the fort stood, on foot.

They therefore headed for the mainland and secreted the kayak and canoe in the thickets of reeds before setting out. Keeler's assumption had been correct: they had gone less than a hundred metres through the reeds when they struck a well-trampled footpath leading in the direction of the Fish River.

The going was easy and quick to a point about a kilometre above the junction of the two rivers, away from the fort's lights, where they faced the great cliff with the sandspit at its foot. They were still covered by the riverside vegetation; but the thought of venturing into the open to ford the shallow Fish was daunting, despite strong factors in their favour. The tower on their side was in ruins, and there were no floodlights above them. The men on the jetty were blocked from view by the cliff proper. This seemed to be their only possible approach to the cliff-face and up into Aussenkehr.

They took their courage into their hands and struck into the open, wading knee-deep across the shallow water. Keeler led, with the climber's rope looped bandolier-fashion about his shoulders, the steel pitons hanging from his belt and holding the Browning at the ready; Gressitt brought up the rear with the UZI; Rill was sandwiched in between. They crossed furtively and silently, dreading at every moment a challenge or a shot from the darkness beyond. A shoulder of the cliff stretched right down to the water's edge on the sandspit side; when they felt dry sand under their bare feet, they raced for shelter. The path led further still into another screen of reeds, where they halted breathlessly.

'We made it!' exclaimed Rill.

'We've been lucky, so far,' replied Keeler. 'But we aren't inside Aussenkehr yet by a long chalk.'

They followed the path along the base of Aussenkehr's cliff. It offered complete cover. They expected the path to continue on round until the jetty and corkscrew summit road came into view. But suddenly it came to an end, and they were facing an impenetrable screen of reeds on every side. They retracted their steps, thinking they might have missed a turn, but there was nothing. On their right the way was blocked by the base of the cliff itself and in every other direction by dense vegetation.

'The path just can't stop here!' Gressitt insisted. 'It must go on! It must have had a purpose.'

'John! Ross! Here – quick! I've found something!' Rill had been poking around the rock face.

'Feel this – give me your hand, John!'

She guided Keeler's hand to a smooth, hard stick projecting from the rock at about knee-height. A few feet higher up was another, and still others leading out of reach above.

A ladder of crude wooden pitons mounted the face of Aussenkehr's cliff.

27

The similarity between these wooden pegs and the ones they had found in the Richtersveld struck them instantly. They were obviously the work of the same old mountain Bushmen.

'This must be Trevenna's original way up into the fort!' said Rill.

'Take it easy,' cautioned Gressitt. 'In the first place, we don't know where these pitons lead – if anywhere – and second, we're all jumping to conclusions.'

'It seems likely,' interrupted Keeler. 'The gang must have lived in this area long before Reutemann showed up and if they stashed away something in Aussenkehr, this was probably their way up.'

'It couldn't be to get to the honey,' replied Gressitt. 'Reutemann would supply them with all the booze they wanted just to keep them happy, you can be sure.'

'We've got to risk our flashlight,' said Keeler. 'If we all crowd close around it, there's not too much danger.'

As they started to form a circle, Gressitt tripped over something in the reeds that felt like wire. He went down on his hands and knees, covered the face of the torch with his hand to mask the light, and switched it on. Some old rusty cable and pieces of rusty iron lay about, concealed in the reeds and vegetation that had grown thick around it.

'I think,' ventured Keeler, 'that wire cable is part of a ladder – a ladder up the cliff! Those bits and pieces are the rungs!'

'Probably left here by the Germans!' Rill said speculatively. 'They probably had a wire ladder up the cliff long ago and Trevenna has used the holes for his pitons . . .'

Gressitt put out the light. 'Let's take a look at the wooden pegs before we jump to conclusions.'

They bunched themselves together to blanket the light. It revealed a series of sturdy wooden pegs, fire-blackened for dissimulation, running up out of sight on the cliff-face.

Gressitt tried to pull one out; it came loose in his hand. Further scrutiny revealed a companion socket to the left, the width of a ladder's rung away. It was clear that the old cable ladder's anchorages were being used for the pegs.

'They're removable,' said Gressitt thoughtfully. 'There must be some reason for this.'

'The cliff is about five hundred metres high,' said Keeler. 'One might as well try to climb the Matterhorn with one hand tied as attempt climbing on these pitons without ropes.'

'But if they are strong enough to support a man,' observed Rill. 'I'm the lightest. Maybe I should go up first and see . . .'

'I'm not taking any risk without proper precautions. We'll use our own rope and pitons.' Gressitt said curtly.

'What's stopping us then?' asked Keeler. 'If this is Trevenna's way up, it's just what we have been looking for.'

'Listen, both of you,' said Gressitt, and they were surprised at the severe tone of his voice. 'We've reached the do or bust point as far as I am concerned. We don't know what is up top, but we do know the sort of reception we'll get from Reutemann if he catches us. What I want to do now is to get a signal to Ron Walker on my transmitter. But to lessen the risk of Reutemann picking it up, I am going to listen first, just in case Ron is trying to contact me. If there is no signal from him within the next fifteen minutes, then we'll attempt the climb.'

It was getting late, and there was just an outside chance that Walker would be trying to get Gressitt.

'He is supposed to go on repeating at intervals if he wants me,' said Gressitt. 'He knows where we are headed, and that I might not be in a position to reply. But if it is important, he'd keep on transmitting.'

They gathered round the mini-transmitter on the sand. Both Keeler and Rill were surprised at the power and clarity of the signals as Gressitt tried to raise Walker. The tiny loudspeaker was turned low.

Gressitt switched frequency. After five minutes of listening to voices in a variety of languages, some incomprehensible, Gressitt returned to Walker's wavelength. But all he got was static. But he continued to search through an infinity of megacycles. Then, suddenly, a metallic, strong voice supervened.

Reutemann acknowledging Heykal. Go ahead, Beryte.

Receiving you loud and clear. Over.

Gressitt sat up straight as if a bullet had passed through him. 'What the hell . . .!'

'*Beryte!*' Keeler was dumbfounded. '*Beryte*! Don't lose him, for God's sake, Ross! Turn up the sound a fraction!'

There was hardly any need to. Either the sender was extremely powerful or it was not too distant.

Heykal to Reutemann. Beryte company on schedule, vicinity Lüderitz. Are Oranjemund hosts standing by? Confirm.

Reutemann to Heykal. Rainbow deadline as scheduled. Japanese reception committee on standby. Socos clear. All systems ready to go. Will signal commencement of party.

Heykal to Reutemann. Signal acknowledged. In the name of our leader, Allah be praised.

Gressitt left the now silent transmitter on for a couple of minutes more, and then switched off. The three of them sat in stunned silence. Gressitt was the first to speak. 'Rainbow . . . iridium; Heykal . . . Allah be praised! It all figures. What with Herington's killer, it all points to the fact that Reutemann is up to his ass in Arabs. And if you ask me, I smell the dirty work of our Great Brother Leader Gaddafi!'

Both Keeler and Rill concurred. After a while, Keeler, who had appeared particularly pensive, started repeating the names *Beryte, Bachir . . . Beryte, Bachir*. And suddenly, as the penny dropped, 'Yes, that's it!' he exclaimed. 'Two clapped out freighters FERRET had been interested in. Same set-up as *Rigel Star*. After some mysterious refit, they suddenly set off from Yugoslavia after lying idle in Split for over a year. Sailed for Ghana under a flag of convenience. FERRET considered them both as likely bets for some insurance swindle, but then decided to concentrate on *Rigel Star*.'

'Okay,' said Gressitt. 'All we have to do now is to work out this nice little jig-saw, and put together the goddam pieces . . . a bunch of Libyan cut-throats, a couple of dicey ships from Ghana, a Jap reception committee at Oranjemund and add a few tons of iridium and a crazy German scientist working out of his Dracula-castle and Bob's your uncle!'

'They must be mad to broadcast openly a barely disguised message,' said Keeler.

'Ultra high frequency, out of range for any but very special sets – like this baby,' said Gressitt, patting fondly his bogus pack of Lucky Strikes. Then, suddenly getting to his feet, he said incisively. 'Listen, we could discuss this goddam puzzle for the rest of the night and still not come up with the answers. The only way is to get ourselves up and into the fort and see what gives.'

'There is another way,' Rill said. 'Get clear of this god-forsaken place and keep plugging away with your radio until you contact Ron Walker. Tell him there is some deadly menace hanging over Oranjemund, what and when we don't know yet and tell him to alert Major Rive . . .'

'My outfit doesn't work that way,' retorted Gressitt. 'My job is to deliver the goods, not to stand on the sidelines with a radio, passing the buck. I have an official mission – to get up into the fort and find out what's going on. If necessary I'll go by myself.'

Unhitching the climbing rope from his shoulders, Keeler said, 'We're wasting time. Let's go.'

'Before we rope up, let me make two things plain,' Gressitt went on. 'We have two objectives. One, to stop Operation Rainbow, whatever that is. Two, to get ourselves out of

Aussenkehr alive after we have done so. Both will take a hell of a lot of doing. This thing is big – very big. So far we've only got an inkling of how big it really is.'

They roped up. Gressitt led, Rill next, with Keeler bringing up the rear.

Gressitt looped the UZI round his shoulders on its strap, secured two grenades in his belt next to his commando knife along with his pitons and hammer. He tested the first wooden peg with his climbing bootees to see whether it would take his weight.

'This reminds me of the Green Berets assault course at Camp Mackall,' he said. 'The difference is, this is for real.'

Rill followed when the rope tautened as Gressitt signalled from above. They could make out his dim silhouette on the rock face against the helipad lights. Then it was Keeler's turn. Gressitt climbed slowly, cautiously, securing the rope firmly for each upward stage. After climbing for about five metres, Keeler was surprised to discover that the wooden pegs gave way to metal pitons. They had decided before the ascent that he, in the rear, would remove the wooden pegs as they went in case they should come in handy further on. The cliff face was sheer; it seemed probable that the rusted wire cables had been a fixed wire ladder used by the old German garrison as a short-cut from fort to river.

On and up they went. It was impossible to see anything below – not a bad thing in view of the drop, Keeler considered – and above only an unending face of rock. They clung on like flies to a wall. As they progressed, the view opened up on their left towards the jetty, but its lights remained out of direct sight, as did the helipad road.

Then – there was a double twitch at the rope, the pre-arranged signal for first Keeler, and then Rill, to close up on Gressitt.

When Keeler joined Rill he asked her what was up.

'I don't know,' she replied in a low voice. 'We can't be more than a quarter of the way yet.'

Rill then went ahead; Keeler noted that the sheer face had given way to a slight levelling off. He had no longer to crane his neck directly overhead to make out the outline of the two figures above him.

When he joined the other two, the grade of ascent flattened still further. To his surprise, Rill and Gressitt seemed to be seated side by side, which would have been impossible a moment before.

When he came within earshot, 'This is it, fellah!' Gressitt told him in a low voice. 'Look what we've found!'

Gressitt and Rill were perched on what appeared to be a ladder composed of metal rungs. It ran up out of sight into the darkness overhead; to their left, it followed up the much easier contours of a saddle of rock which traversed the cliff face diagonally. Attached to the ladder was a thick black polythene pipe which probably brought water from a pumping station near the jetty to the fort itself. The steel ladder was designed to service it.

'Come on up!' went on Gressitt excitedly. 'There's plenty of room.'

There was – they were roosting on a service bay, a square of steel bars fixed into the rock at a point where there was a junction in the water pipeline.

'It's a piece of cake from now on!' exclaimed Rill triumphantly. 'This ladder must lead all the way to the top.'

'Don't bet your knickers,' said Gressitt. 'It's at the top that our problem really begins. Unless the pipeline leads round the back of the fort – which isn't likely – we'll be completely exposed in the floodlights when we arrive.'

Below, they made out the twinkle of fires on Big Belly Island; the jetty was now in sight and also a section of the winding road. They were about thirty metres above the base of the cliff.

On they went. At first, both ladder and pipeline tracked the saddle's incline, but where the angle of ascent became less precarious and flattened out for a number of metres, following the contours of crevasses and gullies, the steel ladder was replaced by fixed steel cables secured to the rock by means of pitons with eyes through which the cables had been threaded – a mountaineering practice with which all three were acquainted. Then, when the face became near-vertical again, the steel ladder resumed. The two methods alternated. The three went carefully, as quickly as they could, not neglecting safety precautions such as stage-by-stage securing of their nylon rope in case one of them should slip. Where at intervals there were further service bays, they rested.

Over their heads the lights grew progressively brighter and once or twice they heard the sound of motor engines. Then Gressitt in the lead, caught a first close-up sight of one of the fort's towers; the ladder, cables and pipeline led inexorably towards the main structure of the building, into full vision of the men whose voices now and again were becoming audible.

Gressitt halted on a ladder section about fifteen metres from the summit and gave the signal for Rill and Keeler to close up. There was no service bay so near the top. They crowded together to hear what he had to say.

'This is about as far as we can go without being spotted,' he told them in an undertone. 'Any suggestions?'

Keeler found himself shrinking involuntarily from the lights overhead. A vigilant sentry, peering over the edge, must detect them. Below, the Big Belly fires now looked as small as stars. He averted his gaze quickly. His bowels felt as though they could drop through the seat of his pants. The pipeline twisted like a big snake towards the surface; Keeler thought he could even detect where it lipped the cliff. The spot was clean under the helipad.

'The higher we go now, the less chance we have,' said Rill.

Keeler, the last on the rope, searched the cliff-face for any possibility. Far to the left was the lighted jetty road – no salvation in that direction. Even if they had wings to fly across the intervening width of cliff, they would still have the problem of making their way up Aussenkehr's highroad. To the right, there seemed nothing but blank rock the whole distance to the Fish River side of the face. He compelled himself to look down again in the direction of Big Belly Island.

As one sights a twig between the eye and a star, he saw for a fleeting moment what he thought was something projecting from the cliff to one side of their ladder, a short distance back the way they had come.

Was it another of the fire-blackened pitons?

He quickly explained what he thought he had seen. 'This could be the final stage of Trevenna's own piton ladder leading off somewhere else than the summit. I'm going down to investigate.'

Rill and Gressitt paid out the slack as he retreated. There was still nothing to see against the backdrop of land and river below. He signalled for more rope, descended further. It was only when he manoeuvred the summit lights into position as backlighting that he spotted a row of pitons leading to the right. The first, within reach of the ladder, had escaped their notice as they passed because of its black camouflage.

Keeler could not make out where the piton route eventually led, but there seemed to be – as far as he could make out – a deeper blackness in the cliff face further on. A cave, perhaps? He was about to signal the other two to come to him to allow him more rope to explore, when a square of light stood out of the rock face about ten metres away on his left.

First the light was dull, then it grew brighter, then it dimmed again. A window! Someone had passed by a window in the rock face with a light!

Without pausing for the usual rope signal, Keeler raced up the ladder to the others. 'There's a window . . .!' Telling them rapidly what he had seen. 'That could be our way in!'

The three of them backed down the ladder together until Keeler once again located the start of the branch piton route leading to the now dark window.

They examined the rock face for crevices into which to drive their own metal pitons in order to gain access to the window. It was as smooth and hostile as a gun-stock. But Keeler kept looking, breathing hard from his full-stretch exertions to find a break in the rock. Then he saw the pipeline running to the summit.

'I've got an idea,' he told the others. 'Let's go on up again.'

The pipeline and ladder angled slightly to the left and higher than they had been before – and nearer the lights. At a point where he judged it nearly overhung the window he had seen, Keeler roped himself down, taking the Blooddrift pitons and hammer with him.

As he descended, his boots struck some rough spots in the rock which might prove suitable for inserting pitons. He was in too much of a hurry now to test them individually. When he reached what he judged to be the level of the window he groped around, but found he was too far to one side – the service ladder side – and a little too high. He lowered himself slightly; his fingers found a crack. He reckoned he must now be on a line with the window but still several metres to the side of it. He hammered in a piton. Then, using it as a purchase, he swung himself like a pendulum on the rope. He dismissed all thought of what lay below him; his jersey was soaked with sweat and fear.

At the extremity of the swing, his foot kicked against the window ledge fronting a deep opening. He hooked it fast, pulled himself bodily to it.

Was it barred?

Keeler's mouth was as dry as a Richtersveld defile. Disregarding a muscle twitch in his right knee, he rested his chest on the sill and explored the aperture with extended hands. His fingertips registered light, flexible stuff – mesh, not bars. You don't need bars, when beneath is a five hundred metre death-dive.

With the sill as fulcrum, Keeler lunged forward with the butt of the Browning. The mesh yielded. He hefted himself up, widened the gap – then he was through.

He was inside Aussenkehr!

28

Gasping for breath from his exertion and with relief, Keeler's actions were like those of a man concussed – apparently rational, but of which later he had only a blurred recollection. Self-preservation was the governing factor. He freed himself of the rope, and gave one brief flick of his flashlight, his nerves tight-strung at the possible return of the man whose light had revealed the window in the first place.

The place seemed to be a storeroom, filled with a miscellany of junk – paint cans, beer crates, cigarette cartons, a paint-splashed length of plastic sheeting, and other bric-a-brac. The door was ajar.

With his Browning at the ready, Keeler moved swiftly across to it, in the dark. It led to a corridor which seemed – as far as he could make out in the darkness – to be a dead end to his right, and on his left to lead towards some dim light and some indistinguishable sounds.

Keeler closed the door softly and returned to the window. He signalled for Rill to descend while anchoring the rope round his shoulders and against the window aperture. He stood with his handgun trained on the door. He could feel Rill's descent by the way the rope jerked. When her feet appeared he guided them on to the sill and then brought her through the bent-back mesh into the storeroom.

She hugged him spontaneously. 'John, you're wonderful! Where are we? Are we safe?'

'For the moment. I'll check again before we bring Ross down. There's a corridor beyond that door . . .'

As he hurried to the door his foot struck an empty beer can.

They both froze. In their tense state it sounded like a grenade exploding. Keeler checked in the corridor; it was as quiet as before.

Rill acted as anchor for Ross's descent while Keeler watched the door. The American's entry into the storeroom was textbook assault course stuff – wary, alert, the rope clear of the UZI and its stubby barrel, and his hand on the trigger ready for anything.

Gressitt clapped Keeler on the shoulder. 'That sure did the trick, fellah! I was starting to get worried out there about ever getting inside. What's this place?'

'Junkroom . . .' Keeler showed him by flicking on the torch. 'The door gives into a passageway – that's where the light came from that showed through the window.'

'Anyone around?'

'I've checked, not so far.'

Keeler eased open the door warily. The corridor remained still.

Gressitt said. 'Listen, this rope of ours is enough to hang us by if anyone finds it.'

'It's our lifeline for getting out again,' Rill pointed out.

'Let me go out again and hide it under the service ladder,' suggested Keeler. 'I can make a way to the ladder. I've already put in one piton on the way up. Hang on to my feet while I fix in a couple of pitons below the window.'

With Ross holding him, Keeler hammered in a couple of pitons, then made his way over the sill on to them, searching the rockface for additional spots. The rope was looped round his waist, firmly anchored at one end in the storeroom in case of a fall.

When he finally made it to the ladder, he concealed the coiled rope and knotted it to provide him with a safety length with which to return along the way he came. He secured the rope-end lightly to the last piton as an insurance against their return. He then reached up, felt Gressitt's iron grip on his hand and edged himself on to the window ledge, and back into the storeroom. After that, he and Gressitt fixed the wire mesh back into position so as to make it appear undisturbed.

Only when he was safely inside did the reaction of having held on by a whisker over the death-drop hit him. He sat down on the stone floor, breathing hard.

Suddenly Gressitt called urgently from near the door. 'John! Get off your ass! Someone's coming!'

'Rill . . .?'

'Here! Quiet! Look!'

The outline of the door grew clearer; someone with a light was coming down the corridor.

'Behind the door – quick!' whispered Gressitt. 'I'll fix him!'

They all crouched behind the open door, Gressitt braced, ready to smash the butt of the UZI down on the head of whoever entered.

Keeler put his lips against the American's ear. 'Unless he spots us, hold it! We don't want to raise the alarm!'

The footsteps slowed, entered the storeroom. They felt sure the intruder would hear their breathing.

However, he was unconcerned. He rummaged about among the miscellany of crates and cartons by the light of his torch and drew out a six-pack of beer cans. Whistling softly to himself, he turned and left, and they heard his footsteps disappearing down the corridor.

'If this is what being on ice in Aussenkehr means, I'm all for it!' remarked Gressitt shakily. 'Beer! Boy, I could use some!'

They all laughed and helped themselves. Never had beer tasted so wonderful. It was German beer, no less!

Then they gathered the empty cans and their wits.

'Did you see who it was?' Keeler asked Gressitt.

'No,' replied Gressitt. 'But he had a gun. Everyone here seems to pack a gun tonight.'

Rill added, 'Even at this late hour the whole bunch of them seem to be up and about. There must be a reason.'

'Could be Operation Rainbow – whatever that is,' replied Gressitt gravely.

'Why not check the transmitter again?' asked Rill.

Gressitt did, using earphones. He shook his head negatively after a short while and added, 'There's no way we'll want to use this radio until we make our way out of here again. I'm going to hide it under some of that junk. We can retrieve it later.'

'Where do we head for now?' asked Keeler.

'The helipad, that's where the action is likely to be,' answered Gressitt.

'And that's where all the lights are too,' added Rill, not without a trace of sarcasm.

Gressitt's near frivolous reply masked a deep underlying anxiety. 'We'll sing the Ballad of the Green Berets for luck.'

Out in the corridor, they headed in the direction their recent visitor had taken; there was a glimmer of light at the end of it. Gressitt and Keeler, holding their respective guns, plus a grenade each, flanked Rill on each side; she kept the flashlight ready for eventual use. The soft soles of their bootees made no sound on the rock floor – the passageway had originally been hewn out of the rock. They crept along, every nerve stretched to breaking point. Soon the floor inclined upwards and they risked the light for a moment. A ramp recently reinforced with concrete, turned to the left; there also seemed to be a narrow archway leading to a tributary corridor, branching in the opposite direction.

They kept to the main passageway. The slope became easier but continued upward – towards the surface. Ahead, they located the source of the light they had spotted lower down; it came from a room leading off the corridor. Then, came the unmistakable rattle of a beer can tossed on to the stone floor, and the sound of two voices.

As they neared the room, they saw that the door was half-closed. The light from inside was too bright for electricity. It was butane gas.

Keeler, Gressitt and Rill froze in their tracks when a metallic voice barked an order – in German. It emanated from either an intercom or a radio.

'Now!' whispered Gressitt. 'Get past while they're occupied!' And they glided past as silently and invisibly as the ghosts of the old fort.

The passageway widened as it rose towards ground level and the helipad lights filtered through small high windows of what looked like a big basement. Under these windows ran what originally must have been a firing-step, the firing slits themselves were now glassed in as windows.

Two flights of steps led from this room: one, in good order and made of wood, clearly led to Aussenkehr's front portal; the other, a dilapidated spiral affair with the odd step missing and with a broken down handrail. This seemed to lead to the unrestored section of the fort facing the Fish River.

Since it was obviously less used than the other, they chose the old stairway. They crept into the open air via a crumbling doorway. All was in shadow. Between them and the helipad towered the bulk of the fort itself. As they stood directly on the cliff-edge, only a shoulder-high wall, with missing sections of brickwork, stood between them and the sickening drop. The wall followed the line of the cliff round to the helipad.

'Over!' whispered Gressitt. 'We'll use this as cover!'

There was not more than a metre or two now between the three of them and the precipice. They edged round hard against the wall towards their objective. At every step the illumination increased. Above them, the fort's quaint candle-snuffer towers looked like so many witches taking off into the night.

Then the helipad was in front of them. The old German parade-ground had been converted into a modern landing-place.

Their attention concentrated on two sights: first, on the Ka-25 helicopter, square and business-like with its quartet of landing-wheels, and then on four tarpaulin-covered trucks, which were parked on the helipad's perimeter. Groups of men lounged about, as if waiting for something.

Keeler mouthed his question silently as he indicated the trucks. 'Iridium?'

Both Rill and Gressitt nodded their heads in agreement.

Rill then suddenly nudged both men, and whispered, 'Reutemann! Reutemann!'

They all froze as they realized how close they were to the fort's main entrance from which the German emerged. They felt as if they could have reached out and touched Reutemann's flying jacket as he strode purposefully out to the trucks. His tough, leather-like face was strained, he proceeded to check the contents of the trucks. He pulled back the tarpaulin of the first vehicle. There was no mistaking the grey-white sheen of the boulder of metal in the back. Rill, Gressitt and Keeler, gasped under their breath. Next, Reutemann checked each truck in turn, easing aside its tarpaulin. In each was a chunk of cleanly cut iridium weighing about five tons.

Rill craned forward utterly incredulous.

And then, as things will happen, disaster struck. A couple of bricks from the dilapidated wall became dislodged and fell with a crash. In her fright, Rill let go the torch, which clattered metallically on the hard surface of the helipad.

Just then, Trevenna appeared in the entranceway on his way to join Reutemann.

The clatter stopped him in his tracks like a bullet.

Keeler threw himself over the wall to get at him and choke his warning shout. But he was too late.

'*Achtung!* Kurt . . .!'

Keeler's impetus took him right on top of the red-head. He lashed out viciously with the Browning butt and clubbed him senseless.

For one moment Keeler caught sight of Reutemann and the men's attitude of stunned amazement; the animation returned and they all reached for guns which must have been close to hand. Keeler risked a potshot. There was a howl of pain.

'Back inside!' he hissed. 'Keep behind the wall! Run!'

An automatic opened up from the direction of the trucks before they had managed even a few paces. Chips flew from the brickwork.

They reached the entrance to the old spiral stairway. 'In!' snapped Keeler. 'I'll cover the rear! Run, run!'

The beer drinkers in the corridor office had heard them coming and were waiting in the basement room. Gressitt opened up on them as he leaped down the steps with Rill at his heels. The place shook with the ear-splitting racket of three automatic weapons in confined space. Then silence, and the awful stink of cordite. It was all over in seconds.

Gressitt, still on his feet, was ramming home a fresh magazine.

From outside, beyond the high windows, came shouts and yells. Gressitt and Keeler waited for the spearhead to come storming down the other stairway. They shoved Rill into the relative safety of the old steps.

Again, the place was swamped by the deafening roar of automatic weapons. Two or three of Reutemann's men came tumbling down the steps.

Then the first shots smashed through the high windows, bringing a shower of glass down on them. Gressitt and Keeler knew their situation was desperate. They were caught hopelessly, like rats in a trap. They realized that a break-out through their underground storeroom would be suicide. They'd never even get as far as the pitons or the ladder beneath the windows.

Keeler went forward at a crouch, grabbed an AK-47 from one of the dead guards, and raced to the firing-step. He emptied it in the direction of the helipad. The sound was reassuring but the results were negligible. Reutemann's men were safely deployed after their first foolish rush. They could now wait their moment to storm the basement.

Gressitt pointed to Keeler that he had only got one magazine left!

A single shot brought down a fresh shower of glass splinters. Gressitt and Keeler now feared that a grenade or two rolled through the old embrasures would put paid to them.

'Ross!' snapped Keeler. 'There's only one chance for us. Can you fly that chopper out there?'

'Some chance! Chum.'

'We just got to do it. It's the only way.'

'We go shooting out the main doorway,' he went on. 'I'll empty these dead guards' automatics while you and Rill make a dash for the Kamov. We're all dead ducks anyway.'

There was not a trace of fear in the American's reply. 'Sure – that's our way! Rill – come over here! Keep low! Here goes: this way! Give 'em all you got, John!'

Keeler whipped up one of the AK-47s, jumped onto the firing-step. All hell seemed to break loose. The noise of his weapon and the return fire blanked out every other sound.

From ground-level, came the chatter of Gressitt's UZI, a bloodhound bark compared to the AK-47's. The helipad was seared by cross-fire.

Then, Keeler threw away his empty gun, raced to Gressitt and Rill. 'Now!' yelled Gressitt. 'This way, kids!'

They sprinted for it, Keeler clutching Rill's hand in one hand, in the other brandishing his Browning. Gressitt now in his element, fired as he ran.

Their sudden move and the swiftness of it, took Reutemann's men by surprise. The first return shots came as they were almost up to the helicopter.

Keeler, first to reach the Kamov's door, leapt at it, and wrenched it open.

He looked into the blued eye of a Stechkin machine-pistol.

29

Behind the weapon was Reutemann. There was death in his face; Keeler's death.

Keeler did the only sensible thing. He dropped the Kapitän. Rill shrank back. As Keeler recoiled, Gressitt cannoned into him from behind. He, too, faced Reutemann in the pilot's seat.

'Drop it!'

Had Gressitt hesitated only fractionally in obeying Reutemann's order, Reutemann would have blown his face in half.

The UZI fell to the tarmac with a clatter.

Men seemed to materialize from everywhere. The truck crews who had clearly kept to their vehicles during the exchange of fire were now on hand, armed, but it was all over. They grabbed Keeler, Gressitt and Rill roughly, while Reutemann sat like a god-like figure in the Kamov with his machine-pistol aimed at them.

Keeler was dragged round by the shoulder to face a newcomer. It was Trevenna, reeling still from the effects of Keeler's pistol-whipping.

'I'm going to break you in half, you bastard!' he mouthed.

Keeler hoped he didn't know he also had a score to settle from the barge-train encounter.

'Trevenna!' Reutemann snapped from the helicopter. 'Hold it. Not now. You'll get your chance later.'

The bright downward-angled lights shadowed Reutemann's eyes in their deep sockets below heavy black brows and gave him an air of brooding menace. The strong lines of his face with its deep inverted V-grooves from mouth to nostril were outlined by his thick black hair. It was the face of a madman.

There was no doubt about it in the mind of the three captives after they had been frog-marched across the helipad to an office in the fort near the basement from which they had made their sally, and Reutemann threw the question at them, 'Where are your parachutes? Where did you hide them?'

All three had been lashed to chairs. Only Trevenna was at the interrogation. But there were armed men – many of them Arabs – at the doorway and further away by the main entrance. 'Shoot, if there's trouble,' Reutemann ordered them curtly.

Trevenna clutched a Makarov pistol; its barrel was lost in his huge paw. The weals where Keeler had hit him stood out under his uncombed red hair.

Before they could reply, Reutemann rapped out. 'And your radio – you must have a radio! Where is it? Search them!' he ordered Trevenna.

Trevenna frisked them expertly. Gressitt and Keeler breathed a sigh of relief that the Lucky Strike transmitter lay buried in the storeroom.

Trevenna found Gressitt's commando knife and Keeler's extra rounds for the Browning.

Trevenna looked inquiringly at Reutemann. They had clearly both played the game of exacting information out of reluctant witnesses before.

'Listen . . .' began Gressitt.

'Speak when you're spoken to!' and Trevenna's fist crashed into Gressitt's mouth. Blood appeared. Trevenna's voice had a higher pitch than might have been expected from such a giant – a derivative of mixed Hottentot-Cornish genes. His accent was as crude as his own mountains. The mixed blood had given him an almost albino-like complexion, and light, pig-like eyes.

Reutemann flicked a glance at his wrist watch. 'I have to know everything. The quicker you come clean, the better for you. Understand? I repeat, where did you land?'

Keeler watched Trevenna's fist as he answered – he thought he might be able to ride the blow if he saw it coming. 'I don't know what you're driving at, Reutemann.'

Reutemann said, half to himself and half to Trevenna, 'We could not have failed to hear their helicopter. They couldn't have used an ordinary aircraft – not for a pin-point drop on such a target as Aussenkehr.'

Keeler shot a glance at Gressitt. Reutemann believed they had been dropped into the fort by parachute!

Reutemann nodded to Trevenna. 'Find out! No, hold it for a moment. When did you leave Oranjemund?' he demanded of Keeler.

Part of the mysterious signal Gressitt had intercepted flashed through Keeler's mind. Was the Oranjemund squad standing by? Heykal had asked. Keeler remained silent at Reutemann's leading question.

Suddenly Reutemann seemed to lose control of himself. He grabbed Keeler by the shoulders and shook him like a rat. He thrust his face close to his.

'Answer!' he shouted. '*What has happened at Oranjemund?*'

The outburst was symptomatic, Keeler realized, of enormous inner pressures inside the man.

He replied, in complete honesty. 'Nothing.'

Keeler's mind was racing. He himself was a skilled professional – in FERRET's interests – at the game of interrogating. To him, the down-the-barrel approach was the sign of a crude amateur. Somehow, he had to extract from Reutemann what Operation Rainbow was all about, and at the same time ensure that the three of them did not lose their skins in the process. Reutemann, he could see, was in a state of extreme tension which might lead him not to guard his tongue as carefully as he would otherwise. The story would have to be extracted in fragments and pieced together later – plus what they already knew from the Heykal signals. How close was the deadline which had been mentioned? The state of full alert at Aussenkehr pointed to its being at hand.

The next question Reutemann barked at him confirmed his suspicions. 'When did you leave Oranjemund? When did you land here? Answer! Answer!'

'Kurt,' interjected Trevenna. 'Let me do this my way. The girl, too. Once I start they won't be able to stop talking. Or shitting.'

'You can't get facts out of an unconscious man,' retorted Reutemann. 'And I need *facts*. The success of our operation may depend on it. I've got to know what these three are up to.'

'It's not the men I'll give the working-over to,' leered Trevenna. 'It's the woman.'

Keep it cool, Keeler, zero cool. That goes for you too, Gressitt.

The red-head made for Rill. 'Trevenna . . .' began Keeler, trying to hold himself in.

The tough's fist caught him between mouth and cheek-bone. The room blurred, swayed. He felt as if all Aussenkehr had fallen on him.

'The time – what time did you land!' the question hammered through his woozy consciousness.

Keeler shook his head numbly.

'Leave him alone!' he heard Rill's voice, at breaking-point. 'Can't you see he doesn't know what he is saying?'

Keeler played stupider than he appeared to be. They *had* to win time! When Gressitt answered in his place, he realized his motive was the same.

'We arrived about an hour ago.'

'Ah, so!' The answer seemed to please Reutemann. He went on. 'Allow also about an hour, give or take, for the flight upriver. So you left Oranjemund about two hours ago?'

When none of them responded, he said to Trevenna. 'There would not be any outward signs in Oranjemund two hours ago – our men are too clever for that. They would have waited until the very last minute before starting . . .'

'You're putting words into their mouths to reply to you,' replied Trevenna with a flash of shrewdness which Keeler would not have suspected. 'Let me beat it out of them, then you can decide what's what afterwards.'

Reutemann and the room came into clearer focus as the cobwebs started clearing from Keeler's mind.

He saw a tangible shudder pass through Reutemann's body as if some untenable thought had suddenly ripped through him. It was followed by a stillness, as sinister as it was threatening.

He spoke directly to Trevenna. 'Trevenna! They started their show out there on the helipad just as the deadline approached! I see it now! That was their purpose! They knew the timing! They're playing dumb! *They know!*'

'I'll soon find out,' grinned Trevenna. 'The girl . . .'

Reutemann thrust his face close to Keeler's so that he could make out the individual blue stubbles on his chin. 'If you have done anything to abort our plan, I'll make you pay for it in a way you can't guess at. What do you know about it – spit it out!'

Gressitt intervened to take the heat off the still-dazed Keeler.

'Plan . . . what plan? I thought you were in the copper business.'

Trevenna's sideswipe rocked Gressitt's chair almost off its legs. It left the American hanging like a dummy on his lashing.

Reutemann's voice rose half out of control. 'The plan – what do you know?'

Trevenna used the side of his hand for a karate chop which reached from Keeler's mouth to his eyes. It half-blinded him. Blood spurted from his nose.

Reutemann grabbed him by the jersey-front and shook him.

'The attack – do you want more?'

Keeler shook his head to clear it – and the blood – but

Reutemann interpreted it as a sign of refusal. He heard Rill's agonized cry. 'Can't you see he doesn't know – none of us knows! Leave him – you're killing him!'

Reutemann and Trevenna switched their attention to her. 'You're a spy! You're a spy for Major Rive! That's who sent you here, isn't it?'

Keeler managed to get his head up. Both men were standing in front of Rill.

Keeler saw Trevenna's paw reach out for the front of Rill's jersey. It tore like paper in his powerful hand. He ripped it from shoulder to waist. Her breasts were exposed and her nipples were erect with fear.

A sudden imperative ring of the intercom froze the scene – Keeler and Gressitt bloodied and stunned, Rill exposed in her chair, Trevenna poised, Reutemann's dark face contorted.

Reutemann turned to the instrument and lifted the earpiece mechanically.

He listened, lifted his left wrist and glanced at his watch to confirm the telephoned time-check.

He said throatily. 'Operation Rainbow deadline – midnight!'

Without any word passing between Keeler, Gressitt and Rill, each had come to the same conclusion. Reutemann would never have spoken so openly in their presence about the pending 'Operation Rainbow' if he did not plan to kill all three of them before the night was out.

30

Zero Zero Hour: CDM Security HQ.

Jiro Izutsu checked his Japanese-made digital watch with satisfaction as he drew up at Oranjemund's double security gate with its flanking fence. Beyond lay the great diamond workings of Consolidated Diamond Mines. Under the flood-lights in the fog the giant sixty-ton dumper trucks, bulldoz-ers and mechanical shovels roared as they moved and dug. The black skins of the workers contrasted with their yellow oilskins and white hard hats. They laboured below sea-level sweeping diamonds from potholes in the bedrock which had been exposed with such laborious mechanical effort – fifteen metres of desert sand overburden. Right against the ocean rose a man-made seawall of sand to keep out the waves. The ochre of the sand, the orange-painted vehicles, the hint of a violet-blue sea – these reminded Izutsu of fragile old prints which had hung in his home outside Nagasaki.

This was not time to indulge in fancies, he told himself abruptly. The job was at hand – he was pleased with his split-second time of arrival after travelling the five-kilometre, ruler-straight road from Oranjemund town. He hoped the other five Japanese under his command would be as punctual.

'Sneezer' Wright – he was hopelessly allergic to desert dust, hence the nickname – heard the sound of the Landrov-er's engine and saw its lights by the gate. He was surprised. The Landrover – he recognized it as one of the General Manager's personal stable – was his second unexpected visitor within the hour. The first had been Major Rive. What was the Old Man up to at this time of night? Wright had asked himself a while before Izutsu's vehicle approached. He knew the Security Chief had been playing bridge at the Social Club – there was never a time when he could not be contacted by his duty staff; his whereabouts was always known to Security HQ situated in a building a little way inside the gate.

Sneezer had discreetly switched off the late-night radio to admit Major Rive. You could never tell from Major Rive's face what was going on in his mind. What was bugging him tonight? Sneezer asked himself. Maybe one of his hunches – and no one could deny that on a famous occasion Major Rive's hunch had paid off when there had been a James Bond attempt to land a plane upcoast and fly out a parcel of stolen diamonds.

Major Rive had asked Sneezer a routine question in passing and driven off to the prefab which housed Security HQ.

Izutsu saw Sneezer start for the gate in order to check his identity. He knew the lay-out and the drill – he had memorized it when he and his five companions had been shown round the workings on various occasions. He smiled to himself as he fingered the trigger of the Makarov which he held out of sight under the dashboard. It was one of the weapons Reutemann had brought from the *Rigel Star*. The pick-up at the arms cache had been ludicrously simple. He and the other five Japanese earlier in the evening had merely driven out to the big pan near CDM's private airfield and unearthed plastic bags of Makarov and Stechkin pistols, AK-47s, grenades, and spare magazines. There were also some sticks of Chinese-made explosive – he wondered who had thought of including that.

On their way back, the Japanese had stopped at the airfield, broken into the unguarded hangar which housed one of CDM's patrol helicopters and a patrol plane, and sabotaged both machines. It had been as uncomplicated as the weapons pick-up – no one had any reason to suspect trouble.

Sneezer Wright unlocked the double gates, and walked

unsuspectingly towards the driver's window. He was further surprised to see one of CDM'S VIP Japanese visitors behind the wheel. What could he want at this time of night – Major Rive?

Sneezer never found out. The smash of the pistol in his face was so savage that he did not even cry out.

Izutsu hefted the senseless body into the Landrover and drove through the open gate towards Sneezer's watchdog cabin. He carefully closed – but did not lock – the gates behind him. Sneezer's half-drunk cup of coffee and a magazine were on the table; there were three telephones – red, white and orange. Izutsu eyed them apprehensively – what if one of them should ring while he was there?

He then acted swiftly, but without panic, as his Red Army terrorist training had taught him. He pinned Sneezer's body on the floor with one foot while he clinically selected the right spot and plunged an AK-47 bayonet twice through his heart. He wiped the bayonet clean between the pages of the magazine. He snapped the bayonet back into position on the automatic – which he had substituted for the Makarov on leaving the Landrover – and drove towards Security Headquarters.

Vic Farrell, who manned the heart of CDM's far-flung radio network at headquarters, had come on duty at nine o'clock for the all-night shift. He rather liked the night stint – the continual bustle of machinery and comings-and-goings throughout the night made it quite unlike the long lonely visits he'd known as a ship's radio operator before getting the CDM job.

Vic had been as surprised as Sneezer when Major Rive had walked in earlier. He knew the Old Man wasn't the sort to make a midnight check just for the heck of it. Vic, too, had heard of Major Rive's hunches but had not experienced them. He and Major Rive had exchanged a few words on professional matters and the latter had gone through to his private inner office. Vic made a pretence of being busier than he was – for the sake of having voices on his receiver, he homed in on a game of chess being played by radio between two far-apart ship operators. He had played long-distance chess often enough himself – he could visualize the chessboard on the desk before him on which stood his powerful transmitter.

This may have been the reason why he did not hear Izutsu's entry. He looked up from his airwaves chess game into the barrel of the Makarov.

Vic's reactions were extra quick. This was one of the reasons why Major Rive had selected him – somewhere, sometime, those ultra-fast reflexes might serve CDM.

But Vic wasn't fast enough. The heavy 9mm slug tore through his right eye into his brain even as his finger reached out for the chicken switch under the desk ledge whose full automatic alert would warn sleepless men listening at secret posts in the desert, on the Oppenheimer bridge entry-exits to Oranjemund, at Alex Bay aerodrome, and aboard any CDM helicopters or aircraft which happened to be in the air at the time. The signal spelt only one message – crackdown. Nothing or no one would move in the Sperrgebiet after crackdown until Security once again gave the all clear.

Izutsu had recognized Major Rive's private car as he had drawn up, but he knew he had to silence Farrell first. He had had to risk the shot in the hope that it would not be heard far away because of the noise of the mechanical works.

He pivoted on his heels as Major Rive's door shot open.

Would he come out shooting? The question flashed through Izutsu's mind, conditioned by years of terrorist brain-washing. He was not to know that Major Rive never went about armed. For a split second he stared at Izutsu's gun and then wheeled to crash the door shut to get to his own private emergency signal which he had devised as a fail-safe for just such a situation as this.

Izutsu's shot hit him in the shoulder, and threw him sideways. Izutsu was on to him like a tiger with the bayonet.

This time he did not bother to withdraw it in order to clean the blade.

Izutsu was in full control of Security Headquarters.

Zero Zero Hour: Namib Desert Station.

Two hundred kilometres north of Oranjemund, in the heart of the Namib desert, Jan Venter got up from his chair in the tiny air-conditioned office-bedroom prefab and went to the door. The secret CDM control post was fenced, and included a small hut to house drums of aviation fuel for the patrol helicopter. Jan had been there five days out of his week's stint, enjoying being away from the wife and kids in Oranjemund; it made him appreciate them all the more when he got back. Wachter and Lassie, the two German shepherd watchdogs, wagged their tails at Jan. They always became friendlier as the week wore on.

The prefab was sited on the lip of a valley in which lay the old diamond ghost town of Pomona. Jan Venter had heard the story that it was from this very ridge that the first German colonists had seen the sand floor of the valley aglitter with diamonds in the moonlight.

He wondered, as he looked out at the wall of fog, why Vic Farrell hadn't come through on the radio to give him the results of the weekly Social Club lottery. His own set was strictly for security use. Vic was a nice guy – Jan wondered vaguely whether he should risk calling him up. He dropped the idea. Security was security – that is the way he had been trained, and this Pomona station was his responsibility alone until he was relieved in two days' time.

On the far side of the ghost town valley, masked from view by the fog, was a cliff overlooking the sea on which were the regimented headstones of an old German colonial graveyard. The headstones had been sand-blasted clean of their inscriptions by the perpetual wind. No one knew – or cared – who they memorialized. That's the way it went in the Namib, Jan said to himself. He turned back inside and went to bed.

Zero Zero Hour: Oppenheimer Bridge.

At Dunvlei Gate, the entry-exit point to Oranjemund at the South African end of the great Oppenheimer bridge, ex-Sergeant Major James Pollock rose from his seat as he saw a car's headlights start to cross the bridge. Pollock was one of the old school. The tough life of the old South West African Security Force had left its mark in his ramrod-straight back, his military speech as clipped as his moustache, and a complexion annealed by a thousand desert suns. Pollock noted, as he went out to hold up his hand and stop the vehicle – that was the way the Military Police had done it in his day and he saw no reason to adopt modern fancy-pants politeness – that the river was coming down; by morning it could be in flood.

Pollock liked the job for the authority it gave him, but he disliked Major Rive's kid-glove approach. Most, he disapproved of the scrapping of the previous security system under which everybody had to be checked through Dunvlei, in and out, and again through X-rays in Oranjemund town itself. In the good old days, Oranjemund had been a town behind barbed wire at night – and wasn't that what security was all about? There had been no talk then that the restrictions had had a detrimental effect on the townsfolk's psyches. Now they had to feel free to come and go at all hours of the day and night – as this car was doing. Where the hell was anyone going at midnight in this part of the world? Pollock grumbled to himself.

Pollock stood in the centre of the roadway, hand upraised. In the old days the driver would have seen a revolver strapped to his side; that was forbidden now, too. But not forgotten, Pollock grinned inwardly. He still kept his heavy .45 in the drawer of his desk only a few paces away, despite an official ban . . .

It was Yoshio Ito's task to seize the Dunvlei Gate. With him in the car was Isamu Kido – they had commandeered the first vehicle that had come to hand near the VIP block of flats when they had emerged with the other Japs for the operation. Two professionals like them were not required to subdue one old soldier like Pollock, but Kido's was the more vital mission. Once they had disposed of Pollock, he would take the car and proceed to seize the control tower at Alex Bay airfield. Unless there was an emergency, the airport always closed at night because of the fog. Only a skeleton staff remained on duty, including the controller, who doubled as radio operator.

The car braked as it approached Pollock. Neither of them ever knew what alerted Pollock – perhaps the overhead electric lights threw a gleam on the Jap terrorist guns, or perhaps Pollock's early years had bred an inborn instinct of danger.

Pollock wheeled, dived for his office – and the .45.

Kido was first out after him from the passenger's side; Ito followed within seconds.

Pollock snapped out his office lights as he raced clear, down a rough ramp and side road to a big roofed-in car park which dated from the time when all private vehicles were prohibited beyond the bridge. As he fled from the office he had punched the emergency button which would tell Security HQ he was in trouble.

Kido dropped on one knee, fired three shots from his AK-47. He purposely conserved ammunition: his own task, at Alex Bay airfield, still lay ahead.

The shots missed; Pollock stopped deliberately, fired. His shooting was good – one of the bullets whanged off Kido's automatic.

Pollock turned to reach the cars. Once in one, he could outpace the two Japanese on foot and sound the alarm. Ito cursed and ground his teeth – the old man was fouling up the whole of Operation Rainbow!

Ito steadied himself, drew a careful bead on the thickset figure stumbling over the rough ground.

The long burst practically cut Pollock in half.

Ito rammed home a fresh magazine and he and Kido hurried back to the car.

'Get going!' snapped Ito, his nerves shot. 'Anyone could come looking after that shooting!'

Zero Zero Hour: The Control Tower.

From Dunvlei Gate to the control tower of Alex Bay airfield (named Kortdoorn, Short Thorn) the distance is about three kilometres.

Fred Brink, the stand-by controller/radio operator, was not as keen as usual to get away from the aerodrome when his shift ended at midnight. He had found a friend, and they were drinking coffee and swapping stories in the control tower.

Fred had come across a genial American – his name was Ron Walker – dossing down in the passengers' lounge. Walker had explained that he had arrived on the afternoon flight from Lüderitz and was headed for Oranjemund. But, he said, his contact there, a fellow-American named Dr Ross Gressitt – the person who would vouch for him in terms of the security rules – was away. Although he had telephoned Major Rive, the Security Chief had been unwilling to admit him on the strength of a call from an unknown person. Major Rive had said he would deal with his request next day. There had been no alternative but to stay overnight in the bare little airport lounge.

Fred Brink toyed with the idea of taking the American home with him – until he remembered Major Rive's steel-blue eyes. He would not throw overboard a good job by contravening security regulations.

Meanwhile, he and Ron Walker smoked and chatted. Walker was careful not to offer Brink a cigarette from his Lucky Strike packet, the double of Gressitt's transmitter at Aussenkehr. Perhaps if Brink had not been so hospitable, Walker on his own might have tuned in earlier – just in case.

Isamu Kido found them like that. He was in no mood,

after the near-miss at Dunvlei Gate, to take any risks. His AK-47 barrel was still warm. He simply walked in and opened fire. It was only afterwards that he regretted being so hasty when he searched the bodies. He knew that anyone who packed a powerful disguised mini-transmitter was no transit passenger. But he established the man's name from his American passport – Ron Walker. He'd advise Reutemann of that once Jiro Izutsu signalled that the whole of Oranjemund was in terrorist hands.

Zero Zero Hour: Oranjemund Power Station.

Mike Ryan wondered how long he would have to go on using the stand-by generators of the power station to keep Oranjemund's machinery supplied. He looked round the pulsating room, clinically tidy. He wasn't even aware of the noise of the thudding diesel. If power from the South Africa grid across the river were restored that was okay with him, he said to himself. If not – as so often happened, when the wind blew down the high-voltage pylons or piled-up sand made them sag and thus endanger the transmission lines – then the old time-tried Oranjemund system was good enough. A little outdated, perhaps, but nevertheless completely reliable.

Katsuzo Nakajima was also an electrical engineer. He stood in the entranceway aiming at Mike Ryan with a Stechkin machine-pistol in one hand, a grenade in the other. He did not want to use either if he could help it. Some part of the plant might be damaged. The power being generated was vital to communication with the *Beryte* squadron and Aussenkehr.

He was therefore not as ruthless as he might have been. Ryan was given the option of carrying on his work at the station under his eye – and his weapons – or being taken outside and shot.

Ryan opted for working.

Zero Zero Hour: The Post Office.

Oranjemund's post office was Haruo Cho's job. Cho was a communications expert; he was intrigued by the Oranjemund telephone exchange. Like Nakajima at the power station, Cho elected rather to walk to his objective through the deserted streets than risk stealing a car. He kept to the shadows, although there was little chance of detection at this late hour.

He arrived at his destination a minute before the deadline.

Just as Nakajima held back on damaging the power station, so did Cho when he found Hendrik Taljaard busy packing up for the night. Hendrik must have been about twenty-three, only a year or two younger than Cho himself. He gave him the same option as Nakajima had offered Mike Ryan. Taljaard, eyeing Cho's hardware – the spare bandoliers hung about his person, grenades at his belt, a machine-pistol and an AK-47 – capitulated. Taljaard had served on the Angola front, he knew what a terrorist was all about.

Cho made him explain the workings of the exchange before he locked him up. The telephone system would be invaluable for contact with the outside world when it came to the ransom demand . . .

Zero Zero Hour: The Social Club.

Mitsuo Shiga walked quickly from the VIP flats across Rill's green lawn to the Social Club. It took only a couple of minutes. Ferdie, the barman, was still cleaning up, but all the guests had gone. In his pocket, Shiga had the official list of guests who had been invited to the reception to honour the international diamond tycoons. Most of them were in the VIP flats adjoining the Japs' own; they would be easy enough to round up.

Ferdie was terrified. He readily supplied Shiga with the addresses of Oranjemund's leading citizens, starting with the General Manager of CDM. Shiga explained to Ferdie the purpose of seizing the Social Club – here he would hold hostage everyone of importance in Oranjemund until the ransom was paid. Ferdie, added Shiga, would look after their creature comforts and provide food and drink. Shiga estimated that the club could hold about three hundred hostages – enough to make a demonstration or, if he had to start shooting some of them, to show the world the squad was in earnest. Ferdie became more terrified – Shiga warned him to stay away from the bar.

Shiga took his checklist and a German microbus the club used to ferry supplies and went off to the address of the General Manager.

Izutsu, the terrorist leader, had realized that the Social Club would be a walkover. But he knew that afterwards Shiga might be put to the test when it might come to machine-gunning some hostages – men, women and children. That's why he had chosen Shiga. Shiga was the most cold-blooded of the Red Army squad.

31

Zero Zero Hour: Aussenkehr.

Reutemann jammed down the intercom on its cradle.

'Trevenna! It's Zero Zero hour! No word from Izutsu! Something must have gone wrong . . .!' He started menacingly towards Keeler and Gressitt.

'Give the Japs a chance!' said Trevenna. 'If they have to take over places as far apart as Alex Bay airfield and Security Headquarters, it's not all going to happen on the stroke of the clock. Izutsu will signal you the moment the operation is wrapped up. There wouldn't be any point doing it before . . .'

Keeler dared not risk a glance at Gressitt and Rill for fear that it might be misinterpreted. But he felt a surge of elation. Now, at least, they knew what Operation Rainbow was all about! Those puppet-like Japs – how could CDM ever have fallen for their cover as diamond mining engineers! They were in fact the worst breed of terrorists – Japanese Red Army. He had been right in believing that the man who had attempted the limpet attack on Herington's kayak had been an Oriental.

Reutemann stopped short, spun on his heel, and called to the door. 'Hamid! Send Ghoga to me – immediately! Niemeyer – where the hell is Niemeyer? He knows Hamid can't understand a word of German!'

Niemeyer came in. He looked more like a scared schoolmaster than an interpreter in Reutemann's polyglot outfit.

Reutemann said to him as a dark-skinned Arab, heavily armed, joined them, 'Tell Hamid here I want him to go to

Schmidt's radio office – now. I want immediate – I repeat, immediate – word of anything that happens at Oranjemund. Schmidt will be too occupied to phone as the signals come in. Hamid himself will bring me the very first signal that Schmidt receives from Izutsu – understood?'

Niemeyer translated. Both Keeler and Gressitt recognized the language – Arabic – although they could not understand it. The presence of Hamid and the other Arabs underscored what they both feared, namely, Libyan involvement. What devilry was the master of international thuggery up to in Southern Africa?

Hamid and Niemeyer went. Reutemann said to Trevenna, 'I told Heykal I'd signal him at midnight. *Herr Gott*, if he doesn't hear he may think the attack has been called off . . .'

Trevenna answered nervously. 'It's only two minutes past midnight, Kurt! Don't panic!'

Neither Keeler nor Gressitt could make any sense of the Heykal – *Beryte* part of it. Clearly, the *Beryte* squadron, as the intercepted message had shown, was on its way to Socos. But squadron! Keeler could scarcely credit the term, knowing as he did that *Beryte* was an ageing, second-class freighter. Nor that she had signalled from the Lüderitz area. How did that tie in with a midnight deadline, just lapsed, of the Japanese terrorist take-over of the main Oranjemund installations? Was the attack aimed rather at seizing control of the world's richest diamond fields? But that left out of account the most important factor of all – those blocks of priceless iridium on the helipad.

What was going on?

Reutemann addressed the three captives in menacing tones. 'If nothing has happened at Oranjemund as you say, you will pay for it. Do you still insist you are not spies? Then why are you at Aussenkehr? I could take you out and shoot you all now – is that clear?'

Gressitt thought desperately for some way of continuing the dialogue without provoking a death-walk. He tried a last

223

desperate gamble and said slowly and quietly: 'Look here, Dr Reutemann. None of us knows what in hell this Operation Rainbow business is all about. What I do know, however, is that you have about twenty tons of the world's scarcest metal, iridium. That's why we're here. I'm in the market for it.'

Reutemann stood back in utter surprise, then burst out laughing.

'*You're* in the market for it – who are *you*?'

Before Gressitt could answer, Reutemann's face went black with rage, as he obviously did a double-take. 'Iridium – how do you know about *iridium*?' He rounded savagely on Rill. 'You little bitch! You're the one who put them wise! *You'd* know! Kurt . . .' Trevenna came forward with a grin, leering at Rill's breast. 'Find out how she found out!'

The look on Trevenna's face frightened Keeler. He said quickly. 'She only found out because I – we – asked her. She identified iridium from a nodule I found in your kayak aboard the barge-train. She knows nothing beyond that.'

Reutemann now stood over her. 'You work for Major Rive! Trevenna, if Rive knows about Operation Rainbow . . .'

Trevenna said with a note of relish in his voice. 'You can trust the Japs to take good care of him.'

'But if Rive knew before . . .'

Gressitt intervened. 'Name your price for the iridium, Reutemann. Then we can talk.'

There was a movement at the door and Reutemann swung round to see whether it was Hamid. It was not. He turned back to Gressitt and asked – with an air of craftiness which made the captives realize that the question was a trap:

'Tell me how far American experiments have progressed?'

Gressitt racked his brains quickly for a reply. What was Reutemann talking about? What experiments? He knew only the semi-classified uses for iridium. Yet, if it had the significance Reutemann obviously attached to it, SAMEX surely would want to know, and he must find out in case he should come out of this alive.

He played the reply boldly. 'Way ahead of the rest of the world.'

Reutemann gave a savage, derisive laugh. 'Shit, Gressitt. You don't know what you are talking about.'

Gressitt tried to save face. 'If you're trying to take a short-cut to the apocalypse with that load of iridium, you'll have both superpowers on your neck before you know it, Reutemann.'

'Short-cut to apocalypse – I like the phrase,' retorted Reutemann. Gressitt's words seemed to strike some latent megalomania in the German. His pose was unrehearsed. His hard, strong profile with chin slightly out-thrust, long hair sweeping back like a helmet to the base of his collar, was the sort of theatrical attitude dictators strike in front of crowds.

'I am Professor Reutemann,' he asserted. 'Nothing can stop me! My invention is the biggest thing the world has seen since the atom bomb! I am the man who did it – I, Reutemann!'

Gressitt said carefully. 'I have the authority to make a financial offer. Let's open the bidding at five million dollars.'

'If you have the authority to offer that sort of money, then you have given yourself away,' retorted Reutemann. He gave full value to the menacing pause after his words. 'Who's backing you? CIA? If so, you'd make my sponsor laugh. Five million dollars – what are five million dollars to, to . . .' he caught himself in time '. . . my sponsor?'

'If I knew who your sponsor was, I'd be able to judge the weight of his offer,' replied Gressitt.

'You're very clever, aren't you, Gressitt?' jeered Reutemann. 'But not clever enough. What is five million? It wouldn't even buy a sub's torpedo tubes!'

Reutemann's slip of the tongue was not missed by either Gressitt or Keeler. Both immediately made the same equation in their minds – submarines, iridium. Where was the link?

Gressitt skidded quickly past the giveaway, hoping that Reutemann himself had not noticed.

'What is your price, then?'

Trevenna broke in. 'Kurt, let's cut all the crap and yak. We know these three are up to no good. All this talk of dollars – it means nothing, you know it means nothing. Let's get rid of them . . .'

Trevenna's intervention seemed to touch some inner chord of power sensitivity in Reutemann. 'I give the orders here, Trevenna. You obey. Understood?'

'They're just yakking . . .' Trevenna muttered.

'*Shut up* until I am finished,' snapped Reutemann. He addressed Gressitt. 'You do not understand. Even if you offered me ten times that amount, I would not be interested.'

'Every man has his price.'

'Not Reutemann,' he retorted. 'The world will remember Reutemann for his contribution to energy long after it has forgotten diesel.'

'Diesel came to a sticky end,' Keeler intervened.

'So will you, my friend – sooner than you think,' replied Reutemann.

'Kurt . . .' pleaded Trevenna, like a dog about to be deprived of its bone.

'Gressitt,' Reutemann went on, 'If you can command five million dollars, you might be worth holding to ransom – along with the other hostages.'

'What hostages?' asked Gressitt.

Reutemann enjoyed playing his cat-and-mouse game. 'You'll find out – soon enough. I'll have to decide whether the other two of you are worth ransoming. If not, you'll be shot.'

At the thought of hostages, his eyes blazed in their deep sockets. He looked at the time again. 'God dammit! What are they up to downriver in Oranjemund, Trevenna? It couldn't have gone wrong – it was all timed, organized to the last detail! I myself planned it all!'

'Nothing can go wrong – any minute now,' Trevenna reassured him yet again. He went on hopefully. 'We can gain time if you let me work over these three . . .'

Just then Hamid came in with Niemeyer the interpreter – like a shark and its attendant pilot fish. The little man uttered one word through Hamid – 'Urgent!' – and handed Reutemann a slip of paper.

Reutemann read it hurriedly. The megalomaniac expression flooded back into his face. He looked about him and said arrogantly, triumphantly, 'Operation Rainbow is under way! Oranjemund and Alex Bay airfield are in our hands!'

32

There was a moment's electric silence – even though the Aussenkehr men had already taken the news for granted. Then Reutemann barked a sharp order to Trevenna.

'Take these three away – lock them up.'

'Kurt . . .!' expostulated Trevenna. 'You're not going to let them live!'

The vehemence of Reutemann's response reflected the razor's-edge tension of his nerves. 'Must I repeat, *I* give the orders here, Trevenna! I say, lock them up! I want a good man to guard them. Put them somewhere where they can't see what is going on.'

'We're short of men – the sons of bitches have already put four of our men out of action and hit another,' Trevenna answered menacingly. 'Where do you suggest we lock them up? There's nowhere that doesn't overlook the helipad.'

'The old storeroom underground – that's safe,' replied Reutemann. 'They'd need wings to escape from there. Hamid can take the door. He's the sort who shoots first and asks questions afterwards.' He turned on the three captives. 'Any funny business, and you know what to expect.'

Gressitt tried a last shot. 'You won't get away with it, Reutemann. As soon as the three of us are missed, the heat will be on you.'

Reutemann strode across and struck him across the face.

'Bah! Bigmouth! Neither you nor anyone else can now stop the action. A little while ago I admit you had me worried. You came here to wreck Operation Rainbow at the Aussenkehr end if you could. You bluff! Nothing – nothing, can stop Operation Rainbow now.'

Addressing himself to Trevenna, 'Untie them. Take them away. And remember I may want to question them again later,' he said pointedly to Trevenna.

Trevenna and Hamid – the latter draped with weaponry like a caricature of the terrorist he was – plus another Arab, marched the three captives into the basement room. Rill took the opportunity to adjust as best as she could her ripped clothing. Beyond this basement the electric light ended. The procession now relied on two butane gas cylinders for illumination.

Keeler half expected Trevenna to take advantage of Reutemann's absence to settle his private score. He obviously thought better of it although he could not resist a savage shove at Keeler and Gressitt as they reached the storeroom door – 'Get in!'

The door banged shut. It took time for their eyes to accustom themselves to the blackness, and their minds to digest the shattering news they had heard. Keeler's head was reeling from exhaustion and the roughing-up he had taken from Trevenna. Gressitt seemed slightly less bothered although it was clear that he, too, had taken a beating. Rill was still in a state of delayed shock which she tried to snap out of by attending to the men's bruised faces. However, she could not do much, without even so much as a drop of water to bathe them.

Finally Gressitt said, 'Either I'm dreaming all this or else we are on to the biggest thing since . . . since . . .'

'Fat lot of good it will do us in the time we've got left until . . .' said Rill angrily.

'Hold it,' Keeler interrupted. 'Can that baboon over at the door hear us?'

'Even if he can, he can't understand English,' she replied. 'Reutemann is mad,' she continued despondently. 'What does it all mean – Oranjemund, Alex Bay, in their hands?'

'He may be mad – he's also dangerous,' replied Gressitt. 'It means that a bunch of terrorists have hijacked Oranjemund. That's what.'

'But why – what's Oranjemund got to offer?'

'Oranjemund just happens to have the biggest diamond fields in the world, honey,' answered Gressitt. 'That would be an answer – if it weren't that there's a joker in the pack in the shape and form of iridium. The jigsaw simply still doesn't fit. That load of iridium on the helipad is worth more than all of Oranjemund's diamonds.'

'Why should Reutemann stage an elaborate hijack when all he needs to do with the iridium is to make a deal with one of the superpowers and live happily ever after?' speculated Keeler.

'Greenbacks Unlimited is SAMEX's other name,' said Gressitt. 'We'd have bought the iridium – at his price. How the hell do we get out of here now? That's the sixty-four dollar question.'

'There's still the way out of that window, Ross,' ventured Keeler.

'We'd be crazy to try such a thing. And in our present physical state,' said Rill flatly.

'More important than that there's that Libyan thug at the door,' said Gressitt. 'Our escape route would be obvious once he spotted the broken mesh out of position. They'd pick us off the face of the cliff like tame canaries. In any event, if we are going to achieve anything, it will be from inside and not outside this goddam Fort. That's the way I see it. I stay.'

As if to reinforce Gressitt's words, the door opened and Hamid peered in. He leered viciously and swung his Stechkin machine-pistol. A couple of grenades and a spare twenty-round magazine hung at his belt as well as a walkie-talkie with a bleeper alert.

'See what I mean?' said Gressitt after Hamid had gone. 'Now – we've all had one hell of a night. It's time we sacked in. None of us is in any shape to tax our brains tonight – we'll work it out in the morning. In the meantime, honey, put your head on John's manly chest and get some shut-eye.'

That is the way they tried to sleep. But Hamid's frequent

irruptions, the continual background noise of engines, distant voices and barked orders, allowed only for fitful dozing.

Keeler was awakened by a prod from Gressitt. It was just after six o'clock. A greyish light came through the window. Gressitt, more restless than the others, with an earplug in one ear was listening to the Lucky Strike transmitter.

The American made a sign to Keeler to check the door and at the same time indicated that something important was coming through on the set. He had been fiddling with it in the hope of intercepting further signals from the *Beryte*.

Keeler edged to the door and put his ear against it, waking Rill in the process. He gave Gressitt a thumbs-up sign.

An overtone of excitement replaced the usually controlled tones of the Cape Town announcer which reached Gressitt's straining ears.

'We are sorry to have to interrupt this programme. An urgent flash message has just been received which we are broadcasting in advance of our normal scheduled news service in view of its serious implications,' said the announcer. 'An unconfirmed report states that the town of Oranjemund, at the mouth of the Orange River, has been seized at gun-point by a number of unidentified men. Attempts to communicate with Oranjemund and Alexander Bay airport have so far proved unsuccessful. We shall interrupt our scheduled programmes to bring you the latest news of what appears to be an unprecedented event in Southern Africa.'

'Reutemann wasn't bluffing,' remarked Rill after Gressitt told them the news.

'I never thought he was,' answered Keeler. 'What matters now is who's behind it.'

Gressitt concentrated over the set as if trying to wring something more out of it.

'We're back to square one,' he observed, listening with one ear to Keeler and Rill and with the other to the radio.

'Oranjemund has been seized – but why? What's it to do with iridium?'

Rill, who had moved up to the window suddenly exclaimed: 'My God, take a look down here!'

Keeler joined her. His stomach turned over at the sight of the drop and the thought of how they had climbed the cliff the previous night. But the spectacle at the foot of the cliff took his breath away. The great sandspit had vanished. As far as the eye could see there was a sea of dirty brown water. The flood had forced its way up the adjoining Fish, and Big Belly Island was half submerged. Most of Reutemann's jetty was under water and the barges and hovercraft were now moored against a shelf of rock where the helipad road debouched at ground level.

'Where do you think our kayak and canoe are now?' asked Rill anxiously.

'There goes our escape route – the water's up to the base of the cliff and over our pitons,' said Keeler.

While Rill continued to stare at the sight, Keeler checked that the window mesh was properly replaced. Their lifeline rope outside was out of sight from inside the storeroom.

Now there was only one possible exit for them – upwards.

Keeler and Rill rejoined Gressitt who stood at a spot where, if Hamid suddenly opened the door, he could quickly slip his transmitter in a pocket.

'Do you really believe Gaddafi could be mixed up in a madcap scheme like this?' she asked Gressitt and Keeler.

'The madder, the more likely,' replied Keeler.

'Reutemann was about to run off at the mouth about his sponsor when he pulled up short,' said Gressitt. 'All the evidence adds up to Libya. Take a load of that guy outside the door!'

Gressitt gave a sign that something significant was starting to come over the radio. Keeler and Rill took up station to watch the door.

'We interrupt this programme again to give further news regarding the armed seizure of Oranjemund,' Gressitt heard. 'United Press International reports that the town of Oranjemund, as well as the main airfield at Alexander Bay and a smaller one belonging to the diamond mining company, have been seized by an unidentified group of terrorists. Their nationality and numbers are not known. There are also unconfirmed reports of shooting and casualties. All attempts to make contact with the town have failed. As a precautionary measure all flights from Cape Town and Namibia to Alexander Bay airport have been cancelled. No comment is available at this stage from official South African sources beyond a statement that the situation is being closely watched in view of the proximity of Oranjemund to the South African border.'

Keeler heard the key turn in the door lock. Gressitt in a flash pocketed the transmitter and its earplug.

Hamid came in, stared about him. Although he had done the same thing many times during the night, all three now felt waves of suspicion emanating from the bearded Arab. He seemed tirelessly vigilant. To attempt to jump him would have been an invitation to suicide.

The open door gave the captives an opportunity to listen for any untoward sound of movement coming from the direction of the helipad. There was nothing.

After Hamid was gone, Gressitt told them of the latest radio bulletin.

'Surely the army will *do* something!' exclaimed Rill. 'There are only six terrorists . . .!'

'For all we know, Heykal's men could have reinforced the Japs,' said Gressitt.

'I wonder,' replied Keeler. 'That clapped-out old freighter could not possibly have got from Lüderitz, where she sent out the first signal Ross picked up, to Socos in that time. Nothing further from Heykal to Reutemann, Ross?'

'No. He'd be crazy to signal now. With that news now aired over the radio, every radio monitor in Southern Africa will be concentrated on the Oranjemund region. You can lay bets that the army and navy are combing the airwaves,' replied the American.

Then Gressitt again held up his arms in a sign that something more was coming over his Lucky Strike set.

'Cape Town coming through again!' he said.

'Here is an important announcement. A broadcast from Oranjemund, monitored by the South African security forces in Namaqualand, states that the town has been seized by a group of armed men styling themselves the Rainbow Group for the Liberation of Namibia. The group has repeated earlier claims that the diamond town itself as well as two airfields are in its hands. The purpose of the broadcast, it was stated, was to demand a ransom of fifty million dollars for the release of a number of captured international diamond experts who are at present in Oranjemund attending a conference as guests of Consolidated Diamond Mines. These include prominent financiers from America, Britain, Belgium, France, Germany, Holland and Switzerland.

The demand states that the ransom must be paid in the form of uncut gem diamonds within twenty-four hours; failing which, execution of the hostages would begin at the rate of one for every hour of delay. In addition the terrorists have announced that civilian hostages have been taken and are at present being held in the Social Club hall in the centre of the town. Estimates are that the hall can hold up to three hundred people. The terrorists have stated that if the ransom demand is not met, hostages in the Social Club will be blown up; following which, execution of the population of Oranjemund by firing squad in batches of fifty at a time will begin.

The terrorists have also threatened that if any attempt is

made to recapture the two airfields, or if any ships approach within twenty kilometres of the Sperrgebiet coast, the hall containing the three hundred top citizens of the town will be blown up. Demolition charges, it is stated, have already been placed in position.

The terrorist broadcast concluded with a final demand for a safe conduct. A plane should be made available to them by the South African authorities, once the ransom demand has been met, to fly them to an undisclosed destination.'

After a brief pause, as if to allow the implications of the news to sink in, the announcer then added:

'Observers in Cape Town say that the ransom demand of fifty million dollars – especially in its unique form of uncut gem diamonds – makes this the world's most ambitious hijack attempt, both in terms of money and the number of victims involved.'

Gressitt passed on the announcement in the same monotone as before. He did not, however, seem to share Keeler and Rill's sense of shock at the news.

'Fifty million bucks!' exclaimed Keeler.

Rill said, with her eyes full of tears, 'I can't stand the thought of what might be happening to all the people I know in Oranjemund.'

Gressitt showed his first departure from his earlier abstracted air when he said gently, 'Cry for yourself, honey – it's also happening to you.'

'Today is Tuesday,' she said sombrely. 'That means that by this time tomorrow executions will begin . . .'

Keeler and Rill were both puzzled at Gressitt's seeming lack of emotional reaction. He pocketed the small transmitter deliberately, unhurriedly.

Then he turned to them and said, 'I believe this whole ransom business is one great bluff to throw everybody off the real thing!'

33

Keeler wondered for a moment whether the beating he had had the previous night had affected Gressitt's senses. The American's face looked gaunt and bruised – like his own – under its unshaven stubble of beard. However, outwardly there was no sign of irrationality.

'But Ross!' exclaimed Rill. 'The radio clearly says . . .'

'I know what the radio says. *I* say this hijack is the biggest con job of all time – you're meant to keep your eye on a preposterous ransom demand for fifty million dollars and a threat to shoot three thousand innocent people. It's supposed to draw the attention away from the real show.'

'Rainbow!' said Keeler. Rill was wordless.

'You said it! That's what this is all about and we three happen to be the only ones to know that. Listen, I lay awake for most of what was left of the night thinking about it. The radio only filled out details of the essentials we had from Reutemann's own mouth. You, me, everyone, is meant to keep his eyes firmly on the hijacking while the real business goes on elsewhere.'

'And what is that business, Ross?' Keeler thought he knew, but wanted Gressitt to spell it out.

'The Heykal signal I intercepted is the key. The ship or ships which make up the so-called squadron is headed for Socos. That is where the action will be.'

'I think you're wrong, Ross!' exclaimed Rill. 'I personally think the purpose of the squadron is to provide back-up for the hijackers. It has a secondary role, probably to land more Libyans.'

'I thought that way myself until I pulled the story to pieces – and put it together again,' answered Gressitt. 'It comes from being mesmerized by the hijacking. The hijacking comes second, the *Beryte* squadron first.'

'It doesn't quite add up . . .' began Keeler.

'It does, John, when you take the times into account. Why didn't the *Beryte*, if it were meant to support the terrorists in Oranjemund, arrive at Socos at midnight, the deadline for Operation Rainbow?'

'I still have lingering doubts that it didn't, despite what John said before,' said Rill.

'I think we should put paid to that one,' went on Gressitt. 'We know for sure that the *Beryte* and whatever other ships were with her were in the Lüderitz area when I intercepted her signal. Moreover, Reutemann himself while waiting for news of the Oranjemund seizure, let slip that he had to signal Heykal to let him know about Operation Rainbow. Add to that the fact that John here says the *Beryte* is a clapped out old freighter, there's no way such a ship could cover roughly three hundred kilometres between Lüderitz and Socos in a few hours. Not even a destroyer at full speed could manage it.'

But Keeler was not yet satisfied.

'Operation Rainbow,' continued Gressitt, '*had* to get started first in order to catch the spotlight of attention. Then would come the real business, which involves *Beryte* and the iridium.'

'It's pure speculation,' said Rill.

'Not when you come to rationalize it,' replied Gressitt. 'The world might be bluffed – for a while – about Oranjemund being held by a bunch of terrorists. We know that there are only six Japs. That they're desperate men, who'll stop at nothing. But even six desperate men can't hold a far-flung area like Oranjemund and Alex Bay airfield for long. That's the reason for their twenty-four hour deadline. Even if the authorities capitulated at this moment, it would be physically impossible to gather fifty million dollars in uncut stones in time to meet their deadline.'

'What does a day's output at CDM amount to . . .?' began Rill.

'It's not relevant, Rill,' said Gressitt. 'The diamonds would have to come from CDM's stockpile in South Africa – wherever that stockpile is kept. *Not* from Oranjemund, that I do know. The whole hijacking is pitched too high to be real.'

Gressitt went on to elaborate his speculations: there had been no direct support from the Aussenkehr end for the terrorists. There were enough armed thugs right here to mount the whole operation. Yet here they had sat on their asses – why? Because the boss man was right here on top of his iridium; twenty tons of the stuff, up there on the helipad above their heads. And what was Reutemann waiting for then? Heykal and the *Beryte* ships. Once they arrived Reutemann would move. Plus the twenty tons of iridium. If they kept their eyes firmly fixed on the iridium they'd have the answers. All the pointers indicated that, although they couldn't prove it. And if Libya was its destination, what was Libya's interest in iridium? From Colonel Gaddafi's track record, the answer would be weapons.

But what sort of weapons? That was the X in the equation.

'Reutemann made a significant Freudian slip of the tongue when he was interrogating us.' It was Keeler who spoke. 'He said five million dollars wouldn't even buy a set of torpedo tubes for a submarine. What was at the back of his mind that made him mention submarines?'

Gressitt shook his head. 'If you equate that with submarines, that means propulsion. Submarine propulsion – using iridium! If Reutemann had invented something along those lines, Gaddafi would be the man to approach as a sponsor – power-mad, anything to kick the Americans in the balls!'

'If we had a chance to talk to Reutemann again we might learn something further!' said Keeler.

'For the sake of your skins, don't give any hint that you know about Oranjemund,' warned Gressitt.

They tried again to listen for some late news. The airwaves were jammed with comment about the hijacking. Then a weather bulletin. A gale warning was forecast for the Sperrgebiet coast.

There was a noise outside in the corridor and Gressitt hurriedly concealed the transmitter.

It was Reutemann and two more guards, apart from Hamid. There was also another man, a German. Reutemann himself was unarmed. His dark pants and zip-up leather top lent him a para-military air. Keeler noted a peculiar emblem on his pocket – three periscopes fronting a rainbow.

The German gave an assessing glance about the storeroom.

'Suitable?' asked Reutemann.

'Ideal,' replied the man. 'It's small enough – the basement room is too big, it would dissipate the blast effect, especially all those windows. This little opening is immaterial.'

'Good,' replied Reutemann. 'This is the place, then. Fix it. I will give you the exact timetable later. You may go, König.'

The man all but clicked his heels as he left Reutemann with the captives.

Then turning his attention to them, 'I trust you had a good sleep and enjoyed Aussenkehr's traditional hospitality?'

'Stuff it!' said Gressitt. 'That's not what you have come here for.'

'Exactly. Last night you were anxious to find out about Operation Rainbow,' he said. 'I can now tell you that the first phase has been successfully completed,' and he proceeded to give them an account of the hijacking which corresponded essentially with what they had heard on the news bulletins and there was relish in the way he mentioned casualties.

He ended. 'When I spoke of hostages last night in relation to yourselves, you know now what I mean.'

Rill no longer had to pretend ignorance of the news and

239

blurted out, 'You can't do this to all those innocent men and women! I know them . . .'

'They won't come to any harm unless anyone is foolish enough to interfere – or resist,' Reutemann said. 'Some did, and they paid the price. With you three, it is different. You came to Aussenkehr with a definite purpose. I intend to find out what it was.' He glared at Rill. 'You are Major Rive's spy!'

'No!'

He shrugged. 'It hardly matters – Major Rive has been taken care of. And . . .' he rounded on Gressitt '. . . so has the American whose papers gave his name as Ron Walker. Our man at Alex Bay airfield found an incriminating transmitter on the body.'

'Major Rive! I don't believe you!' exclaimed Rill.

'You won't get away with it, Reutemann,' snarled Gressitt. 'Ron . . .'

'Ron!' mocked Reutemann. 'You give yourself away, American spy. Last night you offered to buy me out – that is the way you Americans think, in terms of money, always the almighty dollar. You cannot conceive that there are any other things in the world.'

'Such as evil power?' Keeler suggested.

Reutemann threw back his head in a histrionic gesture. 'I have that already! After tonight the world will remember Reutemann!'

Gressitt saw an opportunity to fly a kite while Reutemann was in his present mood.

'What if Heykal doesn't make it tonight?'

Reutemann stared at him and became menacing. 'How do you know that name? What do you know about Heykal – eh? And why shouldn't he make it? Out with it!'

'First it is you who mentioned him last night. Second it looks as if there was one hell of a storm brewing.'

'You know far too much for your own good,' Reutemann went on in the same threatening tone. 'I am giving you one last chance to tell me who sent you to Aussenkehr, and why. Or else ... .'

He made a gesture at the guards' automatics. Their eyes were as hard as their gun barrels.

When no one spoke, Reutemann broke the silence. 'The woman I know is Major Rive's spy. Whatever Rive wanted to find out makes no difference now. But you two,' and he pointed a finger at Keeler and Gressitt in turn, 'there are still things I intend to find out.'

It would, Keeler considered rapidly, make no difference now whether they talked or not.

'I am a marine fraud insurance agent,' he said. 'That's what brought me to Oranjemund.'

Reutemann burst out laughing. 'Marine fraud. And what marine fraud is being perpetrated at Aussenkehr, may I ask?'

'The *Rigel Star*. I wasn't wrong, was I, Reutemann? Socos is a favourite rendezvous in these parts, isn't it?'

'What do you know about a rendezvous?' Reutemann had an apoplectic look on his face.

Keeler decided that it was now all or nothing. Heads they lost, tails Reutemann won. 'I know all about the *Beryte*, too. She was following the *Rigel Star* down the coast. She belongs to the same shady category of ships that I'm interested in.'

'You know all about the *Beryte*!' Reutemann stared at Keeler as if he would bust a gut. 'And because of the *Beryte* you knew to come to Aussenkehr!'

'You can't hope to get away with a load of pure iridium such as you've got,' added Gressitt.

'Who else knows about the iridium?' Reutemann yelled. 'Tell me – or I'll have you taken out and shot, now!'

He wasn't bluffing but Gressitt kept his cool.

'I said before, Reutemann. You'll never get away with it but you and I could still do a deal,' said the American. 'I won't start another auction here. But I'll offer the value of your invention. Face it man, you're up shit creek without a paddle the way things are going.'

'They're going according to plan,' snapped back Reutemann, but now without his previous conviction. 'Operation Rainbow is under way. Oranjemund has been captured. We have hostages . . .'

'Don't bullshit me,' said Gressitt. 'We know all that – you've already told us. So what? Let's talk about the basics behind all the window-dressing – iridium. Specifically, twenty tons of iridium on the helipad above.'

'We know that copper mining was merely a front for your true purpose at Fannin's Mine,' added Keeler. 'Iridium was what you were after.'

Reutemann started forward as if he meant to strike both men; the guards' AK-47s came to the ready to counter any retaliation.

At that moment the man König returned.

'What is it, König?' Reutemann barked. 'Can't you see I'm busy?'

'Sorry, Dr Reutemann, but it's a question of time. We've got to fly the demolition team to Fannin's. If the helicopter doesn't get away soon we can't finish the job – the ground crew has also to rig the gun turret and flare chutes when we get back.'

'Then get going,' snapped Reutemann.

'Another thing,' went on König, looking at Keeler, Gressitt and Rill in turn, as if uncertain as to their continued presence in the room. 'When I get back, I'd like to run an extension lead from the main electric supply down the corridor to this room. We have to have light to see to pack the blocks – the passage is too dark. I'll need to take a connection from it later to do the job.'

'Anything else?' asked Reutemann curtly.

'I'd like to start moving the drums up from below to the helipad for refuelling. The airlift machines are going to need every litre they can take, considering the loads they'll be carrying. There'll also be our own helicopter to refuel.'

'Well go to it,' ordered Reutemann. 'And, König – make

sure there's nothing left of the mine. Especially the shaft.'

'You can trust me!' the man said obsequiously. 'Do you want the mine buildings blown up too?'

'No – there is nothing in them to give away our activities.'

'Yes, Dr Reutemann.' König turned smartly on his heel and went.

The interlude seemed to have given Reutemann an opportunity to get a rein on his anger. He eyed Keeler, Gressitt and Rill. He said in cold, measured tones and with obvious relish:

'You three came to Aussenkehr with the purpose of wrecking my life's work. You have failed. But you have disclosed that you know more than is healthy for either you or me. At first I considered holding you to ransom but you showed yourselves to be too clever to risk that – you realized that iridium, not the Oranjemund hijack, was the real objective. You will pay the price.' His voice went on to assume a strange, double meaning. 'Accordingly, we will have to leave you to the fate of the gods of Valhalla!'

Vice-Admiral Heykal contemplated the coastline. A moment before, the fog had risen with its usual dramatic stage-curtain effect. Heykal almost wished it had remained lowered. Breakers leaped high into the air against the cliffs of Pomona; even with binoculars he could see the spray and spindrift spurting high over the desert dunes.

Beryte was bucking and butting into the teeth of the south-westerly gale. Heykal was anxious. He had about two hundred kilometres to go to Socos and he'd reckoned on *Beryte* and *Bachir* – the latter was sailing in tight company with the admiral, slightly further seawards – making the distance down the Sperrgebiet coast at a comfortable twelve knots. Soon they would be off the coast's leading landmark, the great arch of rock fifty metres high named Bogenfels. But Heykal wasn't anxious about his position, he was anxious about his helicopters – tonight.

He sent for his senior aviation officer. It would be easy

enough to get the machines airborne, the man said looking at the swell creaming in and breaking across *Beryte*'s bows, but would they ever be able to land on deck again, with each carrying a sling-loaded cargo of five tons? Neither Heykal nor the officer knew what the cargo consisted of. They had their orders and they would obey them. Looking at that wild sea and considering the prospect of an open anchorage at Socos, they wondered . . .

A string of flags broke from the *Bachir*'s masthead. The sight made Heykal more thoughtful still. The squadron was observing strict radio silence as would the flight downriver tonight in the fog. He hoped Reutemann knew what he was talking about when he said he would act as pathfinder and lead them to the Socos rendezvous using fog-penetrating flares. The concealed helipads aft in the *Beryte* and *Bachir* also had special fog-penetrating landing equipment to home the helicopters safely. He eyed the wild sea, and wondered again.

Jan Venter spotted the two ships the moment the fog lifted. He was glad to have some company at his secret control post in the desert. He had had a bad night – the usual routine radio calls from Oranjemund had not come through. Venter was worried. It had never happened before, and he'd been at the game for six years. The two guard dogs, Wachter and Lassie, had been on edge, restless, growling at shadows in the fog. Perhaps some of his own worry had communicated itself to them.

He stared at the two ships. They had no right to be so close inshore; he went to the radio to report for a patrol helicopter to check them.

The radio was still dead.

At Dunvlei Gate, the entrance–exit point on the Oppenheimer bridge, Yoshio Ito stared anxiously southwards as the fog cleared. That was the quarter – South African territory –

from which trouble could come. Without the fog he felt naked, alone. Under its cover during the night he had strung half a dozen pieces of Chinese stick explosive among the arches of the bridge nearest him. If he had to blow them, they would serve to block the roadway for a while but the main structure of the bridge with its gigantic concrete piers would need more than a few sticks of high explosive to wreck them.

Ito kept inside Sergeant Pollock's cubbyhole. He thought he could distinguish a group of cars away to his right, but it was too far away to be certain. They'd have binoculars on him for sure, and if they saw there was only one man, they might rush the place, risking a few casualties.

Ito found himself sweating. He checked the AK-47 and laid out his spare magazines closer to hand.

When the fog came down again this evening, Shiga would pick him up and the other Japs and take them to Alex Bay airfield; Izutsu would proceed there directly from Security HQ to assist Kido to hold the airport. From there Reutemann would fly them all out to the waiting ships at Socos.

It would be a long day . . .

34

Keeler banged down the tin mug of tea which, together with bread and jam, the captives had been given for breakfast and went to the mesh window.

'We can't simply sit and wait for that madman to finish us off.'

Reutemann had departed; Hamid had been relieved and the new guard had not kept looking in as Hamid had – perhaps he had not felt it necessary in view of all the activity around him.

'What do we do to get out?' sighed Gressitt.

'Sooner or later they may bring us something more to eat. Then we could jump the guard . . .'

'Guards,' Gressitt corrected him. 'They won't risk one guard by himself – look what happened when they brought us breakfast. Three of 'em. That sort of rush act can end only one way: we're carried out feet first!'

'It's hopeless!' said Rill with a helpless gesture. 'John, you and Ross must simply accept the fact that there is no way out of this trap! Armed men everywhere! They're as trigger-happy as . . . as . . .'

The three of them were still speculating despondently about what Reutemann had said and revealed; there was too much to absorb all at once. All they knew was that it was now eight o'clock, and sometime that night the iridium was to be airlifted out of Aussenkehr to Socos, where the *Beryte* squadron under Vice-Admiral Heykal would be waiting. And Reutemann's reference to Valhalla had not been lost on them!

246

They also knew that all evidence of iridium at Fannin's Mine was being destroyed – probably at that very moment – by a demolition team led by König. They had heard the helicopter take off a while before and Gressitt had caught a glimpse of it through the mesh, heading into the mouth of the Throughway en route to the mine.

Over everything hovered the awful implication that Reutemann intended to do the same to Aussenkehr as to Fannin's Mine. They scarcely dared discuss that possibility; it seemed as if the storeroom had been selected as the ideal spot to pack with high explosive in order to topple the old fort into the river. Reutemann's sinister phrase, *'we will have to leave you to the fate of the gods of Valhalla'* meant only one thing – they were to be given a Wagnerian funeral along with Aussenkehr. It was the sort of act which would accord with Reutemann's madness.

The thought of it made Rill grip Keeler by the shoulders and pull him close to her. 'Why go on beating your heads against the wall? We've only got something like eight hours . . .' Her voice rose.

Keeler said levelly. 'We're going to get out, do you hear, Rill? Our lives depend on it.'

Gressitt added, 'We've still got a joker, if not an ace up our sleeve – the cliff we came up.'

'You don't know what you're talking about!' exclaimed Rill a little hysterically.

Gressitt put his arm round her shoulders. 'You're under the whip – we all are. I know how you feel, honey, but every pack of cards has a joker. The question is when to play it.'

'When – *how* – with that thug at the door?' she went on heatedly. 'Once he'd checked and found the wire mesh removed and us gone, they'd all know exactly where we were. They'd pick us off the cliff face for target practice! We'd never make it, either up or down! And take a look what's waiting at the bottom – a flood! Up, on the other hand, only means another form of suicide . . .!'

Keeler himself clearly saw no way out either. To pacify Rill, he asked Gressitt, 'Perhaps if there's more news from Oranjemund it might give us a lead. Can you risk listening? What about Heykal?'

'Heykal would never signal under the circumstances, but I can give it a try, just in case.'

Rill checked the door; Gressitt also kept his eye on it all the time he used the Lucky Strike set. A shrug indicated that there was nothing.

He switched to Cape Town:

'. . . unless the ransom demand is met by six o'clock tomorrow morning, execution of the hostages will begin,' *said the radio.* 'A new development has been that representatives of the Big Five Western nations have intervened in the hijacking drama and pleas have been directed to the terrorists – whose nationality is still not known – on humanitarian grounds by the United States, Britain, France, Canada and West Germany.

It is also reported that a crack South African anti-insurgency unit has been flown, as a precautionary measure, to an unknown destination in Namaqualand which borders on Namibia to the south. It is accompanied by a squadron of Mirage fighters from the main South African fighter base near Pretoria.

The terrorists have, however, threatened that if any punitive action is taken against them, immediate mass execution of the hostages will begin.

A similar warning has been issued in regard to ships approaching closer than twenty kilometres to the Sperrgebiet coast. However, it is believed that South African warships are in the process of being deployed outside this limit in order to await developments.'

Gressitt switched off and hid the transmitter.

Afterwards, when he had outlined the news, Rill said,

'The news itself all seems as unlikely as our being here, with the same threat of death hanging over us.'

Gressitt seemed abstracted, Then he banged his fist into his left palm and exclaimed. 'I've got it! By God, I've got it!'

'What?' demanded Keeler and Rill.

'Remember that French laser sight we found aboard the barge-train – the TCV 115?' he replied excitedly. 'I've wondered what Reutemann wanted a fancy instrument like that for – now I've *got* it. It's the giveaway to the iridium airlift.'

'So what's new?' said Keeler.

'I couldn't fathom the logistics of how Reutemann intended to fly four helicopters – plus his own – downriver to Socos, loaded to their maximum. Daytime is out – especially now, with everyone on full alert. The choppers would be bound to be spotted – you've just heard how they've moved up Mirages in case they're needed. You can bet that the South Africans have every inch of the river taped by radar. If anything moves – especially a flight of helicopters – they'll know it and intercept them. Moreover, those choppers are going to be so heavy that they'll have to hug the ground all the hundred and ten kilometres to Socos; which in turn means that they will have to stick to the line of the river. It's the logical route to Socos. Reutemann dare not risk their being seen under any circumstances, even by hostages . . .'

'No one could possibly identify the cargo as iridium from the ground,' objected Rill.

'Of course they couldn't,' replied Gressitt. 'But the presence of a whole flight of helicopters of unknown nationality conveying an unknown cargo would certainly arouse the world to the fact that more than a mere hijack was involved. Reutemann – and Gaddafi – daren't risk that.'

'You say Gaddafi – but we don't know for sure it is Gaddafi!' said Keeler.

'I don't – it's an assumption – and a pretty fair one,' replied Gressitt. 'The laser sight is a dead giveaway. They fly the iridium downriver by night – tonight – under cover of the fog and out to Heykal's ships at Socos. Reutemann will lead the other helicopters and sheepdog them downriver and out to sea. The laser sight will enable the other machines to keep station on him through the fog – my bet is that they are fitted with the associated piece of equipment. You remember, I told you the sight couldn't be used by itself? The final proof is what you heard from König – when the Ka-25 returns from Fannin's later today, she's to be fitted with flare chutes. That means that Reutemann will guide the others to their objective by means of flares – pathfinder flares.'

'And how does all this get us out of here?' Rill started to ask but Keeler broke in as if a sudden thought had struck him.

'Ross,' he said, picking his words. 'Are you saying that everything – the whole operation depends on one thing alone, Reutemann's helicopter?'

'Atta boy,' answered Gressitt, beaming. 'No Ka-25, no operation Rainbow, if what I think is correct . . .'

'Then,' said Keeler excitedly. 'We do have a chance.'

35

The Ka-25 returned from its destructive mission at Fannin's Mine at mid-day.

Keeler, Gressitt and Rill heard the clatter of its rotors from the direction of the Throughway and then sighted its undertaker black body against the dun of the ravines as it crossed the brown floodwaters lapping at the foot of the cliff.

They heard it hover above the fort's helipad, and then the engine died as it landed. It was Aussenkehr's turn next!

The morning was the longest of their lives. They were unable to achieve hearing any uninterrupted news bulletins on Gressitt's radio because of continual activity outside the storeroom in the corridor. When the door was occasionally opened by the guard, they had a brief glimpse of men deploying lengths of electric cable. About mid-morning the gloom of the corridor gave way to a brilliant light coming from naked electric bulbs.

Shortly after the Ka-25 had touched down, Trevenna came into the storeroom. Hamid, apparently rested, was with him. Keeler noted again the walkie-talkie clipped to his belt, with his armoury of weapons.

'Out of here!' snapped Trevenna. 'We've got other uses for this place!'

Hamid gestured with his Stechkin. Trevenna's unexpected arrival had given them no time to pocket the Lucky Strike transmitter. It rested where Gressitt had hidden it amongst cartons of other cigarettes. Their last link with the outside world was now gone.

König, the demolition expert, was leading a group of men – all apparently Germans – in the corridor outside. They were standing next to a low flat trolley stacked with what looked like builder's bricks, except they were in buff yellow paper wrappings. Both Gressitt and Keeler knew what they were: TNT briquettes!

Trevenna and Hamid marched the three up the sloping corridor to a room which gave off the basement with the firing-step. It was bare of furniture; its windows faced out across the helipad. A gaggle of mechanics was clustered round the Ka-25, working from scaffolding on the nose and underbelly. A turret with twin Shvak 20mm cannon was about to be installed, converting the machine into a deadly gunship.

Trevenna noted Keeler and Gressitt's immediate interest. 'Don't get any ideas,' he snapped. 'Hamid here has orders to shoot if you try anything.' He glared at them with his pig-like eyes. 'I'd have shot you long ago, if I'd had my way.'

The afternoon seemed to drag even more than the morning. Six hours seemed like six centuries. Hamid was as remote as an automaton, as vigilant as a leopard. The captives watched the crews complete the transformation of the machine. The sun began to dip; the iron mountains behind Aussenkehr emulated their name, the Verneukberge – Cheating mountains – by turning all shades of vermilion-purple in the sunset. The tumultuous chocolate river was threading its way through the gateway of the timeless mountains.

The three prisoners knew that off the river mouth and out to sea, the fog would soon descend.

Vice-Admiral Heykal watched the great purple weal of the fogbank rolling in from the southwest and west. The *Beryte* was running at full revolutions of the new engines they had equipped her with to make her a wolf in sheep's clothing. It was not the engines Heykal was concerned about, it was the hull. How much longer could it stand the awful hammering it was being handed out? The seas were smashing right up to the base of the bridge; out to starboard, *Bachir* also was throwing water all over herself.

Already he was late; he had counted on eighteen knots for the final run-in to Socos, but he wasn't getting more than fifteen at the outside against the run of that savage sea.

Heykal eyed the fogbank. It was all a question of checks and balances, how soon the murk would shut off *Beryte* and *Bachir*. He knew from the news broadcasts that the South African warships were out there somewhere, watching and waiting. They'd have his ships on their radar screens by now, for sure. That wouldn't matter, once the fog was down. Now, more than ever the operation would have to be a quick in-and-out. How long would his helicopters take to fly up-river to Aussenkehr, refuel and load up, and be back again? All that time, his ships would be sitting ducks moored at Socos.

He looked speculatively at the fogbank again. For the sake of Allah – hurry!

Jiro Izutsu had no use for prayer, but he found himself sweating. *Where was the fog?* From Security Headquarters it was impossible to see the ocean beyond the man-made dunes which the bulldozers had fashioned between the workings and the sea. Nothing must go wrong at this last moment – but what if the fog did not arrive as Reutemann and the planners said it unfailingly did? His Makarov, AK-47 and grenades lay on the table, the safety catches off the guns. Izutsu wasn't trigger-happy; he was trigger-high with tension.

To pass the time – he had intended to do it only at the last moment before leaving – he wired a grenade to the big transmitter which was Security's lifeline.

The crying of the infants, the hysterical sobbing of some of the women, and the heat in the over-crowded Oranjemund Social Club was starting to get Mitsuo Shiga down. He checked his watch, glanced beyond the windows. His orders were to leave with the arrival of the fog. If he had had his way, he would have machine-gunned the hostages into silence

253

long ago. He had miscalculated when he had ordered three hundred into the small hall for a whole day in Oranjemund's heat. He had not taken into account the hysterical outbursts – and the puking – the more so when Shiga threatened the hostages with his automatics and the sticks of explosive he had strung about himself. He'd even had to piss in front of the crowd out of fear of turning his back for a moment. It seemed to provoke the women to greater hysteria.

Shiga checked his watch. He'd use the minibus to pick up Nakajima from the power station, Cho from the post office and Ito from the Dunvlei Gate; Izutsu would proceed directly to Alex Bay to hold the airfield with Kido – the fog, sweeping in from the sea, would mask the coastal workings first and give him a head-start on the other Japanese in the town and on the bridge.

The fog, the fog, the fog!

Trevenna returned Keeler, Gressitt and Rill to their original lock-up. He was in an almost genial mood compared to his sullenness earlier in the day.

They saw why, when they reached the storeroom, closely followed by the tireless Hamid.

All the rubbish which had previously cluttered the floor had been pushed into a corner under the window. Against an entire wall and in the centre of the room scores of yellow-wrapped briquettes of high explosive had been stacked to form a neat geometric pyramid. Electrical wires ran from terminals, mating together groups of half a dozen briquettes at a time and linked up with one main central cable. This disappeared tidily through a hole bored in the doorframe into the corridor beyond.

König knew there was enough high explosive in the stack to blow two Aussenkehrs into the river – and perhaps into the Cheating mountains as well. But, since TNT briquettes had no place in the iridium airlift, it seemed a pity to waste those, over and above what were required for the job. König was rather proud of his effort – there might be even less of Aussenkehr left after tonight than there was of Fannin's Mine.

Keeler, Gressitt and Rill had barely time to gasp in horror at the pile of briquettes they saw in the corridor's light before the door slammed behind them. The storeroom was dark; only a glimmer came from the door surround and window, which admitted some of the helipad's reflection.

Rill blanched at the sight of the TNT and said slowly, holding in her emotions, 'You said we had a chance – I hope you still see it.'

Keeler put the best face on it he could. He felt as though his own stomach had no bottom to it. 'We'll have to sweat it out – until the iridium flight arrives.'

That is what they did. They could not locate Gressitt's transmitter in the darkness amongst the piled-up bric-à-brac. Even if they had, it would have proved impossible to listen in. The sight of that massive mound of TNT upset even Hamid's nerve. Every few minutes he snapped open the door to check. Perhaps the fact that he had been forbidden to smoke also had something to do with his unsteady nerves – the previous night on watch he had chain-smoked. The mini walkie-talkie on his belt stayed alive all the time – he had no intention of missing his final order to withdraw.

Fog-time for the coast came – and went.

Next, seven o'clock. It too vanished into the silent mountains. The peaks might almost have been craning their ears for the sound of the helicopter engines from the sea.

Eight o'clock.

There was a sudden burst of angry voices from the corridor. The door flew open. Reutemann and Trevenna and another Arab stood there. Trevenna carried an AK-47 and a savage grin. The fury which suffused Reutemann's face gave a patina of flush to his sallow complexion and seemed to push his eyes further back in their dark sockets.

'Take them away – to the old parade-ground wall,' he rapped out. 'Shoot them.'

255

36

Reutemann's face was closed, impenetrable. His stare was murderous. Trevenna stepped forward gloatingly.

'Wait . . .' began Keeler.

Whatever else he intended – he uttered the first thing that came to mind – was drowned by a bleep followed by a metallic voice which issued from the walkie-talkie of the Arab guard.

'Shut that bloody thing off!' snapped Reutemann. He addressed Keeler. 'You're wasting your breath. I was a fool not to finish you off before! Trevenna! You know what to do!'

Keeler spoke as levelly as he could with Trevenna's gun rammed against his middle. The red-head had a peculiar stink from close up. 'Perhaps we might at least have the privilege of knowing why we are to be shot . . .'

'Don't let him start talking fancy, Kurt!' Trevenna broke in.

'. . . The situation hasn't changed,' Keeler managed to say, in spite of Trevenna.

'*The situation hasn't changed!*' snarled Reutemann. 'You – you three, you have blown Operation Rainbow!'

Without waiting for Keeler's answer, he raged on. 'How did you send that signal to the tanker? You have a radio – you must have a transmitter somewhere!'

'Signal? Tanker? – what are you talking about, man?'

The gun in Reutemann's hand shook with anger. His voice seeemed nearly out of control. 'You – *you* – blew Operation Rainbow! I'll give you a choice. You can die easily, or you can die hard! Tell me!'

'How could we send a signal?' Gressitt interjected. 'What with?'

'You lie!' fumed Reutemann. 'The Jap found a transmitter on the spy Walker! He was retransmitting messages he got from you!'

'There was no signal . . .' Keeler started to repeat. Trevenna's fist crashed into the side of his head. The room wobbled.

'You lie, you bastard!'

'I know that too!' went on Reutemann in the same tone. 'God, I should have beaten the truth out of you as Trevenna wanted to do!' He reached out and grabbed Keeler's jersey-front. It helped steady the swimming room. 'I should have known, the way you went straight to Socos in the kayak in the first place! It was clever, Keeler! Now you are all going to pay for it.'

Keeler tried desperately to keep Reutemann talking. By now he knew his reactions well enough to know that the best way to hold things up was to keep him off balance with some innuendo, which Reutemann would then have to clear up.

'I warned you,' he said with icy composure, 'I warned you that you wouldn't get away with it, Dr Reutemann!' He placed the stress on the word doctor.

'That's it, chief,' intervened Trevenna. 'Now I shoot them!' Again it was the wrong thing for any underling to say.

'How many times must I tell you that I give the orders,' Reutemann retorted savagely. 'Remember that. You shoot when *I* say shoot! – Understand?'

Trevenna backed away a pace from Keeler. There was no chance of falling on his gun, not with Hamid and the other Arab watching every muscle-twitch.

Reutemann's voice remained shot with fury. 'You interfering swine. A few minutes ago I received a signal from Vice-Admiral Heykal commanding the *Beryte* squadron. When he arrived at Socos which he had difficulty in locating because of the gale and fog,' Reutemann, nearly choking with anger, paused for breath. It was a deadly, nerve-shot pause. *'He found Socos occupied!'*

He waited to get over another choking fit and added, 'By a tanker. *You* had her sent there to block the *Beryte* ships.'

Rill said in an anguished voice, 'How can you possibly blame us for a tanker probably delivering oil for Oranjemund . . .?'

'Shut up, you.' Reutemann snapped. 'Somehow or other you three fixed it. I don't know how – it's too late now. That's my last word!' He turned to Trevenna. 'Now! Take them away!'

'That's more like it,' said Trevenna with satisfaction. 'You coming to watch, Chief?'

'Of course. I won't trust these pigs as long as they stand on their feet.'

Keeler moved to be with Rill. Immediately three gun-muzzles swivelled on him. He put his arm round her shoulder. He looked into her eyes; they both knew it was goodbye. There would be no time once up there.

'Move on!'

Gressitt led the procession, Rill and Keeler, arm-in-arm, followed, with Trevenna, Reutemann and the two Arab gun-men in the rear. The only sound in the brightly-lit corridor was the thump of their captors' footsteps and the static-crackle of the walkie-talkies hanging from the guards' belts.

In the firing-step basement, they passed König and his demolition team. Keeler wondered briefly what type of remote control device they would use to blow the destructive charges. A score of impossible escape schemes raced through his mind, but he knew that if he attempted anything now neither Rill nor Gressitt would stand a chance.

They reached ground level. They were marched across the helipad to the old parade-ground wall. The overhead flood-lights were dazzling. A group of ground crew standing by the Kamov watched the procession in fascination.

Trevenna positioned the three captives against the wall –

Keeler on the right, Rill in the middle, Gressitt on the left. Keeler point-blank refused to let Rill go. They said nothing to one another; there was nothing to say.

Reutemann had to play the sadist even to the last. He said with a sneer, 'You will observe that this section of the wall to your right is in pretty bad shape. You may perhaps wonder why.'

Get it over with, you bastard!' retorted Keeler. 'We can do without your private Baedeker.'

Reutemann, however, was not to be put off. 'The Germans used this wall for exactly the same purpose as it is now being put to,' he went on. 'The wall alongside you is full of bullet-holes.'

There was nothing more to say, but Reutemann added savagely, 'I will teach you to interfere with Reutemann.'

He started slowly to step back to be behind the firing-squad. The sound of the safeties of their automatics clicked in the tight silence.

Keeler crushed Rill against him.

A walkie-talkie at one of the guards' belts bleeped imperatively. Reutemann was still in the firing-squad's line of fire. Only when he drew level with them, would it be safe for Trevenna to pull the trigger.

Hamid's companion called out something urgently – Reutemann halted, craned to hear the instrument's message. Trevenna had his AK-47 ready to open fire, but Reutemann still obstructed him.

Then – Reutemann yelled at the guard to turn up the volume of the walkie-talkie.

After listening carefully, Reutemann raised both hands above his head and gave a triumphant shout. It was followed by a yell at Trevenna, still keeping his arms high. Then, slowly, slowly, the muzzle of Trevenna's AK-47 dropped.

Next, Reutemann swung on his heel and strode across to the three captives at the wall. He gestured for the guards to follow.

When he reached his victims, his face was smugly animated.

'Destiny! My destiny!' he said triumphantly. 'I should have known that three stupid, interfering amateurs like you could not stop my destiny. Heykal is resourceful – very resourceful. He has captured the tanker at Socos!'

Keeler felt a nerve kick in one of his legs; relief flooded over and into him. A shudder passed down Rill's body pressed against his. She buried her head in his shoulder. Gressitt stood rigidly still as if he were unable to absorb the idea of their reprieve.

Reutemann went on. 'In fact, now I consider that the Socos operation has been improved by the happening. *Beryte* and *Bachir* are now moored alongside. The tanker will provide a far bigger and more stable landing-deck than either of our two smaller ships could offer – Operation Rainbow is saved!' He rounded on the guards. 'Take them back to the storeroom!' he ordered.

37

An hour later, the first *Beryte* helicopter was overhead.

The arrival of the iridium flight jerked all three captives out of the near cataleptic state which their near-execution had provoked. Trevenna had stalked away from the firing-squad with an oath of savage disapproval; Reutemann had not tried to prevent him. Hamid was back guarding Keeler, Gressitt and Rill. The sight of the pyramid of TNT briquettes had as telling an effect on the Arab as it did on the inmates of the storeroom. Every briquette might have been a mamba ready to strike. Hamid was extremely nervous. Every few minutes he flung open the door, peered in, AK-47 or Makarov pistol at the ready. Even if they had had Gressitt's radio there would have been no opportunity to use it.

'I need time to catch up on myself,' Rill had told the others when first they were back inside. She sat slumped on a beer crate; the others had done the same. The hour seemed both interminably long and impossibly short; they all knew that their last opportunity would vanish when the iridium flights took off.

Gressitt caught the first sound of the choppers in the distance; all three of them rushed to the mesh window to try and catch a glimpse of the machines. Next they heard them directly overhead still without sighting them; then they spotted the navigation lights of four helicopters over the river, circling round in formation over a pre-determined rendezvous-point, which they judged to be Big Belly Island.

Now one helicopter detached itself from the rest of the squadron – they could follow the machines' movements by their navigation lights – and, with spotlight blazing, it headed for Aussenkehr.

Hamid had checked in less than two minutes before.

Keeler swallowed hard, looked at Rill. 'Ready?'

Keeler and Gressitt each grabbed a briquette they had previously selected because of long fuse wires. They dodged behind the door's blind area. Above their heads the helicopter banged and clattered as it came in to land.

Rill took up a position in the centre of the room.

Keeler gave her the signal – 'Now!'

The way Rill screamed, her fake hysteria might have been for real. She was on the borderline anyway, her nerves being taut enough for her to lose self-control.

Hamid threw open the door, masking Keeler and Gressitt, and rushed forward at a crouch with his AK-47 at the hip. Both Keeler's and Gressitt's briquettes crashed down on his head. He went over like a log, his automatic skating across the floor.

Gressitt was on to it like a tiger; he had it trained on the Arab's sprawled figure before Keeler could even manage to get out of his line of fire.

'Get his pistol – shut the door!' rapped out Gressitt.

Keeler snatched the Makarov from Hamid's belt, pitched one of his grenades to Gressitt, kept the other for himself. He closed the door swiftly, silently, after a quick check in the corridor. It was empty.

Rill stood back, deadly pale. 'Is he dead?'

Keeler went to the inert figure. 'No, out cold. He'll be that way for quite a while.'

'No need then to waste time tying him up,' said Gressitt swiftly. 'You all set, John?'

'Yes.'

'Then this is it!'

Gressitt and Rill hurried to the window with Keeler. Keeler pushed through the mesh with one of the pitons which had survived the storeroom's clean-out. Overhead, the *Beryte* helicopter was making an ear-splitting racket over the helipad.

Keeler swung himself onto the window sill while Gressitt took a firm grip of one of his ankles. The really dangerous part was the first step from sill to piton – Keeler could make out the foothold, plus rope, in the illumination from above. It was a question of stepping onto it, unsecured by a rope, and keeping his balance against the rock. If Gressitt let go either too late or too soon, there was nothing to stop him plunging five hundred metres down into the floodwaters.

Keeler threw a glance downwards. An awful wave of sickening vertigo swept over him. He clung on to the window-ledge, cold sweat beading on his forehead.

'John – you okay?' Gressitt's grip was like a steel band round his ankle.

'Fine – now!'

He straightened up, launched his body and one foot into darkness and space in the direction of the piton. As his body arched over, he felt Gressitt let go. At the same moment his free foot touched the piton. He came upright, perfectly balanced, with his hands upstretched so that he was spreadeagled against the rockface. He heard Rill's anxiety-shot call.

'Okay – I'm okay,' he replied. 'I'm going now for the rope.'

He moved cautiously to position both feet on pitons, then with a toe, hooked the rope end he had previously left looped lightly round the piton nearest the window, brought it up, and made it fast round his waist.

He was safe!

Now, with his face and body hard against the rock and his hands held high like a man being frisked, Keeler started to work his way along the row of pitons towards the ladder itself where the bulk of the climbing rope was hidden. He heard the rattling approach of another set of helicopter rotors from the direction of Big Belly Island as he edged along.

It was because Keeler had his face snugged against the rockface and was moving by the feel of the soles of his feet rather than by sight that he did not see the other man at the end of a rope converging on the steel ladder from the opposite direction.

This man moved quickly along another set of pitons – those wooden ones Keeler had spotted previously – from the quarter of the dark hollow in the rock which Keeler had presumed to be a cave. He had strung to his belt a large leather bag.

The helipad's lights picked up the colour of the newcomer's hair. It was Trevenna.

Both men saw one another simultaneously.

Both of them realized in a flash that the one to reach the steel ladder first would be the one to survive.

There was nothing wrong with Trevenna's reflexes. He was on a line slightly above Keeler; he could move quickly and surely by virtue of his rope secured somewhere on the surface and attached to his waist.

He projected himself to swing in what is known as a *pendule* – towards the ladder. His rope had a jumar fixed to it – a Swiss metal clamp which is clipped onto a rope and will slide upwards only and not downwards – thus making the move completely safe. Keeler tried desperately to make speed from piton to piton without toppling off backwards.

Trevenna reached the ladder first – higher than he had anticipated – on the upswing of the rope. It lost him some advantage in time, but this dominating position could prove decisive.

Keeler reached the ladder. He saw the gleam of a knife-blade in Trevenna's hand. He snatched the sharp piton from his own belt to counter Trevenna's attack. If Trevenna had a pistol as well . . .

Trevenna seemed to fumble; perhaps the 'krab' – a friction device used for roping down under control – was sticking or perhaps he found himself off-balance by virtue of the obvious weight of the bag hanging from his belt. Whatever it was, it gave Keeler time to throw himself up the rungs at his man.

Trevenna was a cool fighter. He waited, free of the rope, for Keeler's rush. As Keeler got within range, Trevenna himself dropped down a rung or two and stamped with his heavy boot on Keeler's left hand, the hand without the piton.

The stab of pain made Keeler almost believe Trevenna had hacked his wrist with the knife. He kept his fingers clenched while arrows of red-hot pain shot up his arm into his shoulder.

Trevenna kept his foot down hard, pinning Keeler to the rung. Holding on, he bent down, slashed at Keeler's face with his knife.

Keeler did not make the mistake of trying to get out of range. Instead, like a boxer in trouble, he went in and under his man to body-punch. Keeler's wasn't a punch, it was a savage upward thrust with his piton into the belly of the man above. At the same moment, Trevenna's knife-blade took him across the shoulders, ripping his jerkin.

Trevenna gave a savage cry of pain and rage. He straightened, grabbed for the loose rope-end, jerking convulsively like a marionette on a string.

Trevenna missed the rope. Keeler crushed himself against the ladder to avoid being carried down by the fall of the heavy body.

Then he was alone.

Keeler had sense enough to switch hands on the rungs; after a moment of gasping for breath, he hauled himself up by his sound fingers to the other rope and made himself doubly fast.

The rest of the escape from the storeroom – his own return to the window with Gressitt's rope looped bandolier-like round his shoulders while he used Trevenna's rope as a safety backstop; his hurried explanation to Rill and Gressitt of what had happened; their combined climb to safety in the lee of the helipad wall after he had gone on ahead and secured

Gressitt's rope on the surface near Trevenna's; the roar of two more *Beryte* helicopters coming in to land, the savage pain in his hand and arm – all these had a peculiar episodic character, like an on-off video tape.

To all three of them, there seemed to be a hideous amount of light. They had no need, near the summit, to follow the pipeline service ladder: for secrecy, Trevenna had attached his rope to an old metal gate on the shadowed, or Fish River side, of the fort. Keeler used the same fixture for Gressitt's rope in order to bring Rill and the American to the top.

They lay in the deep concealing shadow of the parade-ground wall. On the other side of it, four naval versions of Reutemann's Ka-25 stood on the helipad with men pumping fuel into them. Reutemann's own machine was parked to one side, the ugly twin Shvak cannon projecting from the nose turret like menacing antennae. Four trucks, each with its distinctive grey-white boulder of iridium, stood waiting for the aircraft to be serviced.

The final phase of Operation Rainbow was about to begin.

38

The walkie-talkie Gressitt had snatched from the unconscious Hamid emitted a warning bleep.

Gressitt pressed the instrument to his ear, keeping the
volume low. First there was the voice of Niemeyer, the
interpreter, speaking Arabic, then German and finally
Reutemann's own voice came through in English.

'The first helicopter is about to load and take off. All truck
and ground crews will join their respective aircraft before-
hand, as previously ordered. No one, I repeat, no one, is to
board the gunship except the pilot and myself. This is firstly
in order to accommodate the Japanese who are at present
awaiting us at Alex Bay aerodrome, and secondly to leave the
gunship as manoeuvrable as possible in the event of trouble.
The gunship will also act as lead aircraft for the rest of the
group and guide them downriver to the Orange mouth . . .'
Gressitt gave a triumphant glance at Keeler and Rill. '. . . The
entire take-off operation is scheduled to take forty minutes –
ten minutes for each machine. In half an hour precisely any
remaining personnel will withdraw from their posts and
enter the last helicopter. Over and out.'

Rill had been massaging Keeler's numb and bruised hand.
She gripped his arm. 'This is it!' she whispered, but she was
trembling.

Reutemann's voice had barely stopped when the rotors of
the first of the *Beryte* helicopters started to turn. Then the
engine fired and it taxied to the centre of the helipad.

The loading operation Rill, Keeler and Gressitt had wit-
nessed at Fannin's Mine was now repeated, but with more
speed and precision. The first helicopter rose a few metres,

then hovered. A cable snaked out from it. Men standing in the back of the truck secured it round the first lump of iridium. The winch cable tightened – like a weight-lifter with legs bent and arms flexed testing his ability to make a snatch. Then a rope ladder dropped from the machine's belly; the truck's crew scrambled up it and out of sight.

The pilot gunned the motor. The cable tautened until it was as rigid as an iron bar. The sound of the engine rose to a scream; with all taps open, the machine rose slowly, ponderously. As it did so, the iridium at the end of the cable swung against the truck's windscreen, smashing it. The winch-wire was put to the same near-maximum stress as the machine itself. Slowly it wound in its load until it was snug against the belly of the machine. At one stage the aircraft looked in danger of yawing into one of Aussenkehr's towers. Then it pulled clear, thundering over the heads of the three concealed in the wall's shadow, and headed for its rendezvous-point over Big Belly Island.

The next helicopter started to move forward to the heli-pad.

'Check your pistol!' said Gressitt in a low voice – he had the AK-47 and Keeler the Makarov. 'At this rate, we'll be needing them soon!'

The take-off drill of the next two machines and their schedule – ten minutes apart was impeccable. They watched their navigation lights join those of the first helicopter circling Big Belly Island. The squadron made a kind of maypole of pulsing lights as they circled over Trevenna's hideout, waiting for the fourth machine, and finally for Reutemann's own to join them.

The last of the *Beryte*'s 'copters moved onto the helipad.

Suddenly Reutemann's voice came over the loud-speaker, crisp, metallic. '*Achtung!* Evacuate the fort! All remaining personnel out!'

Would they check when Hamid failed to show up? Or would Reutemann consider the alternative of sitting on a time-fuse of God knows how many tons of TNT sufficient incentive to make everyone obey orders?

Three figures emerged from the main entrance and jog-trotted across to the apron where the helicopter stood. Their sharp pace was indicative of what was going on in their minds.

Gressitt said quietly, 'This is our cue, you guys! We rush Reutemann's machine as the last of the other choppers goes over our heads – okay?'

'Okay,' Keeler replied. 'Listen Rill, Ross and I will lead with the guns. Keep as close behind us as you can!'

Rill busied herself tying back her hair. 'What are you doing now?' he asked.

'My hair could be a dead giveaway under the lights,' she answered. 'If they see three men running, they may not at first suspect anything, and it may give us more time to reach Reutemann.'

Just then Reutemann's voice once again barked over the loud-speaker as the last of the *Beryte* choppers revved up.

'This is my final order. Firing mechanism for the demolition of the fort has now been activated – it will detonate in exactly thirty minutes from now. Out.'

Keeler, Gressitt and Rill breathed a sign of relief – there had been no last-minute discovery of their escape. They still held the element of surprise.

The split-second loading and take-off routine of the last chopper was as well executed as the previous three. Now the helicopter hovered over its truck, ready to weight-lift the last iridium boulder against its belly.

Reutemann's voice, using the gunship's loudhailer, sounded above the aircraft's rotors. 'Trevenna? Goddam it, where are you? You are to come with me! Get out here – *schnell*, quick!'

The helicopter's winch cable snaked down, the iridium boulder was secured, everybody embarked.

'Trevenna!' Reutemann's harsh, anxious tones were disstorted to a screech by the loudhailer. 'Idiot, where are you?'

The cable to the iridium boulder went rigid as the helicopter's rotors bit. The pilot opened all stops. The helipad was awash with its roar. The boulder started to edge clear of the truck.

It was the signal for the three to come out of hiding.

'On our way!' yelled Gressitt. He jumped to his feet. Keeler threw off the safety catch of the Makarov and followed. Rill raced after him.

They sprinted across the helipad. The slipstream of the helicopter hit them like a solid object. They had a brief, confused impression of thundering sound, blinding light, hard tarmac, fuel stench, looming perspex.

Gressitt tore open the gunship's door.

Reutemann was in the co-pilot's seat, the loudhailer microphone in one hand and with the other he tugged at a pistol in a door holster.

Gressitt reached out with a full-stretch looping swipe of the AK-47 barrel. The savage impact of the blow hurled Reutemann backwards. The pistol went spinning.

There was nothing wrong with the pilot's timing. Being beyond either Gressitt or Keeler's immediate reach, he whipped up the German's pistol from the floor. It came up to fire.

Keeler's Makarov barked twice. The man gave a startled, half-surprised gesture as the heavy 9mm slugs toppled him, still clutching Reutemann's gun.

'In!' Keeler shouted.

Gressitt vaulted aboard to the controls, Keeler gave Rill a leg up. Gressitt shoved the AK-47 into Keeler's hands. Its size made awkward handling in the confined space.

'Get rid of the pilot, John!' snapped Gressitt. 'I can't fly cluttered like this!'

Keeler hefted the pilot's body to the door.

'Can't we do anything for him . . .?' began Rill in a strangled voice.

Keeler gestured at his chest. Both bullets had been killers. 'Nothing,' and he dropped him unceremoniously overside.

Keeler got to Reutemann, who lay sprawled in an unconscious heap at the rear of the cockpit and checked him quickly. The gun barrel had made a savage, bloody weal across his head. He was alive and gasping. Keeler saw that he would be out cold for some time. No time to waste now. He lugged the unconscious body to the rear of the machine and hastily tied his hands with a length of nylon cord which was lying about. Without further delay, he rejoined Gressitt who was already at the controls. 'Out – stone cold. I'll check him again later,' he told him.

Gressitt grinned and indicated the last of the four *Beryte* machines heading to join the rest of the flight over Big Belly Island.

'We'll let him join the others before we take off,' he said. That would probably have been the recognized procedure to follow had everything been going according to plan. 'Thank God there's a radio black-out and I don't have to talk to these gorillas.'

Rill stood in a state of stunned stillness holding on to the headrest of Gressitt's seat. Keeler realized that she needed something to take her mind off what had just happened. 'Rill,' he said. 'We'll be taking off any moment – close that door, will you?'

Rill did as she was asked, but Keeler felt nervous now that his line of fire across the helipad was obstructed, should anyone still come.

'Let's get moving!' he said to Gressitt. 'That load of dynamite down there is giving me the heebie-jeebies.'

'Me too,' rejoined Gressitt. He worked the controls. The engine fired, the rotors started. He gunned her to maximum revs. Over Big Belly Island the lights of the other helicopters were orbiting like choreographed stars; waiting for their leader.

Keeler asked Ross urgently 'How in hell do I fire if I have

to open up on them from the gun turret?'

'No time to demonstrate,' Gressitt replied laconically. 'I'll show you once we get safely underway – a lot of its operation is automatic.' He indicated a small console with dials and lights in front of him. 'That's the TCV sight.'

They put Rill in the co-pilot's seat while Keeler stood behind them.

Gressitt opened the throttle, brought the big machine to the centre of the helipad.

'She moves good,' he said. 'The others up there must be as heavy as pregnant elephants.'

The Ka-25 rose. For a moment it hovered level with the battlements. The Kamov slewed sideways over the cliff-edge with the characteristic sideways motion of helicopters. Gressitt put out the cockpit lights as a precaution against their possibly being spotted by any of the other pilots. It was only a short flight to Big Belly Island – about three kilometres. The tension grew as they neared the rendezvous; Keeler wished again he knew how to work the guns.

Gressitt closed on the circling group at a slightly higher altitude than them.

'Any moment they'll home in on the TCV,' he said quietly. 'The moment they do, I'll head downriver.'

Big Belly Island – a chocolate slab in a chocolate flood – appeared beneath. The other machines drew close, their flashing navigation lights revealing their dark fuselages with no distinguishing roundels. Keeler could see the pilot and co-pilot of the nearest by its cockpit lights.

'They've locked their TCV sights on us – here goes!' exclaimed Gressitt. He banked sharply and positioned himself to head downriver.

'What are those gorillas doing?' he demanded. 'Look out the windows, for Pete's sake!'

Rill slid back the perspex and craned out.

She said, a little light-heartedly, 'Four of them following – like lambs to the slaughter!'

39

The five helicopters, led by Gressitt's, headed downriver. Gressitt throttled back in order not to outpace the clumsy, heavy machines flying in formation astern. They flew almost at zero feet over the dark river; it is doubtful whether they could have hauled themselves high enough into the air to clear the hills flanking the banks safely.

They thundered past Aussenkehr's cliff. The doomed fort perched on top, already looking like the relic it would soon become.

Gressitt was still anxious to know whether they were following okay. If the other pilots had any suspicions about their lead chopper, this would be their last chance to do anything about it.

Keeler checked. 'Line abreast astern,' he confirmed with satisfaction.

Gressitt relaxed and gave the thumbs-up sign. 'I think this ride is going to be a piece of cake!'

'I'm going to have a look at Reutemann,' said Keeler. 'I'm going to risk the cockpit lights. The more light we have on a guy like him, the happier I feel.'

'Let's get well clear of Aussenkehr first,' Gressitt replied.

Just then, there was an almighty explosion, and for a fraction of time they thought something must have hit their craft. Then the whole sky was lit up with an incandescence as bright as if the sun itself had suddenly burst out of the ground below. Aussenkehr! The TNT had done its job. Reutemann had brought twilight to his Valhalla. It seemed incredible to think that only thirty minutes had elapsed since Reutemann had barked his final order to evacuate the fort.

None of them spoke a word. All three knew that there was no time to think of what had been . . .

Keeler took the Makarov, started aft to the main cabin, which Gressitt had illuminated by means of a switch. Keeping his gun handy, Keeler cautiously made his way to the rear. Reutemann lay like a dead man, but breathing in short gasps. Keeler examined the makeshift lashing round his wrists which were swollen because in his hurry he had tied the wire too tight. Keeler loosened it a little. He rolled back one of Reutemann's eyes. There was not a flicker of consciousness. Keeler then dragged Reutemann against the side of the cabin near the main exit.

He returned to the cockpit. 'He's out for the count, but he's as tough as his goddam iridium.'

He instructed Rill to take the Makarov and guard Reutemann once they reached Arrisdrift and the fogline. 'We don't suddenly want him around when shooting could start at Alex Bay,' he added.

'I know nothing about guns . . .' began Rill apprehensively.

'You don't have to – it's only for show,' answered Keeler. 'I've tied his hands securely. It's very unlikely anyway that he'll come round before the final curtain. Ross, now what about that gun turret?'

'I'll give you a crash course once the river straightens out beyond those goddam mountains and I can ease up on the flying,' he replied. 'We've got plenty of time – there's still about sixty kilometres to the fog belt.'

They flew in a northwesterly direction for the first ten kilometres after leaving Aussenkehr until the river came to a sharp left-hand bend. This was its most northerly extremity; from then on it switched south in the direction of the sea, once it had broken free of a series of big S-bends. It all seemed too easy. The four Libyan machines held tight formation on the lead chopper, like sheep being led by a Judas-goat. The flight continued to travel very low so that the river showed as a dark channel against whiter fringes of sand and dun-coloured foothills which reached to its banks.

They flew on. The pulse of the rotors and the impression of boring into a black-and-chocolate coloured tunnel had a mesmeric effect on Gressitt. However, once they were clear of the series of loops in the river, he took time off to instruct Keeler in the elements of firing the gun turret.

The plan was to force the following helicopters to land at Alex Bay aerodrome at gun-point. If any of the machines proved obstinate, Keeler was to fire a burst in its general direction while Gressitt did the actual positioning of the gunship for aiming. Both Keeler and Gressitt considered that the pilots would offer little resistance. They could not escape because of the fog and their lack of knowledge of their surroundings, or of the location of the Socos anchorage. None of them, in view of their massive loads, was in a state to out-manoeuvre the gunship. Once the gunship had landed, Gressitt himself would take over the turret against the Japanese terrorists at Alex Bay waiting to be picked up. If necessary, the gunship would first soften up the opposition by strafing the airport buildings.

The flight proceeded uneventfully. Landmarks passed below – Missionaries' Drift, the Obib Dunes, Blooddrift. Now they were drawing close to Rill's home ground at Arrisdrift. Arrisdrift was the critical landmark. It was here that the fogline began which extended all the way to the Orange mouth.

At Arrisdrift the river twists abruptly to form Big Gut. After that it widens progressively for the remaining thirty kilometres to the ocean.

Keeler and Rill both felt Gressitt's growing tension as Arrisdrift neared. Flying through the fog at almost ground level along the line of the dark river would call for all his skill.

'The others still in sight?' he rapped out anxiously.

Rill flipped open her window. The smell of fog was unmistakable. 'As before,' she replied.

'We're into the fog!' Gressitt exclaimed almost immediately. Wisps spread over the windscreen. Any moment now it would become a solid bank.

Keeler said, 'Rill, go back and check Reutemann again. Soon we're going to have our hands full at Alex Bay.'

Rill left her seat, taking the Makarov gingerly, and went aft. Seconds later Gressitt let out an oath and swung the helicopter hard to starboard as the river bank loomed suddenly out of the murk where it started to form Big Gut.

From the big cabin came a scream and the rush of wind.

'Jesus!' exclaimed Gressitt.

Keeler threw himself backwards out of the turret where he had been studying the lay-out, grabbed the AK-47, and flung himself through the space dividing the cockpit from the rear cabin.

His first thought – because of the single scream and the wind was that Rill had fallen overboard.

Then he saw. Reutemann had Rill by the throat at the open fuselage door. He had a stranglehold round her neck with his right forearm. The other held her Makarov rammed in her side. Blood still oozed from the ugly welt across his forehead. His face looked ghastly. Its sinister lines were etched deeper by pain. Keeler threw up the AK-47 into a firing position. As he did so, he realized what had happened. Somehow Reutemann had managed to free his wrists – probably by sawing the cord against the door catch. He had come round far sooner than could have been expected. The lurch the gunship had given when Gressitt threw the machine into its sharp turn had played into his hands. Either Rill had dropped the Makarov to clutch at something to steady herself or else she had unsuspectingly gone too close, thinking Reutemann still unconscious.

Wind and noise drowned all possibility of speech.

There was no need for it. Reutemann's intention was clear. To shoot Rill or push her overboard, or both.

Reutemann held her as a screen between himself and

276

Keeler's gun. He couldn't fire without hitting her. Reutemann's burning eyes conveyed the message loud and clear: throw down your gun, or else.

Keeler judged the distance between them in a flash. He knew he couldn't get to her in time.

Gressitt's agonized voice came through from the cockpit. 'What the hell's going on back there?'

Keeler called back. 'Keep going! The bastard's got Rill!'

Keeping his eyes riveted on Keeler, Reutemann yanked Rill sideways into the opening. She tried desperately to claw at the fixtures. Her face went blue as Reutemann increased his pressure on her windpipe. Any moment she'd be as limp as a rag doll.

Reutemann made a tight throw-away sign to Keeler with the fingers of the hand about Rill's throat. The meaning was plain: throw away that gun! Here, at my feet! Any tricks, and she's gone!

Keeler made a lightning decision. He'd throw the AK-47 half way. It was cocked, ready to fire. Reutemann had just come round; he'd be sluggish and slow off the mark. He'd have to release Rill to reach the weapon. That might give Keeler time to jump him – even if it meant risking the Makarov.

There was no time for hesitation. Rill's face was purple-blue. Her eyes were starting out of their sockets. She was almost senseless already. She had already stopped her convulsions as oxygen was withheld from her lungs.

Keeler made a gesture of surrender and threw down the AK-47 midway between them. But Keeler had underestimated Reutemann. He saw through the ploy in a flash. His face contorted, part in anger and partly from nausea, he jerked Rill's failing grip from the door. Any moment she'd be on her way to the river below.

Keeler stepped forward and kicked the AK-47 right up to Reutemann's feet. But Reutemann still did not release Rill. Dragging her with him as he bent down, he reached and thrust the automatic behind him with a foot, keeping the Makarov on Keeler. Only then, when the weapon was out of Keeler's reach, did he shove Rill away from him. She fell in a semi-conscious heap on the metal floor. In a second Keeler was at her side – Makarov or no Makarov. The move was fatal. He was now on his hands and knees with Reutemann standing dominatingly upright. He yelled at them. '*Get up!* Both of you – *up!* Into the cockpit!'

As a last desperate attempt, Keeler tried to manoeuvre himself once again to get at the AK-47. But Reutemann was too fast. Supporting Rill, Keeler staggered into the cockpit.

As he reached the partition area, Gressitt glanced round from the controls. He was sweating with anxiety and the effort of flying a strange machine under near-impossible conditions of visibility.

The American looked straight into the barrel of the pistol in Reutemann's hand. He whirled back to the controls. Keeler half-carried, half-supported Rill to the co-pilot's seat.

Reutemann shut the partition door. The wind noise was cut off.

'Keep flying!' Reutemann snarled at Gressitt. His voice was thick, murderous. 'Keep flying, you hear me? Any tricks and I'll blast these two!' He prodded the gun into Keeler's and Rill's ribs.

Keeler threw a desperate glance out the window – where were they? If he could establish their position, there still remained a last outside chance . . .

At an order from Reutemann, Gressitt put on the cockpit lights. The Makarov kept swivelling from Keeler to Rill and then rested on the back of Gressitt's head.

'Any tricks mean death!' he snapped. 'Do you all hear?'

40

The Ka-25 gave a sudden lift. Gressitt gunned the engine hard; the cockpit floor slanted sharply.

The impetus caused Reutemann to step back against the cabin partition. Keeler stumbled against Rill's seat. Out of the window he had a brief glimpse – almost beneath the machine, it was gone in a flash – a long concrete strip with a roadway running across it. The Oppenheimer bridge! They had overshot Alex Bay airfield where the Japs were waiting!

'What the hell . . .!' blazed Reutemann. 'What are you up to?'

'The bridge – just missed it!' Gressitt replied.

Reutemann steadied himself and jammed the Makarov into Gressitt's neck. 'The Oppenheimer bridge! What the hell are you playing at? You've by-passed Alex Bay and my men there!'

'Listen,' snapped Gressitt in reply. 'We missed the bridge by a hair – isn't that enough? I can't concentrate on flying with your goddam gun in my neck!'

'What about the rest of my flight . . .?' Reutemann yelled.

'That's their problem, isn't it?' retorted Gressitt coolly. 'If they're keeping their eyes on the ball and following me, they'll be okay.'

Keeler realized that Gressitt was playing dumb and had deliberately by-passed the aerodrome. Reutemann was now in a fix. By turning back now and leaving the river, he would foul up the one certain means of locating the airport in the fog.

'Don't give me that bullshit!' snarled Reutemann.

Gressitt lifted his hands from the controls in a gesture of impotence. 'Okay – you fly the goddam thing yourself!'

Reutemann's voice was deadly. 'Get your hands back on those, you goddam American spy! You will keep going and fly this machine to the river mouth and then on to Socos – understand! We can fly back later from the ship and collect the Japs. Right now you'll land this machine on the tanker's deck – and you'll do it properly, if you value the skin of your friends, here. Nothing – nothing – is going to stop Operation Rainbow, even if I have to shoot you all in the process!'

But Gressitt didn't give up so easily. 'There's a hell of a cross-wind . . . this machine's unfamiliar . . . the gale . . . How do I know if I can manage?'

'This,' Reutemann said patting his gun, 'tells me you'll manage.'

He then prodded Keeler with the gun barrel. 'And you, you'll manage too. You'll now operate the signal flares for the flight. Get down into the turret; the releases for the chutes are all clearly marked. Every push-button has the flare colour shown on it. When I order you, you will fire four yellow flares when we reach the river mouth, followed immediately by four orange flares. Understood? Then you, Gressitt, will turn a hundred degrees to starboard and carry on up the coast for about ten kilometres. There you will sight the tanker's landing lights and those of the *Beryte* and *Bachir*. Is that clear?'

Keeler tried desperately to fob Reutemann off. 'I've never operated these things before.'

'Shut up and get into the turret,' retorted Reutemann. 'Those flares are visible with the flight's laser sights. They are sensitized to the red spectrum – reds, yellows, oranges. Get going!' He levelled the pistol. 'Now!'

Keeler cast a despairing look at Rill. She seemed about to pass out again any moment. She returned a helpless gesture.

Keeler did as Reutemann ordered. He lay down full-length with his head and shoulders inside the turret. He had noted the clusters of push-buttons previously when Gressitt had explained the working of the guns. Only a cretin would not have had enough wit to press the right button on a given command.

Keeler eyed the quick-firing cannon. What use could he make of such a formidable armament under the circumstances? Even if he risked a burst, what good would it do? The cannon were pointed outboard, with fail-safe trip mechanisms to prevent damage to the helicopter's rotors or fuselage.

It seemed to Keeler that he had not been in the turret more than a minute or two when there was a shouted order from Reutemann up above.

'Keeler! We're over the river mouth! Group four, yellow – fire! Flares away!'

Keeler punched the four yellow switches; away went the flares from the belly pods. The world turned brilliant yellow. The gunship seemed to ride on a cloud of yellow fog.

Then Keeler felt the machine buck. They were above the sea! The air changed density and accounted for the turbulence. The long downriver haul was behind them!

Reutemann's second shout came through immediately – harsh, full of triumph.

'Group four, orange – flares away!'

Keeler fired the relevant buttons. At the same time he tensed his muscles to see whether a backward leap to where Reutemann stood with the Makarov was feasible. His snap assessment told him that he wouldn't stand a chance. With his goal so close, Reutemann would have shot his own mother if she stood in his way.

Five minutes to Socos!

Frantically Keeler cast his mind round. Again, he started to draw up his knees unobtrusively to give him leverage for a do-or-die leap at Reutemann. But the position was awkward; he tried to find another more suitable.

Before he could do so, Reutemann's over-excited voice came through.

'Flare! Green – fire the green flare.'

He had already spotted the ships from his forward-looking position in the cockpit!

Then Keeler himself sighted an elongated, upward-elevated pattern of lights through the swirling fog below.

Landing lights! Those were the special fog-penetrating lights *Beryte* and *Bachir* had removed from their own heli-pads and rigged on the tanker's deck for the benefit of the iridium flight. Keeler could not make out much more beyond them except a shadowy outline of the tanker's upper-works.

Suddenly, a star-shell arced up out of the darkness. It came from the *Beryte*. Its brilliant light showed the group of three ships. It also showed Keeler something else – the mouths of *Beryte* and *Bachir*'s triple missile-launchers and the muzzles of their eight 57mm anti-aircraft guns as they tracked the aircraft. The cannon in the turret – even if he could use them – would be like peashooters against such an array.

'Higher!' roared Reutemann to Gressitt. 'Get above the other craft! Keep circling above them as they go in to land!' He called to Keeler. 'When I give the word, fire a single yellow flare – is that clear? Repeat, a single yellow flare.'

'A single yellow flare,' Keeler repeated sullenly.

Their 'copter picked up altitude and its motion eased as it rose higher above the surface of the sea. It circled, while below the navigation lights of the iridium flight circled also.

Then one of the machines broke formation. Keeler watched its dark silhouette descend towards the lighted landing-deck. It seemed to sway due to the great weight it carried. Nearer the tanker, it started to veer sideways but the pilot recovered and dropped it on the deck with an awkwardness which made it bounce. Men rushed forward and made it fast.

The second and third helicopters made a better job of their landings after Keeler had fired further flares on Reutemann's instructions. The precise timing and logistics of the operation bore Reutemann's trademark.

Now only one iridium machine and their own machine remained airborne.

Keeler felt that before the final flare went down he had to do something or it was the end. He still lay face-down with his upper body in the turret. He held on to one flimsy hope – that with the operation so to say 'wrapped up', Reutemann's vigilance might relax.

In a flash, Keeler drew up his knees, jack-knifed backwards and upwards.

His move did not catch Reutemann entirely napping. The Makarov – unaimed – went off with a shattering roar – but Keeler had already blanketed the weapon by the time it was fired.

His shoulder caught Reutemann; the pistol went spinning. The force of his leap hurled both men together into the rear cabin. Keeler heard the crash of the gun on the metal floor. It skidded towards the open door of the fuselage.

Perhaps the hammering Reutemann had taken slowed him down after all, because Keeler was first up and at the gun. Reutemann followed – by a millisecond. Keeler had no time to shoot. Reutemann crowded him as he rose, off-balance, to his feet. Keeler clutched frantically at a grab-handle by the door to save himself from going overboard. The incoming wind hit him like a mule-kick.

But it was nothing compared to Reutemann's attack. He was on Keeler before he could do anything with the gun and brought his knee into the groin. Keeler's head jerked forward; his world erupted in pain. His pistol-hand also snatched at the grab-handle in an involuntary, reflex action.

Reutemann saw his chance. He grabbed Keeler's pistol-wrist and slipped it through the grab-handle with the gun and half his forearm projecting.

The agony in his groin matched the savage splinter of pain which shot up his arm as Reutemann threw his weight against the bone, using the grab-handle and door-edge as levers.

Keeler knew that at any moment his arm would give. He deliberately unclenched his fingers and let the gun go, knowing that it must fall overboard, and that Reutemann would try to go for it before it did. Reutemann snatched at the falling weapon. As he did so, his head came forward, exposing the same killer-nerve spot at the base of the neck which Keeler had once successfully used to knock Trevenna senseless on the barge.

Keeler hit Reutemann with his free hand. His head snapped forward and struck the edge of the open door.

The wind did the rest.

Keeler's eyes were too blurred with pain to note details of how Reutemann went. He concluded that the slipstream must have got into his loose clothing and plucked him overboard. All he knew was that one moment the man with billowing clothes was trying to kill him and the next, he was gone.

Keeler hung onto the grab-handle, retching and gasping, stars or landing lights wheeling below.

But he managed to get a grip on his reeling senses, hauled himself away from the open doorway and the deadly wind and got back to the cockpit. He saw Rill in the partition doorway, staring at him, numb with terror and shock.

'Oh my God, oh my God, darling!' was all she could say.

'Help me to the seat,' he managed to utter.

Still doubled over, he made his way with her help to the co-pilot's seat.

Gressitt's reaction – or non-reaction – was bewildering. It certainly wasn't the response of a man whom he had just saved from a maniac. He merely stabbed the perspex window and rapped out. 'Look! For Chrissake, look down there!'

The last helicopter was hovering over the tanker's deck at a height of about forty or fifty metres. The iron discipline and landing drill which had been drummed into the pilot and the other fliers was still evident. Instead of going in for a landing as the others had done, he hung back waiting for his go-ahead signal flare from Gressitt's machine.

The pilot wasn't controlling the flight of the machine, however. The iridium was.

The maximum load, plus the gale, proved too much for the winch cable. It had slipped a few metres. At its end, the load of iridium swung like a pendulum, dragging the helicopter sideways and round.

'Boy, is he in trouble!' exclaimed Gressitt.

It wasn't trouble, it was disaster.

The winch cable slipped further as Keeler, Gressitt and Rill watched awe-struck from the gunship. The load plummeted down another ten metres or so.

The pilot made the mistake of holding onto it. He tried to snag the winding-sprocket on the winch. But you can't stop a five-ton bomb once it is on its way. And this was a bomb.

Down, down, it went, dragging the helicopter with it.

It plunged through the tanker's landing-deck as if through plywood. There was nothing between it and the tanker's fuel tanks below.

Taking it all in a flash, Keeler's mind went icy clear as an instant computer read-out. He knew the iridium could be saved.

The deck landing-lights still burned; men raced towards the wrecked helicopter with rescue gear and foam fire extinguishers.

Keeler felt he could almost smell the fumes from the tanker's ruptured tanks.

'Get over the deck – high!' he yelled at Gressitt. 'We've got 'em licked!'

He threw himself into the gun turret as Gressitt manoeuvred into position and fired a flare.

It floated down, a graceful little umbrella of death.

The fumes from the tanker floated up.

At some unidentifiable point in space, the two met.

They told him later that the warships standing twenty

kilometres off the coast saw the flash and shook with the impact.

At Oranjemund, eight kilometres inland, they said the flames leaped through the fog from sea to desert so that for a moment the diamond workings below the sea-walls stood out as in daylight.

The blast shoved their helicopter high into the air, high enough almost for the fog to mask the cataclysm going on beneath. Only Gressitt's cool nerves and superb skill saved the machine. They were unable to distinguish between the double explosions of the tanker and those of the two other ships; the missiles in their launchers contributed their own particular brand of pyrotechnics to the holocaust.

Rill and Keeler held on to each other, sitting on the gyrating floor of the cockpit as Gressitt fought for control. Time ceased to be.

Then it was all over, and the bucking ceased.

Rill had her head buried in Keeler's shoulder. He scarcely heard her words.

'Who does the iridium belong to anyway?'

Epilogue

◆◆

Mud – the same Orange River mud which had covered up Rill's Arrisdrift fossils millions of years ago, proved to be a decisive factor in the ensuing bargaining between SAMEX and South Africa for recovery of the iridium. Experts from the world's most sophisticated salvage vessel, the American *Glomar Explorer* – the very same ship which a few years earlier had successfully plucked a sunken Soviet nuclear submarine from the abyssal depths of the Pacific – flew to Oranjemund shortly after the holocaust.

At Socos, the water being shallow – about fifteen metres deep, the salvage of four five-ton boulders of iridium from the sea-bed would not present overwhelming difficulties. But the longer the salvage operation was delayed, they said, the deeper the iridium would sink into the immense amounts of mud being spewed over the ocean floor by the flooded Orange River, and the more difficult would be the undertaking.

The price the Reagan administration paid for the iridium will never be known. Both sides, however, seemed to have been satisfied; for diplomatic observers afterwards noted a considerable easing of relations between the United States and South Africa. Namibia, it seems, was out of the bargaining at an early stage.

Colonel Gaddafi wisely kept Reutemann's secret to himself. When agents reported that the four Libyan submarine hulls on the stocks at Split were being fitted with conventional propulsion, SAMEX knew that Reutemann's invention had died with him.

There was a smile of satisfaction from those in-the-know at FERRET when the owners of the *Beryte* and *Bachir* filed insurance claims for the two vessels 'lost in a gale off the Namibian coast'.

When American scientists saw the first of the five-ton grey-white boulders emerge from the Socos sea in the jaws of the *Glomar Explorer*'s remote control grab they marvelled, just as the Spanish conquistadores had marvelled long ago at the sight of the unripe gold in the Colombian river sands. Keeler, Rill and Gressitt watched the operation from the deck, not without a certain amount of pride and satisfaction.

Soon after the Socos explosion, South African paratroops descended on Alex Bay airfield. They met with no opposition. When they burst into the control tower, they found all the windows blown out and, among the wreckage, the bodies of the six Japanese Red Army terrorists. They had used a twentieth-century variation of harakiri – a primed grenade held against the head.

As to the ghosts of Aussenkehr, they too were finally laid to rest; along with the battlements and candle-snuffer towers deep down in the Orange River mud, which continued its timeless flow towards the sea.

Gressitt claimed that it had all been part of his job for SAMEX. As for Keeler and Rill, both felt they needed a holiday and a rest before considering SAMEX's offer of a job with that continuously vigilant secret organization.